SARAH CHOI

The King's Heart

*For Appah and Mom
with love and
many thanks.*

Contents

Acknowledgement

Releasing a story series I started when I was 11 and completed when I was 29 has been an adventure, to say the least. Now 34, I find that my dreams have seasons, and this was a fruitful one indeed. The first thanks always belongs to my parents, who loved me and encouraged me in this dream pursuit of mine. Thanks are also due to the many people who gave me feedback, idea brainstorming sessions, and support in some way, shape, or form.

And so, it is with a thankful heart that I write: I hope you enjoy *The King's Heart.* Cheers!

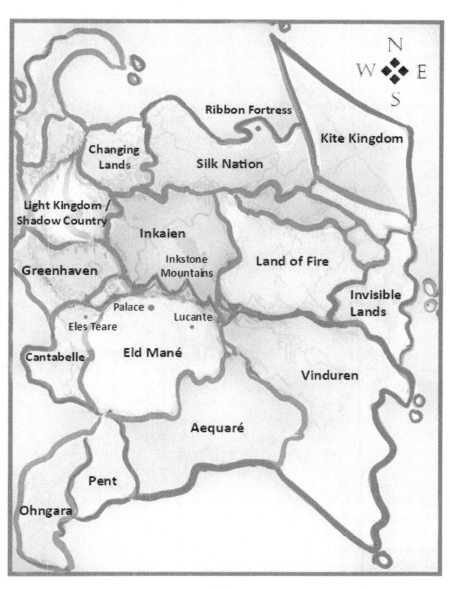

Map

1

Seeing the Unseen

Walking leisurely on the parapet of the palace of Eld Mané just before dawn, Avorne Ehrthann tried his best to size up the ink sign of the day.

Really, it was the ink sign of the last week and a half, and Avorne didn't know what it meant or signified. What puzzled him most, however, was that no one else seemed to see it. Neither Duke Vandek, his uncle, nor Iris, his former tutor and royal gardener could see it. Ionthann, the captain of the guard, didn't see it though he was gifted with an affinity of sight. And even his wife, Queen Renade, hadn't noticed the ink sign behind the palace in the Inkstone Mountains that towered high into the sky.

"Ren, dear?" Avorne called towards an arched window, where he saw Renadé draw out an elaborate line of ink characters and set it deep into the outer walls of the palace.

She was setting up the foundation for an ink portal and had been working on it for the last day and a half.

"Hm." Renadé replied, still engrossed in working her ink enchantment.

She wore rich robes of red adorned with gold embroidery that resembled flames all along the edges. Her sleeves were folded up neatly, and her long black hair was tied half back with a gold pin. The light of the rising sun lit her and her ink enchantment in a golden light, and Renadé bit her lip as she frowned in concentration. The ink line wavered as she became distracted by her husband's voice.

"What is it?" She asked as she kept her ink enchantment steady with both hands.

Avorne took a deep breath,
   took off his crown,
   and ran his fingers through his hair.

Then he studied his crown
   and traced the simple design
   along its edge and asked,
   "Did you notice anything unusual
   about the Inkstone Mountains today?"

He stole a sidelong glance at Renadé.

She turned her head to give a cursory glance towards the mountains with a frown.
   "Aside from the usual ink signs, no, I didn't. Why?"

"Oh…nothing…" Avorne said.
   "I thought something caught my eye,
   but it might have just been the sunlight on the ink."

That wasn't entirely true.

But at this point, the King of Eld Mané wondered if he was seeing things. He didn't insist that it was there to anyone, just as he didn't insist to Renadé that a gorgeous ink sign glittered in the sunlight now. He had mentioned the question to each individual in the palace – once even to a visitor – with more or less the same results. This exchange with Renadé made him conclude he was the only one who saw this intriguing ink sign.

Why? It bothered him that no one could see it. It was such an interesting design, quite different from any other ink sign he had seen. How could he discuss what it might signify if no one else even knew it existed? Also, what did it mean if he was the only one who could see this particular one? Avorne had been discouraged as of late, because try as he might, he didn't know how to bring about the second peace treaty attempt, though he desperately wanted to.

In the last few years,
    the greatest obstacles to the second peace treaty attempt
    had been addressed and taken care of one after another.

They restored Eles Teare,
    the capital city of their
    neighboring country,
    Cantabelle.

Raehn, the singer of the city
    and ruler proper of Eles Teare,
    reclaimed her
    position,
    power,
    and sign
    of authority.

They finally rescued Valéon,
    their ally from the first treaty attempt
    who held the original peace treaty draft
    from the Ribbon Fortress
    in Silkairen up north.

And with the help of the Ribbon Princess,
    they restored Valéon's wings and voice
    and began reconciliation
    with the current Ribbon Queen,

Sylasienne.

There were still
    nightmare outbreaks
    in various countries,
    but on the whole,
    the people of the north and south
    were open to the idea
    of a second peace treaty attempt.
    Avorne wasn't sure what accounted for this change in sentiment. He had
asked his uncle, Duke Vandek if some underlying manipulation influenced
the opinion of the masses, but Vandek had shaken his head.

Vandek's only comment had been,
    "People's memories are short.
    And everyone knows it's easier
    to defeat a nightmare
    with the support of others;
    they're just too proud to admit it."

Perhaps.
    But Avorne wasn't sure how to get started.
    He also wasn't sure who to ask for help.

Everyone looked to him for answers,
    as he was now King of Eld Mané
    and had dealt with two nightmare outbreaks:
    once in the south when he was a prince,
    and once in the north, when he was king.

Somehow those two experiences had earned him
    the reputation of being *the* expert in defeating nightmares,
    which wasn't even close by any stretch of the imagination.

Avorne knew the truth.

He had survived the first nightmare
   with the help of many
   northerners
   and southerners.

And he had barely defeated the second nightmare
   with the help of a young Legend, other allies,
   and a stubborn, guilt-laden friend
   who suffered a severe bout of amnesia.

But despite this,
   the unspoken expectation
   of his people and even rulers
   of the surrounding nations held strong:
   if anyone could single-handedly bring about peace
   between the north and south and push back the nightmares
   that plagued their lands, it was Avorne Ehrthann, King of Eld Mané.

On good days,
   that absurd expectation
   amused Avorne to no end.

On bad days,
   it weighed upon him
   like an anchor dragging
   him to the bottom of the sea.

In one of his more discouraged states,
   the King of Eld Mané had made
   a desperate wish on a dandelion:
   Show me a sign for good.

So I know I'm on the right track.
So I can have the strength
to do what I need to do,
and the wisdom to do it well.
So I know that I'm not just wasting my life
trying to achieve something that
was never possible in the first place.

Beholding this ink sign that no one else could see,
  Avorne remembered that wish.
  He also had no idea what to do with it.
  This wasn't the sign he had been looking for.
  He had been thinking about something more visible and noticeable.
  Like a call to arms to start the peace treaty.
  Or a request to discuss peace between the north and south.
  What about a declaration of loyalty or a vocal commitment?
  Or a mysterious but timely appearance by a Legend
  who could spearhead their efforts and lead the way?
  An ink sign in the mountains behind his palace that only he could see
was none of those things. In fact, Avorne wondered what good it could do.
It was beautiful, yes. But useful? He eyed it from where he stood, studying
the way it stood gleaming in the Inkstone Mountains, lit up by the rising
sun. Not so much.

  Avorne sighed and found a white dandelion globe growing in between
the cracks of the stone parapet. How convenient. He bent down to pick the
flower and spin it between his fingers. He considered a slight amendment
to his last wish, but before he could gather his musings into a coherent line
of thought, he heard Renadé make a noise of alarm and say,
  "what in the world?"

He spun towards her to see
  the characters on her inkline
  ripple and pulse in

an unnatural fashion.

It was as if the characters
    were being squeezed
    by an invisible hand
    into a fist
    over and over
    again.

The lines that had been laid
    on the palace's stone walls and parapet
    became distorted,
    flaring and stretching,
    dimming and shrinking.

Even as he ran towards Renadé,
    who struggled
    to maintain the inklines
    with preventive measures,
    Avorne saw the unfinished ink portal open.

Out of it tumbled a mess of torn paper,
    splintered wood, tangled thread,
    and a man surrounded in disjointed ink lines
    that spun around him in frantic orbit.

At first, Avorne had a double take.
    The kite made him think of Darkon, the King of Kites.
    But then the ink made him assume it was Raiidran, the Ink Prince.
    In fact, it was neither Darkon nor Raiidran.
    Renadé recognized the man before Avorne did.

"Tal?!"

She whipped an impromptu set of inklines
around her broken ink portal to hold it in place,
and rushed to extricate him from the mess he had arrived in.
"Are you all right?"

Well, Avorne felt less embarrassed about not recognizing their unexpected
visitor after realizing who it was. Of course Renadé would know her
older brother when she saw him. Slightly relieved, but still puzzled and
concerned, Avorne followed to see if he could assist.

"I'm fine,"
   Tal answered as he winced and stood up shakily.
   The robes he wore as advisor to the Ink Prince
   were covered in twigs, leaves, and dirt.

But ignoring his disheveled state,
   Tal just glanced towards Avorne
   with an apologetic look.
   "Did I break anything?"

"Aside from Renadé's ink portal?" Avorne answered,
   "Only your kite, by the looks of things. What happened?"

Splinters of wood lay strewn across the parapet,
   and torn paper fluttered from the wind
   that blew in through the still open ink portal.
   There were characters of ink that seemed to just barely
   keep the fragments of kite together in inky stitches.
   Avorne had never seen a kite in such bad condition before.

"I don't know," Tal shook his head.
   He gave Renadé an appreciative nod
   as she spun a quick ink charm

to wrap around his wrists and hands,
which sported minor bruises and cuts.
"It was flying fine, and then it wasn't.
I was traveling above Greenhaven when the kite…"
Tal grasped for the word he was looking for.

"Malfunctioned?"
Renadé suggested.

Tal nodded. "It startled me so much,
I reached for the nearest
ink portal I could
without thinking.
Sorry about
bursting in on you
like this, Ren."

Renadé just shook her head.
"It was an emergency. I'm glad you're in one piece."

"Me too," Tal replied.
Then he asked Avorne,
"How are your kites here?"

"Fine," Avorne answered.
"The system Darkon set up has been steady for years.
None of our kites have experienced anything like this."

"We can ask Darkon," Renadé suggested.
"We have a meeting with him this afternoon."

"That's right." Avorne had nearly forgotten.
"What would I do without you, Renadé?"

9

She smiled.

"Forget more things, probably.

Speaking of, let's eat breakfast."

Leave it to his queen to make sure he stayed on top of all of his responsibilities and stayed in good health. Avorne grinned.

"Right. Why don't you and Tal head to the dining hall first? There was one thing I wanted to see first – something that caught my eye."

Renadé frowned slightly and looked once more towards the Inkstone Mountains. But she didn't question him and instead led Tal away in casual conversation. Tal followed her without comment. So did that mean Tal couldn't see the ink sign either? Avorne sighed once the two left the parapet.

He looked at the ruined kite and ink portal,

then at the dandelion he still held in his hand,

which almost looked like a golden globe

in the light of the rising sun.

The ink sign that only he could see was still there, unapologetically bright and bold. It looked like a crystallized rainbow caught in a watery trellis. Beholding the unaccountably cheerful sight, Avorne found words for his wish amendment:

The sign is great.

Not what I was looking for,

but I'll take it.

Still, it would be nice

to not be the only one

who can see this.

If it's not too much,

please find someone

who can help make

this second peace treaty a reality.

If there's anyone out there
   who has a heart and vision
   for this like me,
   send them my way.

Because I don't know where to start,
   and I can't do this on my own.

2

Message

When he envisioned his life after captivity, Valéon never imagined the possibility of being a messenger. He had always considered that he would return to serving some family of nobility, even after the deaths of his Lord and Lady Pondragai, whom he had served faithfully until the end nearly twenty years ago. Maybe even serving in his original capacity as keeper of the Pondragai Estate and its extensive library collection. But what he found when he did return to the Sky Realm after being rescued from the Ribbon Fortress was quite different.

The Pondragai Estate
had been
dismantled
and
dissolved
completely.
There was nothing
and no one
to return to.
His service was no longer needed.
The message had been quite clear,
though no one brought him

formal word,

acknowledgement,

or direction.

In a state of loss, Valéon sought the domain of the Sky Maiden, who had once resided within the Pondragai Estate, when she had brought the young, infant Halas to Lord Leutheros and Lady Laehna to raise. Had it been twenty years ago, Valéon would have thought it inconceivable to enter into the domain of a Legend to speak to her directly. But that was two decades ago. He had been a timid, yet loyal servant then. He was no longer a servant. And though his loyal and faithful disposition remained, he had long grown out of that timidity.

Without much difficulty,

Valéon located

the golden gateway

of the Sky Maiden

and entered her domain.

He hadn't been there in quite some time.

When he approached her where she sat cross-legged on her bed,

bent over a notebook in concentration,

he knelt before her on one knee,

folded his wings neatly upon his back,

and rested a hand upon hers that held a pencil.

"Hello, Crystal."

It felt odd addressing her by name instead of by title,

but Valéon forgot about his awkwardness

as soon as she lifted her head

and beheld him with surprise and delight.

"Valéon?"

The young Legend put aside her notebook

and enveloped him in an enormous hug.

13

It was a minute before she let go,
took him by the shoulders,
and asked,
"How have you been?
Are you all right?
Have you visited Emily?
She misses you tons, you know.
She never says a word these days, but I can tell.
She asked to have a description of you for Christmas.
I know it's next week, but I'm going to give it to her early
and write her something else for then.
Actually, it's funny that you showed up now…
I was just finishing my last sentence."

For a moment,
　　Valéon forgot everything
　　he wanted to ask the Sky Maiden.

He used to have visions of the Sky Maiden
　　when he was captive
　　in the Ribbon Fortress
　　in Silkairen.

They were at his lowest moments
　　when he floated between
　　consciousness
　　and unconsciousness,
　　drifting between pain and sleep.

His voice had been extracted at the time,
　　so he had never been able to speak with her directly.

Honestly, Valéon had been afraid

that she was some
hallucination
induced by
the nightmare-ridden
Ribbon Fortress
or its nightmare-plagued
queen.

The entrenched nightmare
had conjured up terrible
visions and lies
that to this day,
Valéon fought
to get out
of his mind.

He told no one of what he struggled with.
He was too ashamed to admit
that he hadn't been able to overcome
these things even after a year of freedom
and being reconciled with Sylasienne,
the Ribbon Queen restored.
He didn't want to inflict poor Sylasienne
with any more guilt than she already felt
towards her treatment of him in the past.

To this day, she treated him like family, always checking on his well being
and his happiness. They talked for hours on end about dream lore, which
Valéon enjoyed immensely and considered it as compensation for the years
they had both suffered in the nightmare's clutches.
It was because of this
that Valéon felt that
admitting his struggle

would only burden
others unnecessarily.

Who wanted to hear
of the horrors
of the former
Ribbon Fortress?

Of the ribbons and needles
that had pierced him
and embedded
themselves
into his flesh
to control
his movements
against his will?

Of the extraction
of his voice
through a procedure
of bloodied needles and ribbon
that made his throat burn for days?

Who wished to know
of the Ribbon Queen's despair
that deteriorated into
her isolation and madness?

Who desired to know
of the methods of torture
inflicted on him,
the way his wings
were torn from his back

in agonizing manner,
the humiliation
and degradation
that had stripped him
of dignity and hope?

No one.
Not even him.

Valéon wondered if he could erase
the memories and the pain.
So far, he found
no solution,
no remedy.
But he was presented with one when Crystal looked into his eyes and studied him closely. She diagnosed his predicament without knowing a thing about what he had gone through.

"You're drowning in problems, aren't you?
Ones you can't tell anyone else about?
Halas practically wore that look all the time.
And Emily always gets that look too; she started it.
She looked that way today at the Paperweight Café.
She won't tell me what's going on. She never does.
She listens to everyone,
helps them even when she's got nothing left to give,
doesn't say a word about how it stresses her,
and then she burns herself out. Every time.
She's got to stop doing that.
And she tells *me* to draw boundaries…"

Crystal sighed a long sigh after that long outburst and shook her head.
"Older sister or not, she's terrible at asking for help.

Hey, Valéon, could you do me a favor?"

Valéon blinked.
  Somewhere,
  a deep ache
  within him
  was put to ease
  as he bowed his head and said,
  "Gladly. What do you need?"

"Can you give Em this?"
  Crystal tore out the paper from her notebook,
  folded it in quarters,
  and handed it to him.
  She must have noticed his curiosity,
  because she blushed and admitted,
  "It's a new description.
  I haven't written in so long,
  I think I've lost my edge.
  But I really liked working on it;
  it made me think I could come back to writing characters again.
  And then you showed up and made my day.
  I almost thought you were Halas, but then I noticed your wings.
  I'm *so* glad Emily helped you get them back on again."

Valéon just listened. To know that the Sky Maiden held this much affection
and to see it openly expressed comforted him. It was as if all the things
that Crystal hadn't been able to tell him for the years he was in captivity,
she told him now. Then she gave him another huge hug. This time, she
whispered softly to him, her breath tickling his ear.

"Tell Em that she needs to take time for herself. If she keeps living day-
by-day for other people, one day she's going to wake up and realize she
never lived her life. I don't want that. She's got dreams of her own, and I

want to see her reach them."

    Returning the embrace, Valéon murmured,

    "You know, Crystal, you could write what you just said.

    It would be easier to pass on the message that way."

"I know," Crystal said, finally letting go.

    "But it's better if you say it.

    Besides, she misses you.

    You should stop by and say 'hello,' like you did for me.

    If you're visiting on business to deliver a message,

    then what's to stop you two from catching up on life afterwards?"

    At that, Valéon paused. He saw Crystal tilt her head with a questioning look to prompt him to say what was on his mind. He ruffled his wings in admission before saying,

"Odd that you should mention business…

    I actually came here to ask you

    about what you thought I should do,

    now that the Pondragai Estate

    has been dissolved,

    and Lord Leuthe,

    Lady Laehna,

    and Halas

    are gone.

I have nowhere left to go,

    nothing left to do."

Crystal's eyes teared up slightly, but she said,

    "You'll always have a home and a family.

    It might be different than your first,

    but it can be just as good and special.

    Besides, you still have

lots of places to go
and lots of things to do.
Go find Emily, and ask how you can help.
She needs you. More than you know."
She lightly tapped the paper she had given to Valéon.
"And since this is the first message you're delivering,
I'll make an exception. You can read it; it's about you anyway."
With yet another hug, Crystal sent Valéon off on his first assignment in years. But soon after leaving the Sky Maiden's domain and coming back to the Sky Realm once more, Valéon took a moment to pause and open the paper Crystal had entrusted to his care. Standing atop a cloud, with the wind picking up around him, Valéon gripped the message tight as he read:

After years of unspeakable suffering and hardship,
the living legacy of peace between the nations looks to the future.

With his wings and voice restored,
Valéon enters a new stage of life and searches to fulfill his purpose.

He is a message of reconciliation and restoration to all who will listen.
He is a messenger to all who need a reminder that hope lives and speaks.

Who will heed the messenger's call?
Who will listen to his voice?

Make way for the beloved messenger,
whose message is peace.

It moved him,
and Valéon hastily wiped away
his unexpected tears,
taking care not to ruin the paper
that held such kind words.

The Sky Maiden was not gifted
  with a voice of power
  or an affinity with words or ink,
  but that didn't make her message
  any less powerful.

That was exactly
  what he had needed.

That single paper gave him
  purpose, meaning, and direction.

For so long, yet another piece of paper
  had done the same for him.
  Only back then,
  it had been
  the peace treaty draft
  that he had kept safe until
  he had been able to pass it off
  to another keeper in a dream.

With the peace treaty draft no longer in his care,
  Valéon had felt like a part of himself was strangely missing.

This new message did not replace the void within him in the same way,
  but it did fill him with a new feeling,
  like there was still much in his life that he had to do before he was done.
  All this had come from Crystal. How could he ever repay her? Valéon
didn't know. But he was grateful. It made him proud to be of the sky and
to have the Sky Maiden as the Legend of his homeland. And it made him
glad that he now had a reason to seek out Emily, or the Ribbon Princess by
title. Valéon hadn't mentioned it to anyone either, but he missed her too.
It would be nice to visit Emily again, see how she was doing, give her this

21

message and tell her what Crystal said, ask what she needed.

For some reason, as he flew in the air, his wings beating steadily to bear him to his next destination, Valéon thought about the last sentence he had read in Crystal's message.

Make way for the beloved messenger,
  whose message is peace.

Valéon couldn't get it out of his mind,
  and he couldn't help but wonder:
  did that mean that their
  second peace treaty,
  which hadn't
  materialized
  as of yet,
  was
  on the way?

He certainly hoped so.

3

Crisis

S tanding on a cliff overlooking the sea,
     Darkon, King of Kites,
        beheld the sky, land, and sea
   as kite after kite fell around him.

They dropped from the sky, through the clouds,
   swept in one direction or another by the wind that whipped across the
land.

Some kites plummeted into the sea
   and were lost to the ocean's depths.

Others were washed up on shore.

Yet others crashed onto the rocky cliffs
   or above in the landscape of green hills.

Had he been younger and more inexperienced,
   the King of Kites might have panicked,
   rushed to gather his advisors,
   called for assistance at once.

But Darkon had been ruler of his beloved kingdom for over two decades.
  And though all visible signs seemed to pronounce this situation a crisis,
  the Kite King was loath to lose his head over this mysterious occurrence.
  It was not an isolated case, this loss of kites.
  It was a condition that was pervasive throughout the kingdom,
  and it affected kites of nobility and kites of commoners alike.

To say the citizens
  of the Kite Kingdom were alarmed
  would be an understatement.

The people of the kite
  prided themselves on their self-sufficiency,
  boasting they were the only people in all of the North or South
  who could afford to have a King more absent than present in their
  country.

As citizens, they were fiercely loyal
  and defended their King and his efforts
  to encourage the peace efforts through their independence
  and ability to conduct their lives and business on their own.

This was the first time in twenty years
  that the people had requested
  the presence and guidance of their King,
  pleaded for him to come, in fact.

Darkon gripped the letter that he had received until it crumpled in his fist.
  It had been delivered to him by Queen Katarina,
  his faithful wife, beloved queen, and most trusted advisor.

In her desperate efforts to reach him, she had traveled through half
  of the neighboring countries on a series of failing kites.

Every time one lost its life and fell to the earth below,
she had summoned another to take its place.

Katarina went through a dozen kites to reach him,
and had nearly crashed her last one into his kite,
as it too, failed like the rest.

Thankfully, Queen Katarina had brought with her over two dozen kites
and was able to bring them both back to their kingdom in one piece.
Of course, they had no kites left by the time they returned.

But at least they were back.
At least he was back.
Darkon took in a deep breath. He knew his citizens awaited his word
with anticipation and baited breath. They were such a reserved and private
people, no one would dare to approach him directly to ask an explanation
or demand a solution. No, they would quietly wait for his pronouncement
and obey his command without question, as they had always done. And
that was what concerned Darkon the most.

He almost wished there were some outburst of outrage or panic to quell.
At least then he would know the condition of his people, hear the state of
their minds and hearts. But they were too much like him. Too dedicated
to aiding others to admit that they had reached the end of their rope. Too
proud to slow down and rest. Too ashamed to give voice to their pain.

Deep within him, Darkon knew what they knew. He had no answer.
He didn't know what was wrong with his nation and its kite epidemic,
and he didn't know what to do about it.

But Darkon also knew that his people drew their strength from him.
More than anything, they just wanted him to be close.
If nothing else, they were comforted by his presence, glad to see his face,
relieved to hear his voice, even if he had no remedy to offer.

The King of Kites tried to fight the terrible bout of dread
　　that swept into his chest like the incoming tide, wave after wave.

He tried to fend off the fears and doubts that dropped into
　　his heart and mind like each of the kites that continued to fall from the
sky.

According to Katarina, this wasn't a nightmare outbreak,
　　like so many countries of the north and south now fought to keep at bay.

According to August, his eldest son, this wasn't a case
　　of a lack of diversity or variation in craftsmanship.

According to Griffin, his middle son, this wasn't a case
　　of a kite rebellion, for the kites held no breath or life in them when they
fell.

According to Den, his youngest son, who had miraculously memorized
　　the entirety of the kite archives before it had been lost,
　　there was no historical record that could account for this occurrence.

So what exactly was he dealing with?
　　Darkon attempted a cheerful hum to stay his anxiety
　　and bent down to examine a kite that had knocked into him
　　before tumbling down to his feet.

Kites were the livelihood of his people.
　　Kites supported their economy, provided transportation,
　　assisted in keeping the flow of trade steady,
　　and helped build good relations with other countries.
　　The reliability and high quality of their work was the hallmark of their
nation.
　　Darkon picked up the green kite, held it up to the wind and gave it a

gentle hoist to see if it would take to the air and fly. Nothing. The kite was lifeless. Darkon turned over the kite in his hands, examined it for any tell-tale signs of damage, illness, or corruption. There was no mark of disturbance, no nightmare strands attached to the kite. It was as if the kite had been fine and then somehow reverted to the state of the southern kites that couldn't fly, expand, or shrink on their own.

And then he realized that he was late for a meeting. He had promised Avorne and Renadé, the King and Queen of Eld Mané respectively, that he would come to discuss beginning the second peace treaty attempt. He had been on his way down south to Eld Mané as well, until Katarina had intercepted him and turned his course back for home.

Well, it was too late now,

and he had no way of sending word of what had happened.

By the looks of things, there weren't any kites that were at full capacity.

Darkon took in a deep breath and let out a long sigh.

He needed help, and he didn't know how to go about requesting it.

Fortunately, he didn't have to consider it for long. His thoughts were interrupted by the sound of running footsteps and a hasty call.

"Hey Dad, I got an idea!"

Darkon turned around and almost got bowled over by his oldest son, who took a hold of his shoulders and grinned from ear to ear, though he was sweating and out of breath. It was August. As the eldest and responsible son, August rarely acted on impulse without thinking, so this display of enthusiasm took Darkon by surprise.

"What idea?" Darkon asked, eyeing August with a puzzled look.

He noted the windswept state of his son's chestnut hair that was usually combed neatly and fell about his shoulders in graceful waves.

"Did you run all the way here from the palace?"

"More or less," August took in a gulp of air and tried to catch his breath. The royal purple robes of his son had somehow remained meticulously clean – without crease or wrinkle – even after being subjected to all that

27

sudden activity.

Darkon couldn't help but chuckle,

"Why didn't you send Griffin?"

Of the three brothers, Griffin – the second son – was the strongest and fittest, the kite tamer of the family. As the first son, August crafted the royal kites and released them into the sky, and the third son, Den was the one who took the tamed kites and organized them in the archives. The running joke within the royal family was that instead of being endowed equally with talent, strength, and intelligence, each prince was given only one quality to steward. Or as August, Griffin, and Den claimed, the eldest got all the craftsmanship, the middle got all the brawn, and the youngest got all the brains.

"He's trying to be helpful," August scowled.

"Right now he's with Den, sorting through the archives we lost. I swear Grif is more trouble when he doesn't have any kites to go chase and wrestle with. He's making a mess. But you know Den. That kid's got more patience in him than two dozen kite lives and then some. I don't know how he does it. But anyway, I've got an idea."

"Which is…?" Darkon waited for the answer.

"We should request the presence of the Ribbon Princess," August answered, as he unwound a bright blue sash from his waist over his robes. He offered it to his father, and the gold threads woven in with the blue gleamed whenever the sunlight broke through the clouds.

"August." A sigh escaped from Darkon.

"That was years ago. You were all boys back then.

The Ribbon Princess was a child as well.

You've all grown. Emily is a year shy of thirty.

She has her own domain to maintain, her own to look after.

We can't just conjure her up at our beck and call."

Darkon did not say that as Ribbon Princess and Legend of Silkairen,

Emily was practically a cousin to them in her life philosophy.

She helped everyone, never said no,
　　and couldn't ask for help even if she needed it.
　　She was prone to taking on too much for too many people for too long.
　　Emily was the last person Darkon wanted to ask for help.

"But she came when you needed her most last time,"
　　August was undeterred. "She was the one who rescued Valéon.
　　And she helped you all to defeat not just one, but two nightmares.
　　Emily's not called a Legend for nothing.
　　And I understand she has plenty of responsibilities. So do I.
　　She's only a bit younger than me; we've got six years between us.
　　But she gave us her word, as Ribbon Princess and as a friend.
　　Don't you remember what she said?"

Darkon shook his head and took the bright blue sash from his son.
　　He remembered, but he wasn't sure if those words
　　could hold strong and true in the face of a crisis like this.

Misunderstanding the silence,
　　August began to say,
　　"She said –"

Darkon cut off his son's gallant attempt to remind him
　　by giving voice to the promise he received
　　from one he considered to be the daughter
　　he always wanted but never had.

"If you ever need me, just call.
　　I'll be there. No matter what."

"So let's call," August prompted him.
　　"If not a time like this, then when?"

Hesitating, Darkon confessed,
    "I can't find it in myself to ask for help."

"Then don't ask,"
    August said it as if it were
    the easiest conclusion to draw.
    "Just call."

Leave it to his oldest son who loved the Ribbon Princess with his entire being to convince him to call. Darkon gave a half-hearted grunt of acknowledgement before lifting the blue sash closer to his face.

And there,
    he spoke the name
    of the beloved Legend of Silkairen,
    their neighboring kingdom.
    "Emily."

With that one word,
    the blue sash shimmered in the Kite King's hands
    before fading completely.
    There. It was done.

Darkon looked at August and confided in his oldest son.
    "Do you think she'll come?"

August just gave him a look.
    "Dad. It's Emily. She always does, even if she's up to her ears in other people's emergencies...though I'm hoping she's learned how to deal with that by now. She'll show up. And when she does, you should tell her what's going on. If you don't, then I will. Because she won't know how to help if she doesn't know what the problem is."
    Darkon shook his head in amazement. Since when had August come

to sound so much like the Ribbon Princess? Still, it comforted him to see his son speak so wisely and firmly. It gave him hope about passing on his kingship to August someday in the future. Darkon felt relief fill the space where anxiety once weighed him down.

"Well, I suppose Katarina, Griffin, and Den would love to see Emily too. I better think of what to tell her when she does come."

4

Declining In Order to Accept

Sitting on the third step from the bottom of the stairwell connecting the kitchen to the second floor living quarters, Emily took a break from her shift at the Paperweight Café. Her coworkers rushed in and out of the kitchen, filling and taking out orders or bringing in dishes to be washed. Brook stood by the sink, faithfully washing the dishes that were piling high beside her on the counter. Alex, who was helping out for the holiday rush, stood by the oven, half-singing and half-whistling the latest pop song, while checking on the brownies. Luke and William argued in fits and starts, acting completely unruffled whenever they went out to wait on the customers, and then picking up their dispute from where they left off whenever they returned to the kitchen. Jess, their manager, was upstairs taking care of bills and updating her many lists.

Lavender, Luke's younger sister, had settled next to Emily on the second step from the bottom and was relating her high school woes. Listening to this, and trying to convince this usually peppy and self-assured sixteen-year-old that anyone who asked you to do their work for them was most definitely not a friend, Emily wondered if anything she said was sinking in.

"Can you just…talk to her?" Luke had asked her in desperation as they worked the counter and tables together yesterday. He'd been tugging on his sleeve so much in the past few weeks that Emily had worried he'd wear a hole in it if he kept at it. Luke had been a childhood friend and neighbor for many years. And while he had a flair for the dramatic and tended to exaggerate things, from his annoyance with William to his descriptions of women he adored, Luke was also an overprotective brother. Luke would rather die than admit in front of Lavender that he was worried about her. Emily knew that. She also knew that Luke thought his little sister was falling in with the wrong crowd because of a boy she liked at school.

"But if I don't do their work,

then they won't let me sit with them at lunch,"

Lavender was saying.

"And then I won't have a chance to say 'hi' to Cory."

According to Lavender, the girls in the "in" group at school had all been trying to get Cory to notice them all year long, but he didn't seem to be interested. The other day, he had been assigned to be Lavender's lab partner during chemistry, and the two of them had hit it off really well. Cory had said he liked Lavender's style, and thought she was one of the smartest girls in class. After that, the girls had zeroed in on Lavender and tried to get her to hang out with them.

"So you worked with him on a lab,"

Emily said. "A lab is a lab. Not a date."

"But he came to sit next to me in class after that,"

Lavender pointed out.

"He's been coming for two weeks.

He even talks with Jamie and Lynn.

They like him too.

They were super surprised that he joined.

People treat me differently now.

It's like everyone actually sees me."

There were so many things Emily could have said to that.

That having a friend that bumped your social status into favor

could be just as easily lost as it was won.

33

That you couldn't judge someone's intent
through two weeks of interaction.
That friendship – and romance –
was something that took time.

But what Emily said instead was,
    "If this were some other classmate,
    would you ditch your friends
    who love you for who you are
    to go with other people who say
    they'll only be friends with you
    if you to do their homework?"

Lavender was taken aback,
    and she bit her lip before looking down. "No."

Emily felt sympathy for the girl.
    "I bet it's nice to be noticed. It feels good, right?"
    "It feels great," Lavender murmured.
    "Well, don't sacrifice who you are for that feeling."

She offered her best piece of advice.
    "Find a better solution. You're smart. Use those brains, girl!
    I know you'll find a way without compromising yourself."
    Emily was glad to see Lavender perk up at that.
    She knew she had succeeded when the girl jumped up, skipped over to
Alex to ask for a brownie, and then intercepted Luke, who had entered the
kitchen again, with a tight hug.
    Luke, intent on continuing his argument with William, got distracted by
this burst of affection from his sister, and just patted her awkwardly on the
back while holding up a tray of empty dishes. Meanwhile, he shot Emily a
bemused look as if to ask, "what did you say?"
    Emily shrugged with a smile and gave him a thumbs-up. They'd see how

things panned out, but Emily let the informal counseling session go. She
had plenty of other things on her mind.

Henry had called,
    asking if she'd be up for watching a nature documentary with him
    if he brought a batch of homemade Christmas cookies.
    He'd been fine for the most part,
    but he still got depressed around the holidays,
    because his younger brother,
    who died in a car accident years ago,
    had been an enthusiast for fun festivities,
    cheerful decorations, and making baked goods.

Abby had sent her a series of messages throughout the day:
    mad at mom and dad – again. can i spend the night with you?
    never mind, they apologized a bajillion times
    said they'd buy me a new cello…i hope they don't.
    twice is enough, and this one is already mad expensive
    i just wish they'd show up for once
    how hard is it to come to a concert that's 2 hours long, i mean, really
    and i nailed my solo. got a standing ovation and everything -
    how cool is that?
    Crys came even though she's cramming for finals,
    said it inspired her to write
    and she stopped by at the café before and
    said it was packed and super busy.
    anyway, i just needed to vent…i'll be fine. how are you?

Emily messaged back:
    Congrats on the standing ovation!
    Sorry I missed your performance.
    Café's crazy. I'm fine.
    You sure you're okay?

She had to smile at the instant reply:
    you're exempt cuz you've come
    to all my other concerts.
    i'm good.
    oh, and don't listen to
    everyone else's problems.
    love you, bye!

Her attention was brought to the creaking boards of the second floor.
    Jess, her manager, called from the top of the stairs, "Ribbons."

"Yeah," Emily responded automatically
    to the nickname for her that had stuck at the Paperweight Café.

It wasn't absurd that it was a reference
    to the ribbons Emily wore in her hair;
    it was absurd that it had become
    such an endearing way of addressing her.
    Especially because no one knew it was a reference
    to a title and position that Emily held elsewhere.

No one knew about the Ribbon Princess here,
    and Emily was content to keep it that way.
    But it was strange how that nickname brought to memory
    adventures in another place
    with another set of friends
    every time she heard it.

Emily stood up and pocketed her phone.
    "What do you need?"

"Come to my office,"
    Jess replied with a nod of her head.

"It'll only be a minute."

Emily blinked
   and said,
   "sure."

She went up the creaky wooden stairs, walked down the hall until she reached Jess's bedroom that doubled as an office. It had three file cabinets on one side of the wall, a couch, a laundry basket, and a desk with a chair.

   Jess rearranged lists on the bulletin board on the wall, and took the time to retie her long black hair into a ponytail. As she did, she eyed Emily and asked,

   "How would you like to cover some extra shifts in the next few weeks?"

Emily shrugged.
   "I can cover whatever you need me to."

Jess adjusted the red apron that had "#1 Boss" emblazoned at the front over her white collared shirt, crisp dark jeans, and high heeled boots. Then pursing her lips, Jess frowned and said,
   "Let me rephrase:
   Can you afford to work extra hours in the next few weeks?"

Jess plopped onto her couch,
   crossed one leg over the other
   and leaned back
   to rest her left arm on the back cushion.

"I heard your chat with Lavender.
   I was there when you waited on Ryan and Vincent this morning,
   and asked how Ryan's Dad was
   and if the doctors figured out what was going on.
   I heard you call Katarina after and ask if she needed anything,

37

even if it was just a hospital visit."

Jess kept going.

"The other day, you reminded your parents to attend Abby's concert
   and tried to convince them that being home for Christmas
   would mean more to your sisters than sending them on a cruise.

Last week, you got a call from an acquaintance having relationship trouble.
   The week before that, it was someone who struggled with bad spending
habits
   who was trying to pay off their credit card debt.

Last month, it was a friend dealing with depression and anxiety.
   Then there was the time you counseled someone who had eating
disorders
   and a suicidal tendency on top of that.

And you listen to Luke, Alex, and William all the time. Even Brook."

Emily found herself at a loss for words.
   She thought she had done a decent job
   keeping the issues she was dealing with
   separate
   and
   in seclusion.

For the most part, the people she helped didn't know of the others she
counseled informally, and she preferred to keep it that way. She didn't
realize how much her manager had picked up on, just by being in close
proximity.
   Jess sighed,
   "Ribbons, I don't know where your reserves of patience come from, but

frankly, I'm amazed you're not a walking basket case. You're going to hit your limit."

Emily managed to cobble together a reply.
"Did you just offer me hours and advise me not to take them?"

Jess didn't flinch.
"I'm offering you the same as everyone else. I get that your decision matrix is highly influenced by being the oldest and responsible one in your family and social circle. But at some point, you need to consider yourself."

This permission to decline lifted a weight off of Emily's shoulders, and she said,
"It would be best for me to keep my set hours and not take on anything else."

Jess approved,
"Good. Now, there's one more thing. It's about taking off the weekend."
She waved away Emily's look of protest with one hand.
"We'll be fine. I'm giving a few paid vacation days in addition to the ones everyone already scheduled in. We had a good year. With our surplus, I have enough to put into savings and be extra generous."

"I don't know what to say,"
Emily said.

"The usual 'thank you' will suffice," Jess grinned.
"Do my heart good, Ribbons.
Treat yourself to something special.
I don't know what that would be, but I bet you do."

Emily thought for a minute and said,
"Well, there *is* an invitation sitting on my dresser drawer

that's waiting a long overdue response.
I've wanted to go, but things keep coming up."

"Don't wait for it," Jess advised.
"Make room for it.
Or you'll never get around to it."

"Thanks," Emily grinned.
"You know, for having a hard-as-nails reputation,
you sure have a soft side.
You have the makings of a good counselor."

Jess snorted.
"Don't kid yourself.
I don't have your patience.
Never did, never will.
I'll stick with my expertise instead."

"Which is…"
Emily began.

Jess pointed to the "#1 Boss" apron she wore
that had been lovingly and jokingly bestowed upon her
by Luke and Alex last year for Christmas.

"Maintaining my hard-as-nails reputation, Ribbons,
maintaining my hard-as-nails reputation.
It's not easy being number one."

Emily laughed at that.
"No, it's not. Where would we be without you?"

"Unemployed," Jess didn't hide her amusement.

"Or employed somewhere else. Hopefully that."

She became serious as she added,

"And I'd be stuck with a failing family business that I inherited after my folks passed away. But what am I saying? You're making me sentimental. Get out of here."

"Right,"

Emily smiled.

"Back to work."

"Actually, your extra vacation hours start now."

Jess didn't wait for Emily to express her surprise and just said,

"Go to the hospital, Ribbons.

Take care of what you have to take care of,

and you'll feel better about treating yourself without feeling guilty."

With a thankful heart, Emily did just that. She left for the hospital immediately. It was a short visit. Scott had just fallen asleep after being subjected to a battery of tests from the doctors, and Katarina was at his bedside while they waited for results. Emily didn't even have a chance to ask Ryan's mother how she was when she was given a little bright blue bundle.

"What's this?" Emily felt something wrapped in all the bright and soft woven cloth.

"Just a little something for you," Katarina replied.

"We've been meaning to give it to you for a couple weeks,

but with so many hospital visits, we never got to wrap it."

"He'll be fine," Emily heard herself saying with conviction.

It surprised her almost as much as it surprised Katarina, but in the back of her mind, Emily remembered her friends who claimed she had a voice of power. She remembered how they said her words were a gift, even if she didn't understand what she was saying or the reason why.

41

"Scott needs rest. Besides, he'd rather be with you at home
    than on another business trip halfway across the world during Christmas.
    He'll be on his feet again soon enough. Until then, take good care of him."

Emily found herself buried in a tight embrace.

"I'll do just that," Katarina promised.
    "I'll let you know if we hear anything from the doctors.
    Thank you for coming. I'll let Scott know that you stopped by when he's
awake."

"Actually, before I go," Emily paused.
    "Was there anything you two wanted for Christmas?
    It's been so crazy, I haven't had a chance to get anything for anybody."

Katarina took in a deep breath.
    "Well, Scott said earlier he wished he could visit the Kite Kingdom again
    to see how the three sons of the King and Queen of Kites were doing,
    and to see how the Ribbon Princess had grown as well."

"I could ask Ryan, Vincent, and Crystal
    to write something for you two," Emily offered.

"It isn't their story to write,"
    Katarina pointed out.
    "It's only yours to tell."

"Well, I'll see what I can do about that," Emily said,
    thinking storytelling was not in her comfort zone.

But she suggested, "The next time we all get together maybe.
    At my place, with you, Scott, Ryan, Vincent, and Crystal.
    But I'll have to find the right adventure to tell first."

With that, she said goodbye to Katarina and left, relieved to get away from the smell of hospital that still lingered on her clothing as she walked to her car in the parking lot.

After driving home to her apartment, Emily called Henry while still in the car and left a message on his voicemail.

"Hey Henry, it's Em. That's fine with me.
How about Monday night after work?
Let me know either way. See you."

All the while, she had been unwrapping the gift from Scott and Katarina. By the time she hung up and put her phone in her coat pocket, Emily found that the gift sitting on her lap was actually two gifts, instead of one.

The cloth "wrapping" was the most beautiful, bright blue scarf that Emily had seen. Delicate strands of golden thread were interwoven among the blue threads, and Emily took a liking to it immediately. And at its heart, nestled safely between the silky folds of scarf, lay a book. With a matching color scheme, the book's cover boasted a deep blue jacket displaying yellow-gold lettering for its title which read, *Gold: Leadership at Heart*.

Opening it to look inside,
she caught sight of Scott's handwritten note on the front cover:

To our Ribbon Princess, who was born to be a leader of the highest caliber:
 Today, we celebrate your heart of gold.
 Proud to be yours,
 The King and Queen of Kites

Closing the book, Emily brushed her fingers along the spine. She turned the book over, glanced at the book blurb accompanied by endorsements and praise. She peeked at the inside flap of the jacket cover that provided the author information. Apparently, this was the same author who had written *Bold: Leadership for All Times*, a longtime favorite of Emily's.

What a timely gift. Emily wrapped the scarf around her neck and gathered her things from the car. The entire way up the elevator to the top floor, she held the book in her arms like it was a treasure. When she got out of the elevator and walked down the hall, Emily realized that someone was waiting outside her apartment door, leaning casually against it.

For a fleeting moment, she wondered if Henry had come by unannounced and not gotten her message about meeting on Monday. But then she registered the silver hair, the enormous wings, and the silks and scarves that still held them onto the back of the visitor who waited at her door. It didn't dampen her surprise though.

"Valéon?" Emily hadn't seen Valéon in months.
    "What are you doing here?"

The widest grin took over Valéon's face
    as he held out a piece of lined paper that had been folded into quarters.
    "Crystal sent me to give this to you. And she wanted me to tell you something,
    but why don't we go inside first? It's freezing out here."

Emily smiled and handed him the key to her apartment.
    "You could have waited inside."

"After you advised me not to pace in other people's hallways?"
    Valéon took the key and opened the door with amusement.
    "I'll stick with your advice."

"That was when we had first met,"
    Emily grunted as she followed
    Valéon into her place
    and shut the door behind her.

"Before I knew about you

or your world
and everything else.

Now we're..."
    She flipped on the lights and felt a comfort
    settle in her chest as she finished,
    "friends."

"That we are," Valéon agreed
    as he helped Emily get out of her coat
    and hung it up in the closet for her.
    He handed her the folded paper.
    "Read this while I get the tea ready."

"Oh, so we're doing tea now?"
    Emily raised an eyebrow as she looked up at Valéon.

"Why not? I waited a long time," Valéon shrugged.
    "And you look like you could loosen up and relax.
    Or do you live on the edge of exhaustion every day?"

"Ouch," Emily said.
    "I'm looking worse than you, is that it?"

"You're the one who said it, not me,"
    Valéon said as he moved into her kitchen.

Had he just ruffled his wings at her?

"Show off," Emily shook her head
    and a tired laugh tumbled out of her.
    "Where have you been all this time? I've missed you."

Valéon pulled out one of the chairs at the small,
    battered, wooden table for two and said emphatically,
    "Save the questions. We've got all night. So settle down and read."

"Yes sir," Emily didn't know why it felt so good to accept that offer,
    and she wondered about how nice it felt to be treated this way,
    with care, close attention, and affection.

And for the first time in months,
    Emily allowed herself to rest in the presence of her friend.

5

Hope in Paper and Flame

Avorne wasn't usually one to worry.
    That was Halas's well-known habit.

    And while Avorne dearly missed Halas,
who had been dead for a few years now,
he wasn't quite sure he wanted to pick up
on his half-brother's unproductive habit.

But he was concerned that Darkon hadn't come
    for their meeting like he said he would.

The Kite King was always punctual
    and consistently arrived on a cheery note.

It had been over three hours,
    and there was no sign of Darkon anywhere.

And seeing the state of the kite
    that Tal had crashed
    through Renadé's ink portal,
    Avorne couldn't help but envision

Darkon's kite failing
while en route to Eld Mané.

Recruiting Tal to help Renadé fix the broken ink portal from that morning,
   Avorne also asked if they'd make a few adjustments in the ink lines
   and open it into the Kite Kingdom.

It would be a bit rude, Tal and Renadé both informed him.
   Especially since it would be similar to having someone
   coming to the palace here without any warning, like Tal did.

But this was Darkon, Avorne reasoned with them.

He had a hard time imagining the Kite King being angry at anyone.
   Besides, Avorne felt he could afford having Darkon upset at him
   if it meant that he knew his ally was alive and well.

It seemed that he wasn't the only one who was worried.
   Renadé and Tal didn't take much convincing at all.

In unison, they raised the ink lines they carried off of their skin
   and twisted the ink characters into the appropriate configuration.

When the ink lines were laid out and arranged upon the portal,
   the ink around the gateway glowed bright blue, then violet.

It opened into the Kite Kingdom.

The sight it revealed
   made Avorne's stomach
   wrench.

Kites fell from the sky filled with clouds,

down upon the grassy hills,
past the cliff side by the sea,
and into the ocean.

What was going on?

He stepped through the portal before Renadé or Tal could protest.
A kite nearly struck him in the head as he did,
but Avorne just clutched at it and held it out before him.

"You shouldn't be lifeless like our kites in the south,"
he murmured to the limp kite.

"You should be flying in the air, full of vitality and life.
What happened?"

"Nothing that you need to concern yourself with,"
a strained voice spoke from a distance.
Avorne looked to his side, and beheld Darkon, King of Kites. The older
man was dressed in his usual kingly garb, a colorful patchwork coat, over a
plain shirt and pants, complete with worn black boots. The wind blew the
kite king's neatly combed brown hair into a tousle that sometimes blew
into his matching brown eyes. But what struck Avorne most was that no
trace of a smile was on Darkon's face. For the first time, the Kite King
looked tired and harrowed.

"Darkon, are you all right? Are you in some sort of trouble?"
Avorne fumbled with his words, lifted the kite in his hands as he offered,
"Can I help you in any way?"

"I'm fine. I can take care of this," Darkon replied tersely.
"You can help by going back to Eld Mané
and figuring out the next step

for the second peace treaty attempt without me."

"Without you?" Avorne balked.
    "Darkon, it's been twenty years
    since the first peace treaty attempt.
    The world won't end if we wait a little longer
    and get your kingdom up and running again.
    You're an integral part to our peace efforts.
    You've helped us from the beginning,
    even when we were of the south
    and you of the extreme north.
    I'm not doing this without you."

"Yes, it's taken twenty years
    when it should have succeeded the first time,"
    Darkon didn't hide his bitterness.
    "There's no time to waste.
    You're the best bet we've got to mend what never should have been
broken.
    I'm sorry I missed our meeting, but you're fully capable
    of taking the first steps on your own. I...
    I'll join you when this is resolved."

"Why not let us help?" Avorne tried again.
    "You've helped us countless times in the past.
    I'm not sure what we could offer you,
    but we're more than willing to assist in any way we can."

Darkon shook his head,
    firmly took the kite out from Avorne's grasp.

"No, Avorne. Go home and figure out how to begin
    the second peace treaty attempt.

That's where your responsibilities are,
not here."

It was the first time that Avorne found the word "stubborn"
rise to his mind as he beheld his old friend and ally.

That same persistence with which Darkon provided so much support
to outsiders had somehow transformed into a stubbornness
to refuse help now. Avorne couldn't understand why.
Why would anyone decline help? Especially in the face of such dire need?

Avorne knew as well as Darkon did
that the Kite Kingdom was in big trouble.

"Your crisis
might be resolved faster
if you let others help,"
he began to say.

Lucky for him, Darkon's refusal was interrupted
by a man some years younger than Avorne
who came running towards them.

Avorne recognized him to be Darkon's oldest son, named August.
They both nodded their greetings to each other
and shared a look that begged, "Can you do something?"
and a silent "Sorry, I tried," regarding Darkon's mood and plight.

"August, you really should just send Griffin next time,"
the worried look on Darkon's face
was replaced by the slightest amusement
as August tried to catch his breath.

51

Avorne was relieved to see a remnant
　　of his friend's good disposition
　　still alive and present.

"I should get going then, I suppose,"
　　he hadn't meant to barge in on Darkon like this,
　　and he really didn't want to stress his friend out more by staying.

"Come as soon as you can,
　　and I'll see what I can do on my own until then."

"You working on peace treaty efforts?"
　　August looked at Avorne with great interest.

"Well…we're trying," Avorne gave a shrug.
　　"I'm at a loss on how to start."

"That I could help you with,"
　　Darkon replied
　　and a smile finally
　　came upon his lips.

"The first stipulation for our new peace treaty efforts,"
　　he stretched out his right hand
　　and let it pan over the horizon,
　　"shall be built on these two words…"

Darkon held up his first finger
　　and then his second
　　as he spoke each word.
　　"No ink."

Avorne felt comforted to witness

the Kite King's dramatic flair once more.
He also understood where Darkon was coming from.

Northern ink had thrown the first peace treaty efforts into chaos
and killed a good portion of both northern and southern representatives.

Under the unfortunate influence of nightmare outbreaks,
ink had become a symbol feared and detested in the south.

It had taken years for people to overcome their prejudice against
those from Inkaien, or Ink Country, for that very reason.

It had also taken some time for the people of Eld Mané to accept the fact
that Renadé, their queen, was an ink prodigy of that same dreaded
country.

Some years ago, Avorne had asked his newly wedded queen
if she had ice in her veins and steel in her bones
to be able to withstand the disapproval of so many citizens.

Renadé had only laughed and said their words were nothing
compared to what she had faced as a child up north in her home country.

She wisely mused that public opinion was subject to change,
and that given enough time or the right circumstances,
people could begin to welcome this alliance between the North and South.

She also informed Avorne that her blood was blood,
and bones just bone, same as his.
"That's what makes us human after all," she had said with a shrug.

"Beneath our affinities is flesh and blood.
We hold the heart, mind, and soul in common."

"No ink," Avorne agreed with a nod to Darkon,
    though he still wasn't sure how to proceed from there.

But heartened by Darkon's willingness to assist
    even in the midst of such a stressful situation,
    Avorne said, "Thanks, Darkon."

Then, he found an offer coming out of his mouth
    that he hadn't even seen coming.

"Our kites at our palace are fully functional,
    so if you want to take those
    until you figure out what's going on,
    feel free to do that."

"Wait," August spoke up before his father had a chance.
    "Your kites are still flying?"

"On their own, as they should be," Avorne confirmed.
    "Tal's is completely busted, but he wasn't using one of the royal kites."

"But how?" Darkon finally managed to get a word in before his son.

"Maybe they just haven't gotten affected by whatever's going on here,"
    Avorne suggested.

"Or maybe there's a pattern to the ones that are still up and running.
    Did you give us a special shipment of kites
    the last time you changed out the kites in the system?"

"They did,"
    Renadé finally poked her head through the ink portal,
    and stepped through all the way.

54

"I suppose here is as good a place as any to have our meeting,"
　　she smiled as she bowed her head in respect to Darkon and August.
　　Then she held out her hand, palm side up,
　　and spoke to the tiny kite that rested in it.

The kite expanded,
　　flew in and out among them with a flourish,
　　and then hovered just in front of Renadé, expecting a command.

Exclamations of surprise came from Darkon and August both.
　　August was the first to step towards the kite
　　and tentatively reach his hand out towards it.

"May I?"
　　He turned to Renadé for permission to examine the live kite.

"It's your craftsmanship,"
　　Renadé smiled.
　　"Go ahead."

August took the kite and gently rested his hand upon it.
　　The kite nudged him,
　　glided up along his arm,
　　and settled just by his shoulder and shivered.

It was as if it sensed the plague of kites around it
　　and wanted to stay as safe as possible.
　　But it also pulsed with soft light,
　　like embers that still held the promise of fire within them,
　　even without flames present.

"If I recall correctly," Renadé said as she took Avorne by the arm gently,
　　"This batch of kites were made specially to be fireproof.

With all the fires sweeping through Vinduren, east of us,
   there was concern that our kites might end up burning along with the
land."

"These are the kites that we made
   from the paper manufactured in Kalos Fyrian?"
   Darkon murmured. He reached out for the kite,
   and it willingly let itself be picked up and held by its king.

Kalos Fyrian,
   better known in the south as the Land of Fire,
   was the neighboring country to Inkaien, or Ink Country.

"I believe so," Renadé answered.
   "Because most of the fires were stemming from the firewalls
   that came up unexpectedly around there,
   we thought the kites would be a good defense and symbol of neutrality.

I'm not sure if it worked, but most of the fires didn't come across the border.
   The most serious case was Duke Vandek's estate in Lucante
   almost burning down, but the flames mysteriously withdrew
   when one of the estate kites flew around the manor."

"So if kites made from the paper of Kalos Fyrian are still alive,
   then you could craft a few kites from that same material
   to serve as emergency transportation until you can
   get the other kites up and running," Avorne said hopefully.

"But we don't have any more of that paper in stock," August said.
   "It's the most expensive, and for good reason.
   No other paper exists that can wrap fire and not burn.
   It's a prized specialty good."

"Then a visit to Kalos Fyrian is in order," Darkon concluded.

"The firewalls are still up around the country," Avorne pointed out.
    "It's been eight to ten years since they set their borders ablaze.
    We haven't heard from the royal family or a single citizen in that time
either."

He was surprised to have a sealed scroll
    handed to him just then by Renadé,
    who procured it out of the sash
    that she wore around her waist.

"What's this?" Avorne asked.

"A word from Vinduren," Renadé said.
    "Came this afternoon.
    Take a look at the seal."

Avorne did.
    He was shocked to find
    the symbol of a musical note
    intertwining with flame.

"Is this the seal of Ezra Blazewick and Amelia Featherfall?"
    As one who had been taught by Iris,
    royal gardener and his personal tutor,
    Avorne recognized its significance immediately.

Ezra Blazewick, a prince of Kalos Fyrian long ago,
    was the first king of the Dream Realm,
    and Amelia Featherfall, the princess of Vinduren in that same age,
    was the first queen of the Dream Realm.

They were known for suffering from the same illness
    that at the time had no remedy.

It was rumored at the time
    that while Kalos Fyrian held a list of ingredients for a potential cure,
    Vinduren was the only land in which the plants for the cure could be found.

But because of the tension between the north and south,
    no one tried to pursue the impossible endeavor until
    Prince Blazewick wrote a letter to the Princess Featherfall,
    asking for assistance. Of course, Princess Featherfall wrote back.

And so, in an exchange of letters and various gifts,
    the two rulers not only came to love each other dearly,
    but also discovered the basics of dream lore together.

Legend told of a miraculous healing that took place
    in the process of assembling the cure,
    but more miraculous than that was the alliance
    that formed between Kalos Fyrian and Vinduren through that trial.

Afterwards, in their union, the two rulers created a royal seal
    that would forever declare their commitment to each other,
    personally and nationally.

That was this seal that Avorne beheld on the scroll now.
    He ran his fingers lightly over the wax note and flame.
    He hadn't seen a letter from Vinduren or Kalos Fyrian with this seal
    until today.

Whatever message was inside,
    he knew it had to be significant.

"Well, don't just stand there," Tal called
   as he stepped through the ink portal at last,
   hauling the remains of his own kite behind him.
   "Open and read it already."

To Darkon and August, Tal said,
   "Do either of you happen to know
   a good kite doctor in your area?
   My poor kite could use one right about now."

Avorne half-listened to the helpless chuckle that rose from Darkon
   and the discussion that ensued,
   but went on to break the wax seal,
   open the letter, and read:

To the most esteemed Avorne Ehrthann, King of Eld Mané –

Greetings in the name of Eladan.
   May He grant you bold melodies for this time.

I write to ask if I may kindly borrow one of your kites,
   which are rumored to be immune to fire?

If your kites are indeed fireproof,
   then they will be made of the same type
   of paper this letter is written on.
   You can see for yourself that it does not burn.

Under normal circumstances,
   I would have requested this of the Kite Kingdom,
   as kites are their hallmark and specialty.
   But I'm rather pressed for time,
   and thought I could ask you,

59

since Eld Mané is closer in proximity.

For the past few weeks,
　　I have been hearing cries for help at the northern border of Vinduren.
　　It's beyond the Inkstone Mountains and coming from the other side
　　of the firewall in Kalos Fyrian. No one else in my country can hear the pleas,
　　but I can, and I can't ignore this with good conscience anymore.

It is my intention, if you are willing this small provision,
　　to travel through the firewall on a fireproof kite
　　and come to the aid of Prince Elias Blazewick.
　　He has always been a good friend and ally,
　　and I know he would do the same for me
　　if I and my country were in a similar state.

I do not ask for more than a single kite.
　　I suspect a nightmare outbreak is responsible for this,
　　and I aim to go to the source and see for myself.
　　I understand you have plenty of responsibilities
　　and have no wish to waste your time.

If you could let me know either way,
　　I would very much appreciate it.

My thanks to you and all that you stand for,
　　Falleyne Featherfall, Princess of Vinduren

With Renade looking over his shoulder, Avorne read it twice,
　　just to make sure he followed the contents of the letter.
　　He did; the current Princess of Vinduren was quite clear.

For a fleeting moment,
　　he envied the apparent ease

with which the princess wrote.

Writing was something he avoided as much as possible.
  It was hard enough to express his thoughts out loud,
    not to mention organize all his thoughts coherently on paper.

But that feeling was quickly replaced by empathy
  as he considered the princess's predicament.
    No doubt it had been difficult for her to reach out to him,
  especially when she had so little to go off of except her own affinity to
hear.

Those of Vinduren could hear music and song
  everywhere and in everything.
    They heard melodies in people and places,
    harmonies in things and each other.

But to hear something that no one else could hear…
  well, Avorne could relate.

He thought of that mysterious ink sign behind his palace
  in the mountains that no one else could see,
    and he felt he understood the princess of Vinduren completely.
    Because of this, he found himself handing the letter to Darkon.

"You may find a way to help
  and be helped at the same time," Avorne said,
    a bit surprised at his desire to help Princess Featherfall.

This was the first substantial interaction he had encountered
  with Vinduren in all his years as King of Eld Mané.

He already had all sorts of ideas forming in his mind

to help both Princess Featherfall and Darkon,
but for the sake of preserving his friend's dignity,
Avorne just gave a gentle prompt.

"Take a look, and tell me what you think."

6

Unexpected Admission

In Emily's kitchen preparing tea,
Valéon observed his friend
with a growing concern.

While he understood that Legends had much to take care of in their
domains,
he had trouble accepting the fact that the Ribbon Princess
could be so worn out and be in complete denial about it.

Valéon remembered the domain
called the Paperweight Café
where Emily spent most of her time working.

He was aware that she took on a guardian-type of role
among the others there, but he hadn't known a Legend's domain
could take such a toll on the Legend themselves.

What had she been doing?
She didn't say.
And that bothered Valéon the most.

He tried to prod her gently to say something,
 asked a question here or there,
 waited for her to open up.

But she didn't.

Emily wouldn't say a word about what was weighing so heavily on her mind. Valéon recalled Crystal's lament about how Emily wouldn't tell her what was going on. That Emily never did. That Emily listened to everyone, helped them even when she had nothing left to give, didn't say a word about how it stressed her, and then burned herself out. Every time. Valéon had to agree with Crystal, too, that Emily was terrible at asking for help.

It made him wonder.

How could he help someone who didn't know how to ask for help?

Without embarrassing them?

Or making them feel uncomfortable?

If it had been anyone else, Valéon would have just left them to their own devices and let them be. It wasn't his problem, after all. It wasn't his business either. He had no desire or right to meddle in such private matters.

But this was Emily,
 who had returned his wings to him
 when he was a captive
 in the Ribbon Fortress
 under a queen corrupted
 by a nightmare.

This was Emily,
 who had provided him with a refuge and safe harbor
 to recover from the dark enchantments
 that had bound him to the Ribbon Queen's will.

This was Emily,

who talked to him as a close friend
from the first moment she had met him
even when he had no voice,
and treated him with dignity, respect, and love.

He couldn't just leave her.
Not like this.
Not in this state.
And for a moment, Valéon just looked at his poor friend in this sorry state and wondered if it was so very hard to ask for help. Valéon had been without his voice for years, since it had been taken from him – literally extracted from his throat. For years, he had wanted to call out for help from anyone, but had been unable to do so, and it had been a silent agony like nothing else. Valéon found it ironic that those who were still in possession of their voices seemed just as incapable of asking for help.

Valéon wasn't sure how to proceed, so he decided to stick with the basics. He prepared tea the way Emily liked it, the tall mug filled with steaming water, a light steeping of the tea bag, and two spoons of honey, mixed well. He handed hers over, sat down across from her with his own mug of tea, and waited for her to finally relax.

He almost laughed when he heard the first words out of her mouth.
"So how are you?"
It was as if she had been trained to ask that single question and then listen for hours after. Valéon knew better than to fall into the same pattern of behavior as everyone else.

He just said,
"I should be asking you that."
He noted the irony of this reversal.

Emily shrugged.
"You still can.
After you answer.

How are you?"

Valéon shook his head, let out a resigned sigh.

"I'm trying to find a purpose outside of my former role as personal attendant and keeper of the estate library. I miss Lord Leuthe and Lady Laehna and Halas, but I can't grieve their loss forever. They wouldn't want me to. But they were my life. It's hard to reorient myself after regaining my freedom. That's why I visited the Sky Maiden in her domain. And she of course, sent me to you with that."

He pointed to the message he had delivered to Emily.

"What do you think?"

It made him curious as he watched color flush Emily's cheeks as she looked away and down at the description.

"It's...well..."

Emily took her time to think about what to say, drinking her tea in the meantime.

"Your message is about the peace efforts, right?
That second peace treaty attempt
that you and Avorne and Darkon
told me about last time?
I want in on that.
I've wanted to all year.
It's just that things came up.
A lot of things."

"What things?" Valéon asked.

He didn't realize what effect those two small words could have on the direction of their conversation. It was as if he had unclogged a stream bogged down with foliage, and now the water could flow properly. But whatever water had been held back came in floods and torrents.

The first was a list of people

that Valéon did not know or recognize.

The second was a list of problems,
    where only the names of the issues were identified:
    anxiety attacks,
    eating disorders,
    depression,
    suicide,
    estranged family members,
    dysfunctional relationships,
    lawsuits,
    financial trouble,
    death in the family or loss of a loved one,
    gossip,
    bullying,
    car accidents,
    drug addiction,
    alcoholism,
    marital issues,
    struggling children,
    myriads of health problems,
    passive aggressive friends,
    bad parenting,
    escapism,
    workplace challenges,
    home challenges,
    social challenges,
    and more.

Valéon got lost in the names of identified issues alone.

He tried counting them as Emily listed them and got lost somewhere around twenty seven. He rounded up to thirty just to keep the number even. How was it even possible to keep track of that many people and their corresponding problems? Also, why was Emily in possession of all of this knowledge?

"Are you telling them you're available for counseling?"
   Valéon finally managed to ask.
   "Because if you are, you should stop."

Emily laughed into her mug as she was taking a sip and choked on her tea. After coughing, wiping her eyes, apologizing, and laughing some more, Emily said.

"I don't say anything about counseling.
   I say 'hi, how are you?'
   and then I get,
   'my son is failing at school'
   or 'my friends won't talk to me'
   or 'I can't stop my spending habits,
   could you help me?'"

"Tell them 'no,'"
   Valéon said.

Emily stared at him then.
   "How do you say 'no' when you're the first person they've come to for help?
   It's not like I'm looking to be a therapist.
   If people paid me every time they came, I'd be a millionaire."

She paused and then corrected herself,
   "A billionaire."

"But they're not,
   and if they're coming to you with that sort of thing,

then you should tell them to go find professional help.
Do you *want* to listen to all of their issues?"

Emily sighed and looked into her mug.
"No. I just do. They need someone to listen."

"Do you have the time and the energy to listen to all of these people?"
Valéon asked almost desperate on behalf of his friend.

Emily shook her head.
"Of course not.
But I can't say, 'Sorry, I can't listen,
because I just talked with someone who's trying to pay off their debt,
and convinced another person out of contemplating suicide,
and comforted another who lost their child to cancer,
and that was just today, not this week.
That would be a complete breach of trust on multiple levels."

"You can say 'no' without having to explain yourself," Valéon argued.

He found himself laying down each point of his argument
as if he were dealing her a hand of cards.

"You need to say 'no,'
and take care of yourself.
The world will not fall apart
if you step away to rest.
All those people can find someone else.

They should.
It's not healthy for them to rely on one person.
And it's not healthy for you to take on their burdens.
Plus, half of them are just coming to complain;

they're not planning to change.
And the ones who do change don't come repeatedly."

"Tell me something I don't already know,"
Emily said numbly and took a long sip of tea.

It was as if she were so deep
into her predicament
that she knew everything
that was wrong about it
but still couldn't come out.

"As your friend,
I think you've spent enough time
living your life for the sake of others,"
Valéon was taken aback by how firm his counsel was.

He attributed this to his voice of power
and concluded that Emily needed to hear it this way.
He went on,
"You're almost thirty.
Have you even lived a life for yourself for a week?"

Emily said nothing for a minute before murmuring,
"I'm not going to answer that."

"Your sister said –" Valéon began.

"Of course Crystal put you up to this,"
Emily shook her head.
"Why am I not surprised?"

"Your sister said,"

Valéon repeated more softly this time,

"that you've got dreams of your own,

and that she wants to see you reach them."

"Did she?"

Emily looked genuinely surprised and touched at the same time.

She cupped her hands around the mug to warm them and asked,

"What do you say to that?"

"I stand by the Sky Maiden," Valéon replied.

"As I always have.

But if I were to add my own thought to Crystal's,

it would be that it's not just what you do that's important.

It's also about what you don't do.

Because how can you do what you really want to do

if you can't say 'no' to the needs of others?"

Emily stood up then. She backed the chair she was sitting in out and walked out of the kitchen. Valéon wondered if he had come on too strong and had struck a nerve. He had only said what she needed to hear, probably what no one else could say, given that they didn't know Emily's situation. He didn't worry long, however, because Emily was back after a minute, holding a cream-colored card in her hand. She came up beside him and handed it to him silently.

He noted the calligraphy design all along its edges, and then read the three lines each written by a different hand:

There is no need to write, only a desire to listen and watch.

Just say the word and it shall be so, your presence a gift...

To behold as a witness a beautiful promise.

Valéon held the card and then glanced at Emily.

"What's this?" He asked.

"The tangible form of the offer you, Avorne, and Darkon gave me," Emily answered.

"It's the invitation to the second peace treaty efforts. And my answer is 'yes.' I said 'no' to a whole lot of other people to make room for this. Took a blasted year to do it, but I'm better late than never. I want to come to your second peace treaty. When is it? Did I miss it? Can you show me where it was and how it went if I did?"

Valéon felt his heart skip a beat,
  and his mouth went dry.
  Of all things that Emily wanted…
  she wanted this?

Valéon looked up at his friend,
  who wore her brightly colored patchwork silk robe
  over her long-sleeve collared shirt and blue jeans.
  Her chestnut locks were pulled back
  half up and half down by a ponytail in the back,
  and she had a bright blue ribbon tied into it.
  She met his gaze with her unflinching green-gold eyes,
  and waited expectantly for his reply.
  Valéon had none available.

Instead, he wrestled with the fact
  that she had just admitted to him
  that what she wanted above anything else
  was to attend the second peace treaty attempt,
  which wasn't even taking place in her world or domain.

She could have easily chosen spending more time with her friends or family,
  delving deeper into a hobby,
  or pursuing a romantic relationship with a significant other.
  After all, it seemed that there were a good number of young men
  who seemed to be rather taken by her as of late,

as Valéon observed from the pile of Christmas gifts
that hadn't yet made it to the couch in her small living room area,
but still sat on the kitchen counter.

And he didn't know what prompted him,
but Valéon pointed to the small mound of gifts with a cheeky,
"Are you sure you wouldn't rather
find a worthy suitor for your hand in marriage?
How about Luke? Or Henry?"

He laughed when he was swatted lightly on the shoulder.

"Valéon!
That's...no.
Just...no.
And be serious!"

She let out a sigh and said,
"Because I really mean that
about the second peace treaty.
I want to know how it went."

Valéon became sober at that, and said.
"I know. There's only a slight problem."

"What?" Emily asked.

He took in a deep breath
and tried to find the best way to explain the situation to her.
Valéon couldn't think of a way to make it sound any better,
so he just told Emily the truth.

"There hasn't been

a second peace treaty attempt.
There still isn't one.
Nothing's happened
ever since you left."

7

Allowing a Small Exception

Above all else, Darkon, King of Kites, wanted to be left alone.
He did not want the aid of a younger southern king,
    who didn't understand the workings of the Kite Kingdom.

He did not want the sympathy of a lesser-experienced ruler,
    even if that lesser-experienced ruler
    was the son of his first true southern ally,
    the late Queen of Eld Mané, Annette.

And he did not want
    the probing questions
    and careful attention of Avorne,
    who even without an affinity
    of perception or influence,
    somehow managed to get involved
    in everyone else's business
    without meaning to or trying.

Avorne was a good friend,
    but he didn't know how things were done here in the North.

The only problem
    was that in one blunder of great political magnitude,
    Avorne had pointed out Darkon's prevailing issue
    and offered a solution to remedy it.

Darkon still felt the sting of Avorne's suggestion
    that there may be a way for him to help and be helped at the same time.

But as he read the letter from the Princess of Vinduren
    that had been meant for Avorne's eyes alone,
    he knew Avorne was right.

Never mind that the way Avorne had come unannounced
    broke the silent but understood expectation of the Kite Kingdom
    that one never offered help unless one was asked directly.

And never mind that Avorne had just handed him
    a personal correspondence that was not meant for him,
    but could hold the key to helping his kingdom to recover again.

This could help.
    And he needed it.

Darkon took in a deep breath and let out a weary sigh.
    Really, he was just tired, embarrassed, and very uncomfortable.

He had no desire to meet anyone in this state,
    especially when his usually disciplined cheerfulness
    was worn completely ragged around the edges.

He hadn't meant to be so terse with Avorne,
    who was just trying to be supportive.
    It was just hurt pride,

which made him feel foolish.

He was older and more experienced.
　If anything, it was up to him
　to swallow his discomfort
　and set a good example
　for the upcoming generation.

He thought of his son's simple solution of,
　"You don't have to ask. Just call."
　And it made him ashamed
　that he would have to receive
　such prompting in the first place.

At times like these,
　Darkon wondered what he was doing
　as ruler of this enormous kingdom
　and how often he fell short of his title as "king."

This made him realize that Avorne
　probably felt the same way about Eld Mané
　and the expectation of seeing to the success
　of the second peace treaty attempt.

In small part,
　Darkon pressed Avorne to pursue
　the second peace treaty attempts so firmly,
　because he himself was at a loss of what to do.

Other rulers would have pushed back
　and claimed it wasn't their problem or responsibility.

Avorne had embraced it entirely,

though it was most certainly not his responsibility
to spearhead the peace efforts alone.

The difference between Avorne
 and everyone else,
 in Darkon's opinion,
 was perspective.

Everyone else who had been involved in the first peace treaty attempt
 considered this second peace treaty attempt
 to be a constant reminder of their first failure.

It was, in essence,
 a disaster that the next generation inherited
 from the first with no choice or say in the matter.
 Naturally, no one else wanted to be the one "in charge."

But not Avorne.
 He took on the second peace treaty efforts
 like it was a child he had adopted
 and was raising up to be the heir to the throne.

Darkon briefly glanced over at Renadé
 and wondered if the queen of Eld Mané
 was still unable to bear any children of her own.

Eight years of marriage
 and still no royal sons or daughters.
 At thirty six, she was just a year older than August.

It was one thing to be childless.
 But to be of the royal family
 and to not be able to bring forth a royal heir...

well…

Darkon considered his wife and three sons
　　and felt his heart go out to Renadé and Avorne both.

No doubt the two of them felt strained and under pressure
　　from the mounting expectations around them.

"Avorne," Darkon murmured softly.
　　"Didn't you have a birthday recently?"

Avorne coughed.
　　"Is your next question
　　going to be how old I am?
　　I'm not going there."

"Do you feel that old?"
　　Darkon grinned.

"Ancient,"
　　Avorne confessed.

Darkon laughed.
　　"If you're ancient,
　　what does that make me?"

"Beyond ancient,"
　　Avorne smiled and admitted,
　　"Forty.
　　Just a few months ago."

Darkon scoffed.
　　"Forty is not ancient.

Sixty five, maybe.
Or seventy.
But not forty."

"Tell that to Renadé,"
Avorne pointed to his wife.
"Her teasing is relentless."

"Only because I love him,"
Renadé gave an innocent shrug.
"I only tease people I like."

Darkon shook his head.
All that pressure,
and yet the King and Queen
of Eld Mané remained close,
like the paper of a kite
to its wooden frame.

For most other couples,
this would be the perfect condition to fall apart and separate.
But then again, Avorne and Renadé were not like most other couples.
Perhaps it was witnessing this steady relationship that gave Darkon
renewed hope.

And so, Darkon handed the letter back to Avorne and said,
"You need to reply to this, since it was addressed to you."

"That's right," Avorne nodded.
"But I could send you with that fireproof kite to Vinduren.
What better way to start the connection between you and Princess
Featherfall?
I can say that I happened to receive her letter when I was meeting with

you,

and that while I'm currently occupied with the second peace treaty attempt,

Darkon, King of Kites is willing to offer his service and assistance at this time."

"That…" Darkon trailed off.

"Could work," August finished for his father.
  "If you can get into Kalos Fyrian,
  then you could ask for a shipment of fireproof paper
  after explaining our situation."

"No, that part I got," Darkon qualified.
  "I just wanted to make sure I heard correctly."

He studied Avorne carefully and repeated,
  "currently occupied with the second peace treaty attempt?"

"Well, that's what you want, right?"
  Avorne looked somewhat unhappy.
  "I don't know why everyone expects me
  to bring about this peace effort,
  but I'll do my best."

"Is it that difficult to start?"
  Darkon felt sympathy for his younger friend.

"No one expects you
    to roll out
    a complete proposal
    in a week,"
    he pointed out.

"It feels like they do," Avorne admitted.
  "It's like everyone is waiting
  to vicariously succeed through me,
  and it's nerve wracking."

Darkon felt a twinge in his chest,
  knowing he was guilty of doing just that.
  "What would make it easier for you?"

"A vision of what reconciliation would look like.
  A place to display it.
  A verbal commitment from those who want peace.
  Words backed by action.
  Some sort of guidance or direction...
  I don't know," Avorne sighed.

"Why does everything have to be so abstract?
  Everyone says they want peace,
  but no one can tell me what that would look like."

"They can't explain something they haven't seen," Darkon said simply.

"Well, I can see something,"
  Avorne's shoulders fell slightly,
  "it's just no one else can."

Darkon didn't miss the confused expression
  on the faces of Renadé, Tal, and August.
  He was just as confused as them,
  but something in him prompted him
  to address Avorne's discouragement.

"If you can see something

no one else can see,"
Darkon said,

"Then it's your
    responsibility
    as leader
    to make
    your
    vision
    a reality."

Avorne wrinkled his nose at that.
    "You're sounding like my mother."

Darkon laughed.
    "That's because we're the same generation.
    But you're not the only one.
    Queen Annette told it to her peers as well.
    What was the exact wording again?" he mused.

"What you see is your responsibility,"
    Renadé offered.
    "Seems like it was a favored piece
    of wisdom she shared with everyone.
    Even future and upcoming queens."

"That's great in theory and all,"
    Avorne began.

"But even if I speak what I see,
    who will believe me?"
    Avorne asked.

"It's invisible
　　to everyone
　　but me."

"Just because you can't see it,
　　doesn't mean it isn't there,"
　　Darkon reminded Avorne.

"Take the Invisible Lands for example.
　　It may not be seen by our eyes,
　　but that doesn't mean the nation doesn't exist."

He watched as a light came to Avorne's eyes,
　　and discouragement was replaced by a cautious excitement.

"Just like the Sunshade House,"
　　the King of Eld Mané mused.

"Exactly," Darkon nodded.

He recited part of the Sunshade House's conditions,
　　"All who seek this place shall find it."

"All who take refuge here shall be safe..."
　　Avorne murmured.

With renewed enthusiasm,
　　he took Darkon by the shoulders and said,
　　"Thank you. I have something to go off of now.
　　Hopefully I'll have something to present by the time you come back.
　　If you need anything..."

"I'll let you know," Darkon couldn't help but smile.

He decided to make a small exception regarding this entire incident
and his way of dealing with issues and said, "I'll ask."

Darkon wasn't sure why Avorne looked so pleased,
 but he was glad that as the King of Kites,
 he had reached a place of understanding with the King of Eld Mané.

The way he saw it,
 if they could overcome their own differences now,
 then their nations – perhaps all the north and south –
 could follow suit one day in the future.

8

Choice

"What do you mean nothing's happened since I left?" Emily asked.

She fully expected Valéon to tell her
that the second peace treaty
had been conducted
and was a success.

She thought the answer would be along the lines of,
"It was amazing. Sorry you had to miss it.
Here's what it was like."

Instead she had learned the exact opposite.

She went from pacing her small kitchen in front of Valéon to settling on the couch in her equally small living room next to Valéon at his prompting. Maybe her agitated pacing reminded him of the time that he used to pace her hallway before she found his wings and gave them back to him. Or maybe he was just tired and wanted a comfortable place to sit and provide her with explanation after explanation. So sitting on her couch and resting her feet on one of the lower shelves of her bookshelves that lined the wall opposite her, Emily found herself asking the same question repeatedly:

Why?

Why had nothing been done?

Why had no one tried to make progress on something that was so important?

Why had no one taken responsibility to lead the peace efforts?

Why, when Valéon was the living legacy saved, was nothing being done?

The list that Valéon gave her was just as long,
    perhaps even longer than the one she had relayed to him
    when he asked what things had kept her from coming.

There was something about the prevailing sentiment of the people,
    which had only just begun to favor peace efforts.
    Then there was something else about the political boundaries,
    northern and southern differences,
    complications and more nightmare outbreaks.

More specifically,
    Avorne was doing his best to continue the peace efforts,
    but he was only king of one southern kingdom.
    And while most of the south thought highly of the King of Eld Mané,
    there was one southern country called Vinduren,
    which was divided in opinion.

Half of the country wanted war
    with the Land of Fire, Kalos Fyrian,
    the country immediately north of their border
    past the Inkstone Mountains.

The other half wanted peace,
    but were hard pressed by the fact
    that fires from Kalos Fyrian had destroyed
    a good deal of their crops.

This had gone on for almost ten years.

Vinduren's current ruler, Princess Featherfall,
    was a firm supporter of the peace efforts
    and kept her country from declaring war by sheer will power.

Meanwhile, those of the first peace treaty attempt
    were struggling with bad recollections of the first failed attempt.

Most were uncomfortable talking with Valéon
    or spending extended periods of time with him,
    because he was the living legacy of the first peace treaty draft,
    who had suffered in the hands of both the south and north.

Some ignored him as if he weren't there
    so they didn't have to face the aftermath of the failure.

Others would overcompensate
    and be extra kind and attentive towards him,
    because they felt terrible about what had happened
    but couldn't find the courage to apologize.

"I don't need an apology," Valéon confessed.
    "It would be nice, but it wouldn't change what happened.
    The best apology would be seeing this second peace treaty come to life.
    At least then everything that I went through would be worth it."

But he didn't dwell on that sentiment.

Instead, he went on to explain Darkon's challenges.
    Valéon told her about a failure of infrastructure
    in the Kingdom of Kites of which Darkon was the ruler.

Emily felt her stomach turn at that
    and immediately thought of Scott in the hospital.

What was the diagnosis?
    Was it a nightmare?

Valéon's answer made her feel ill.
    It wasn't a nightmare.
    No one knew what it was.

The Kite Kingdom said nothing
    of their troubles to the countries around them,
    and though the condition grew worse,
    they did not call for aid.

"The main problem is a difference in priorities," Valéon explained.

"Darkon considers his country's problems his own,
    and that the most important thing to address is the peace effort.

Avorne considers providing help as the first priority,
    and the peace efforts can wait.

That's a fundamental difference
    in northern and southern philosophy."

That was it for Emily.
    For all the listening she had done in the past year,
    Emily couldn't take any more. She had reached her limit.
    She was so glad that Jess had sent her home on more or less a mandatory holiday. She wasn't sure what she would have done if it were Henry or someone else she was talking to. But because it was Valéon who sat next to her explaining the situation, Emily held up her hand to stop him.

"Can we call it a night?"
    She suggested.
    "My head hurts."

Valéon looked at her like he knew exactly what she felt like and nodded.
    "We can figure out what to do tomorrow."

Then he asked, "Are you sure you still want to come?
    You could always wait until things get better."

She laughed.
    "Between you and me,
    when is that going to happen?"

Emily nudged him in the shoulder as she got up from the couch.
    "I'm coming. If not now, then when?
    Besides, I want to step away from everything here.
    Get my perspective back. Maybe this is the break I need."

It was a strange but familiar comfort,
    having Valéon back at her place again,
    sleeping on her couch.

Though her head throbbed
    with all of the new
    and additional issues
    she was now aware of,
    Emily was glad
    that Valéon had come.

For one, it was nice to know
    that she wasn't the only one laden with the burdens of many.

For another, it was wonderful to have
    a friend who was, for the most part,
    detached and unrelated to all
    the things that she was dealing with.

He was
    her independent perspective,
    voice of reason, and sanity check.

It occurred to her as she went to bed
    that she might also be the same for Valéon.
    Her last thought before falling asleep
    was how thankful she was to be home
    free of any people commitments.
    All clear. What a relief.

That night she dreamed that she was at a crossroads.
    But instead of a few paths,
    there were thirty roads to choose from.

A high-ranking
    soldier in uniform
    stood at the center.

"Which path will you take?"
    He asked her when she walked over to him.
    "Choose well, for you can only travel down one."

Emily looked for a sign post and found none.
    "How can I choose when I don't know
    the names of the roads or where they lead?"

"Ahh…"

the soldier nodded in understanding.
"Good question. Not everyone asks.
I will show you. May I?"

With that, he sat down and motioned
for her to sit down across from him.

Then he drew out a cloth from his inside coat pocket
and unfolded the cloth upon the ground,
revealing a set of worn, black cards.

The soldier picked up the cards, shuffled them,
and then laid them out face down between them.

He lay down three rows of ten and began turning them over.

The first card at the top right corner revealed
blood red lettering that read,
ANXIETY ATTACKS

The second was
EATING DISORDERS.

The third was
DEPRESSION.

Then,
SUICIDE
ESTRANGED FAMILY MEMBERS
DYSFUNCTIONAL RELATIONSHIPS.

LAWSUITS
and FINANCIAL TROUBLE

followed.

The next was
DEATH IN THE FAMILY
LOSS OF A LOVED ONE
followed by
GOSSIP
BULLYING
CAR ACCIDENTS.

By the time the merchant flipped over
DRUG ADDICTION
ALCOHOLISM &
MARITAL ISSUES,
Emily understood that each card
was a road on this crossroads.

She also knew the rest of the cards
without needing to see them flipped over.

"Stop."
She put her hand over the soldier's hand
as he finished flipping over
STRUGGLING CHILDREN
and had started on
HEALTH PROBLEMS.

Emily took in a deep breath.
"I don't want to go down any of these roads."

"Those are the only paths,"
the soldier didn't say it unkindly.
In fact, he spoke to her as if he was quite fond of her

though they had only just met.

"None of them are for me."
    Emily distinctly felt that he expected her to answer this way.

"I listened,
    but I will not follow suit."

She collected the cards one by one
    and handed them back to the soldier.

"I choose
    a
    different
    path
    than
    what
    surrounds
    me."

"And what path will that be?"
    The soldier asked.

"May I?"
    Emily reached out her hand for the deck of cards.

The soldier handed them to her willingly.

As the cards transferred from his hands to her,
    Emily said, "I choose the path of leadership."

The deck of cards shimmered
    and turned bright blue,

clear as the sky.

There were slight designs
   of delicate gold
   all along the edges.

Emily smiled and laid out four cards between them.
   "The path of leadership has four directions, and they are..."

One by one,
   she turned over the cards,
   from left to right.

The first card read,
   STRENGTH.

The second card read,
   HONOR.

The third card read,
   WISDOM.

And the fourth card read,
   KINDNESS.

The four golden words gleamed in the bright sunlight.

Looking at the soldier, Emily said,
   "Leadership at heart is
   strength, honor,
   wisdom, and kindness.
   I choose this path."

"Well said and well chosen."
    The scene around them wavered,
    and the crossroads
    with thirty paths
    now had just four.

Not only that,
    but the soldier was a soldier no longer,
    but a white wolf that shone like sunlight on snow.

"Because you have
    treasured this path in your heart above all others,
    you will find allies to help you in every direction.
    I will be the first.
    Follow me."

With that the wolf dashed off
    down the road named STRENGTH.

Emily gathered the cards back to her hand
    and pursued the shining wolf
    with a growing joy that matched the sun and sky.

She woke up that morning with that joy pulsing within her.

Emily felt like she had
    that clear sky and bright sun
    infused into her bones and blood.

The first words out of her mouth
    as she opened her eyes was,
    "What was that?"

She kicked back the covers and sat up in her still sleepy state.

As she did,
   something –
   no,
   many
   things –
   fell from her bed
   to the floor.

Cards.
   Blue
   with gold designs
   all along the edges.

They spilled over
   and littered the bed
   and floor around her.

Emily's heart beat faster.
   Weren't these the cards she had dreamed about?

She picked one up, turned it around, and read, STRENGTH.

She picked up another, and it read, HONOR.

Then came WISDOM,

and after that, KINDNESS.

Emily shivered.

Each card had a word

written on it
in gold lettering.

Emily read each one as she picked them up:
THANKFULNESS
DETERMINATION
HOPE
JOY
LOVE
UNDERSTANDING
PEACE
PATIENCE
SELF-DISCIPLINE
TRUST
THOUGHTFULNESS
SELF-RESPECT
CONFIDENCE
COURAGE
JUSTICE
GLADNESS
BEAUTY
FORGIVENESS
HEALING
ENCOURAGEMENT
MERCY
DISCERNMENT
PROTECTION
FAITH
GENTLENESS
GROWTH.

There were thirty cards in all –
long, slender, and smooth.

Emily felt a lump in her throat
   as she realized that each card
   corresponded to an issue
   she had listened to in that year.

It not only offered a solution to that problem,
   but it also showed Emily the qualities
   she had gained while providing counsel.

It was a rather overwhelming discovery,
   so Emily was relieved when Valéon appeared at her doorway
   asking if she wanted to eat.

Of course the answer was "yes."

Emily gripped her new set of cards
   and was thankful for this unexpected
   but very much needed gift.

She would ask Valéon what he thought at breakfast.

Not wasting a minute,
   Emily hurried to get washed up and ready.

She couldn't remember the last time she had been this excited.

9

Invisible Architecture

Avorne returned to his palace at Eld Mané alone.

In a way, he was relieved.

Tal had asked to go with Darkon to Vinduren to Princess Featherfall, saying that he was interested in offering his services as well. Avorne had been shocked to learn that Tal knew the Princess of Vinduren personally. Apparently, Tal owed a great debt to her, but didn't want to say what it was exactly.

Avorne didn't pry, only saying,

"If you owe her, then go.

I'm not stopping you."

He was also thankful that Darkon hadn't objected and even admitted looking forward to catching up with Tal along the way as they delivered Avorne's written response to Vinduren by fireproof kite.

As for Renadé, she had been asked to stay for a short while to assist Katarina, the Queen of Kites with finding a way to preserve the kites that had fallen in good condition until they could be brought back to life or appropriately retired. Avorne was glad Renadé had agreed. He knew that Renadé always liked a new challenge to keep her skill with ink in shape.

But the true reason

Avorne was so pleased to come back alone

was because he wanted to investigate
something on his own
without worrying about
what others would think
or say to him in the process.

This wasn't something he wanted input on,
    and Avorne knew that if he wanted to check out his hunch,
    he better do it while he had the precious time and privacy to do so.

While talking with Darkon,
    he had been visited by an idea:

What if the ink sign that only he could see
    in the Inkstone Mountains wasn't an ink sign at all?

What if it was some sort of invisible architecture
    like that of the Sunshade House?

Avorne knew that the Sunshade House had been designed and built by a
rather famous architect from the Invisible Lands, who wanted his legacy
to be seen. The architect had made the house so it could be seen on the
Borderlands between the Light Kingdom and Shadow Country if it was
actively being sought. Anyone who looked for the Sunshade House could
find it and enter the place for refuge.

So in his mind, Avorne thought it wouldn't be too different to consider
what he saw as the beginnings of invisible architecture. Perhaps he was the
only one who could see it because he was looking for something that could
help him with the second peace treaty attempt.

He flew to the site of the beautiful structure
    by one of the palace kites,
    and when he arrived,

he took his time walking around
trying to examine it more closely.

It had changed while he had been gone.
Instead of being a huge dome,
it appeared like the beginnings
of some enormous castle-cathedral.

It was still made of the same glistening,
see-through material
that seemed to have
rainbows trapped
in watery walls.

Avorne thought it looked even more magnificent than before,
and found himself more and more intrigued.

What was this made out of?
It wasn't ink or water.
It wasn't wood
or stone
or glass
either.

The substance this was made out of
was completely foreign to Avorne.

They did say that the Invisible Lands
held the most advanced forms,
materials, and methods
for crafting their cities
and buildings.

Avorne had only heard about it;
    he had never seen any of it himself,
    since the Invisible Lands were extremely private –
    even more so than the Kingdom of Kites.

He rested his hand upon it
    and the entire structure
    rippled and pulsed in response.

Avorne wondered if there was a door for him to enter and go inside.

At his thought,
    an extensive entranceway began to form,
    taking shape from the ground,
    rising up around him,
    and then over his head.

Two double doors solidified before him.
    They had no handles or knobs to take hold of.
    Instead, in the center was a bizarre keyhole.
    A complete circle was engraved in the middle, one half on each door.

Just above the circle,
    in letters that gleamed gold were the words:

> *What lies at the center of a king's heart?*
> *Name the secret of his joy and crown:*
> *Turn the key to unlock the vision and enter.*

Avorne trembled as he
    remembered his amended wish on the dandelion
    that he had made earlier that morning,
    remembered asking for someone

who had a heart and vision like him.

Was someone on the other side of this mysterious sign?
  It certainly seemed so,
  from the way the place seemed to change
  with Avorne's slightest thoughts.

It was as if someone was designing
  a place for him specifically,
  tailor-made to help him.

Who would do such a thing?
  And why?
  What for?

Well, there wasn't much else to do except to try to go in.
  Avorne studied the words one more time.

What lies at the center of a leader's heart?
  Name the secret of his joy and crown.

Avorne took off his crown and traced his fingers
  along the inside engraving which read,
  A KING IS NOTHING WITHOUT HIS PEOPLE.

Surely it couldn't be referring to his crown...Avorne frowned.
  No one knew about what the inside of his crown said.
  Well, a few did, but other than them, it was a well-kept secret.

How could this place know about his crown?
  But because this whole situation was already abnormal,
  Avorne decided to suspend his disbelief.

After all, he reasoned, if this sign was only visible to him,
and was responding to his presence and his thoughts,
then maybe it was connected to him more deeply than he knew.

For a moment, Avorne felt like he was back in the Dream Realm though he was awake. But looking at this set of double doors with a keyhole shaped like his crown made him wonder. The fifth gate of the Dream Realm was opened by placing his crown inside of it and speaking the five words to unlock it, right?

Maybe this place had the same sort of workings and reasoning as the Dream Realm. Avorne decided to try his dream reasoning instead of natural reasoning.

With both hands,
he carefully placed his crown
into the circle, like a key into a keyhole.

Then as he began to turn it clockwise,
then counter-clockwise, he said,

"People are at the center of a king's heart.
They are his joy and crown.
Because a King is nothing without his people."

There was a series of clicking sounds,
and then the keyhole disappeared,

and the crown dropped back into Avorne's hands.
The doors opened of their own accord,
and Avorne stepped in.

What he saw shocked him.

On the stained glass patterned floor
   was the image of a golden crown with
A KING IS NOTHING WITHOUT HIS PEOPLE
   surrounding it like a ring of light.

And sitting in the center of the entire design,
   was a young woman
   completely unaware
   of his presence,
   poring over
   an enormous
   set of blueprints.

She wore a lavender coat
   with white flowers embroidered
   all along the sleeves and edges.

Underneath, she wore
   a dark blouse and pants.

Sprawled out in a mess around her were
   scrolls and crystal tiles of some sort.

She rested one elbow on her knee
   as she sat cross legged
   and propped her head up with her hand
   as she studied the papers around her.

Her pale, silver-white hair
   made Avorne wonder if she was from the Sky.

But her attire was most definitely from the Invisible Lands. Those of that
country tended to prefer wearing colors that were lighter in color, whites,

grays, pastels and the like. Although the dark colors beneath her coat seemed odd; was she secretly in mourning?

But remembering that once he had taken on a disguise pretending to be of the Invisible Lands, Avorne thought it would be safer not to assume he knew where this individual came from or what she was doing here.

Avorne cleared his throat to get her attention and said, "hello there."

A surprised yelp came from the young woman
as she glanced up and saw him standing there.

"Who are you?
How are you here?
How did you get inside when there's no door?"

Avorne just pointed to her.
"You've set this up in the mountains
just behind my palace. I'd like to know the same.
I'm Avorne Ehrthann, King of Eld Mané."

Seeing her alarmed expression as she stood up,
he rushed to say, "No need to address me by title.
I don't like them. Never did. Still don't. I'm here by accident.
I've seen this for the last week and a half. No one else can see it.
Am I going crazy? This is really here, right?"

She gulped
and then nervously ran her fingers
through her silver-white hair.

"You're not going crazy. This is really here.
I'm Mirae. Mirae Hope."

She seemed very aware of his royal attire and crown
    and gave an awkward bow before saying,

"You're standing in my life's work.
    I needed a safe place to finish,
    and this was the best I could find.
    The mountains are the natural divide
    between the north and south.
    It's a neutral zone.
    I need neutral."

So many questions flooded Avorne's mind.
    He just went with the first.

"When I thought about coming inside,
    a set of double doors appeared.
    Somehow my crown was the key to unlock them."

Avorne couldn't help but blurt out,
    "Did you design this for me?
    Because it sure seems like you did,
    even though I don't know you."

Mirae flushed pink at that.
    "It isn't for anyone," she said.
    "I'm doing this for myself.
    I've been working on it since I was ten."

Avorne had a hard time believing this.
    She did it for herself, she said,
    and yet clearly in the center
    of this enormous reception hall
    was the design of his crown

and the words engraved on the inside of it.

"Then why…"
    Avorne asked.

"I originally designed it for my leaders,"
    Mirae admitted.

"When I still worked for them
    in the Invisible Lands as an architect.
    I tried to give it to them as a gift,
    but it went completely wrong,
    and they suspended me
    because I broke a bunch of
    social conventions
    to present this to them.
    I designed it so it would help bring their dreams into reality;
    that's the tailoring aspect of this place.
    I engineered it to bring to life
    and personalize their unique desires.
    Apparently I did it so well,
    they said it was inappropriate
    and sent me away
    telling me to come back
    once I got my thinking straight
    and vow I'd never be capable of doing something like this again."

She looked pleasantly surprised to neutrally explain
    something that had once been gut-wrenching to express
    and seemed to take comfort in that.

Mirae continued.
    "Thing is, I felt like I was dying a thousand deaths every day there.

That was what drove me to work so hard on designing this place.
It was my lifeblood. Still is. Besides...I did get my thinking straight,
and my prevailing thought is I don't ever want to go back. Plus,
I'm very capable of doing something like this. I'm still doing it.
And I've gotten better. I've improved in technique, skill, and
construction. I guess you're proof of that."

She gave him a shy smile and shrug.
   Then she shook her head and murmured.

"Why am I saying all this?
   It's got to be the inbuilt design.
   I didn't know it was so effective.
   Maybe that's why it freaked everyone out."

Avorne, on the other hand, was at a complete loss for words.
   He felt like Mirae had looked straight into his heart
   and addressed everything he wondered about
   but hadn't been able to express.

It left him feeling quite exposed,
   much like the times he did when he used to speak with Halas,
   who could perceive his emotions and address him directly
   though he never said a word.

But this was on a completely different level.

Avorne hadn't expected all of this
   so suddenly from a person he had just met.
   Did this place really let you talk with someone
   as if you had known them for years
   when you just met them?

It seemed so,
   and Avorne was a bit unnerved
   by how easily he was getting to know
   this talented but exiled architect.

But Mirae laid out the blueprints of her own history willingly, perhaps because he was the first one to see her work and enter, so Avorne did his best to listen and understand. He suspected there was more to Mirae and her work than she was letting on, that it ran deeper than the incident that had led her out of the Invisible Lands.

Avorne also sensed that he needed to address a few things on behalf of those leaders who were no longer present. Granted, Avorne didn't know them or their prevailing philosophies regarding governing people. He didn't know the complete story and doubted he would receive more from Mirae, who seemed to have resigned herself to a life of obscurity and insignificance based off of this supposed failure.

Avorne was bothered by this.
   It didn't seem right or fair
   to relegate someone with so much potential,
   and clearly a lot of heart and intelligence,
   to a status of permanent failure
   and good for nothing.

Moreover, Avorne understood
   that as the first leader
   who had stepped into
   Mirae's handiwork
   since that bad experience,
   he had a responsibility to set things right.

If not for those leaders,
   Avorne thought,

then at least for the sake
of the young woman
who poured her heart out to him now.

So Avorne ventured to ask,
   "What exactly about this did they think was inappropriate?"

"The intimacy."
   Mirae said.

She pointed at the stained glass floor,
   then the rest of the surrounding walls and windows.

"Everything here
   takes your deepest desires
   and tries to bring them to life.

This place is meant to
   encourage you
   to pursue
   your dreams.

It allows those in it to speak together as if
   they're teammates, friends, and family
   even if in reality they're strangers
   who have only just met.
   Kind of like how we're talking now."

"And that's somehow…wrong?"
   Avorne asked puzzled.

He had half a mind to say he wished
   he had had one of these places for years,

especially for the peace efforts.

"I don't know.
　　Apparently it makes people very uncomfortable.
　　It's the way I've always talked with everyone, so it's normal for me.
　　I suppose they thought I stepped out of line when I spoke
　　like a teammate, friend, and family member
　　when they considered me a nobody.
　　Maybe they were right.
　　I should have just kept my mouth shut."

Mirae looked at Avorne and admitted,
　　"I love all my leaders.

At first I thought it was just my leaders in my homeland,
　　but everywhere I've been,
　　I've loved the leader of that place.

It doesn't matter what
　　country or nation,
　　north or south,
　　king or queen or even Legend.

Sometimes they hold philosophies of life
　　and beliefs I don't understand or agree with,
　　and I still love them. I don't know why.
　　I think it's a curse, this fondness I have for them,
　　this desire to be loyal to them, to uphold them no matter what."

"It's not a curse," Avorne said at once
　　to negate that sentiment. "It's a blessing."

In his mind, he dared to wonder

where Mirae had been all this time.
He could have really used her love and loyalty
to keep his morale afloat in the last few years.
He tried to express what was only just becoming articulate in his mind.

"You're not a nobody.
It's your leaders who are nobody without you,
because…well, we're standing on my belief right now,"

Avorne pointed to the bold lettering of
A KING IS NOTHING WITHOUT HIS PEOPLE.

"Yeah, well…" Mirae sighed.

"I pretty much ruined my promising career because of this.
They made sure of that. So this time, I'll do it right.

No one can tell me it's inappropriate when
I'm designing a tailored resource for myself.

I'll finish,
prove to myself that I'm capable of achieving
this dream of mine, and then figure out
what to do with the rest of my life."

Avorne paused.
"You're not planning on giving this to any leader?"

Mirae shook her head.
"I gave up on my leaders.
I'm not doing this for them anymore.
I'm doing this for myself. That's it."

"If you're doing this for yourself,
    then you're a leader." Avorne said.

He watched her tear up at that comment and look away.

He added gently,
    "And speaking as a leader myself,
    I think it's brilliant.

Maybe your leaders didn't want it,
    but I've wanted something like this for a long time.

Stick close by. Stay here and finish your work.
    I'll make sure you stay safe, and I won't say anything.

Though I might stop by every once in a while
    to see what you come up with if you don't mind.
    I could use the inspiration."

"You think so?"
    Mirae seemed to perk up at that.
    "Inspiration for what?"

Avorne took in a deep breath
    and decided that he would trust this young woman
    with the burden that had weighed so heavily upon him all these years.

"The peace efforts.
    I'm trying to realize the second peace treaty attempt,
    and I need help making it a reality."

Mirae's eyes grew wide
    and her jaw dropped open.

Avorne laughed.

"That's how I feel standing here looking at your work."

It took a minute before Mirae was able to shyly offer,

"I'd be honored to provide you with inspiration for the peace efforts.
If..."

She looked away, rubbed the palms of her hands on her coat nervously,
and then played with the buttons on the front of her coat as she went on.

"If you'd like...I can offer up this place for the second peace treaty if you
haven't decided on a venue or location yet. It's very flexible and able to
expand, accommodate, and personalize. This place can do a lot of things.
I haven't even figured all of it out yet. But it is designed to give you a
glimpse and vision of what could be, even though it doesn't exist yet. And it
provides you with the tools you need to go out and make it a reality. Maybe
you'd like to consider it?"

Something about the cautious eagerness and tentative offer touched
Avorne. He wondered about Mirae's willingness to offer her work again to
yet another leader, without knowing if it would result in the same painful
experience as the last.

He answered softly,

"I would love to consider having the second peace treaty attempt here.
For now, though, I'd like to develop my own vision to share with others,
so I'll keep it private until then."

He looked around at the brilliant stained glass walls
that already seemed to shift and change,
ready to tailor itself to his needs.

Avorne murmured,

"This is your heart, isn't it?"

Mirae nodded.

116

"Well, you've got a king's heart,"
   Avorne said, both impressed and comforted
   at this tangible expression of something
   usually invisible to the natural eye.

All of a sudden, Mirae's expression changed.
   "That's brilliant!" She exclaimed.

"What?" Avorne asked,
   not knowing what had accounted for the change in mood.

"Now I know what I'll name this place!"
   Mirae beamed at him.
   "The King's Heart."

This time,
   it was Avorne's turn
   to fight the tears
   that came to his eyes.

For the first time in years, Avorne felt like he was equipped and ready to begin preparations for the second peace treaty attempt. He wasn't sure how this was all going to work out, but he was glad that he had seen this sign that no one else could see, and met the architect who had lovingly designed it for her entire life, despite her initial failures. He also thought that if he could work in a place like this with a person like Mirae, he could actually start and get somewhere.

10

Bridging Dreams and Reality

Valéon wasn't sure what to make
of the deck of cards
Emily placed before him during breakfast.

They were long, smooth, sleek, each bright blue with gold.
He riffed through them and counted thirty cards in all.
He flipped them over and read a few of the words
that were lettered in gold on them as well:
COURAGE, THANKFULNESS, TRUST.

Valéon studied Emily with a keen look
and wondered at the clear change
in her demeanor since last night.

Those three cards certainly did seem
to reflect his friend's current attitude.

Questions rose in his mind as he looked the cards in his hand.
What was this?
Where did they come from?
What were they doing in her possession?

When did they appear?
How did they appear?
Why did she pass them to him without a word
but with a clear unspoken expectation?

Valéon decided to start at the beginning.
What was this?
She shrugged and nodded to the cards
as if to say it was pretty obvious they were cards.

Where did they come from?
She told him it was a dream.
That got his attention.

What were they doing in her possession?
She met someone while dreaming who had the cards first,
but the cards had changed when they passed hands to hers.

They ate for a minute,
munching buttered toast
and cereal,
drinking
tea
or coffee.

At that moment,
Valéon was reminded of the time
when Emily had asked him
a series of questions
to learn more about the situation they were in.

It had been when they were trying to restore his voice,
and Valéon wondered if this was what Emily had felt like,

asking question after question,
and receiving answers,
but very limited ones.

How had she not gone crazy while trying to piece everything together? It occurred to him that Emily had an ocean of patience when it came to assisting others, and for the first time since they had met, Valéon realized that she was using that ocean of patience to wait for his help.

It was clear that Emily had no idea what the significance of the cards was. She was aware of how unusual it was to dream about something and to have it manifest in the waking world, which is why she had brought them to him. But other than that, Emily had no frame of reference to understand what had happened. Valéon decided that he would have to do his best to gain the clearest picture possible by asking good questions.

Even if they inhabited different worlds, they all dreamed right? The workings of the dream realm could be the same. Valéon had never helped a Legend make sense of their dreams in their domain, and he wasn't sure how much of his understanding would apply. But he could try to filter the information he received through his preexisting knowledge about the workings of the dream realm and go from there.

So Valéon asked Emily to describe the dream
from the beginning to the end.

She explained the crossroads
with thirty roads and no signpost,
the high ranking soldier
who asked her to choose a path,
and her question of how she could
without knowing where the paths led.

She told him about how the soldier laid the cards out between them and turned them over one by one, bringing to light the issues she had described to Valéon the night before. She showed the way she had stopped the soldier from continuing and declared she chose a different path, the path of leadership. And Emily said the cards had changed in her hand and turned into the cards he held now. She ended with the crossroad that changed to have only four roads, and how the soldier had turned into a white wolf and led the way down the path called STRENGTH.

Valéon had to remember to eat at Emily's prompting. Part of him was moved that Emily had trusted him with a dream so personal. Part of him was taken aback by how vivid and clear the dream elements were. One in particular was the high ranking soldier. Valéon tried to find out more about what he looked like from Emily, but was disappointed she didn't remember.

"I just knew he was a high ranking soldier.
    Very noble, very brave. And kind.
    He wasn't even surprised when
    I said I chose a different path.
    It was like he expected me
    to diverge from the norm,"
    Emily said.

Then with a wry smile, she asked,
    "So what's the interpretation?"

Valéon shook his head.
    "What's to interpret? It's self-explanatory.

You're at a crossroads now with
    everyone you've been supporting,
    and you need to respond to the demands
    upon your time, energy, and focus.

Each person expects you to help them,

and for the first time you've said 'no'
to everyone and decided to pursue your calling.

You're called to be a leader,
  though your vision has been obscured
  by the issues you're bombarded with.

You have yet to explore what that calling
  of leadership looks like for you specifically,
  but you know to begin with
  strength, honor, wisdom, and kindness,
  because they define your heart
  for the people you will lead.

You already have the promise
  that you'll have allies
  wherever you go
  and whatever you do
  while seeking to fulfill your purpose.

The first path you've chosen leads to STRENGTH.
  I can only imagine the others will lead to
  HONOR, WISDOM, and KINDNESS.
  You're on the path to become a leader."

Valéon wasn't sure why Emily looked at him the way she did in wonder and amazement, as if he were some mystical fortune teller who had conjured up a favorable future out of thin air. It made him uncomfortable, because he just considered himself to be a good friend who happened to have fifteen years of additional life experience under his belt compared to Emily.

It was true he had learned much of dream lore from Sylasienne in their time spent together in the restored Ribbon Fortress, but that wasn't anything particularly spectacular. But since his younger friend seemed

convinced that he could read her heart and mind, which he most definitely
couldn't, Valéon pointed out,
   "Your dream is pretty symbolic.
   It defines you and your situation clearly
   and in a way unique and meaningful to who you are."

He handed the deck of cards back to Emily.

She took the cards from him
   and fanned them out in her hands,
   flipped them over,
   studied them from every angle possible.
   "But why did these come to me?"

"My guess? You'll be needing that
   where we're going," Valéon suggested.
   "Not just for yourself, but for the people you'll meet.
   Plus, it's a tangible reminder of who you're called to be.
   Much like your scarf and book,"

Valéon nodded to the blue and gold scarf
   that Emily wore around her neck
   and the book on the kitchen counter
   that was titled *Gold: Leadership at Heart.*

Everything was blue and gold
   and matched in theme and color.
   Valéon tried not to laugh at the very clear signs
   of his friend's life calling that remained
   completely unrealized by Emily herself.
   It amused him that it took someone outside of her domain to recognize
this.
   He had a growing thought that perhaps Emily was discovering her new

purpose just as he was. And Valéon was comforted to think that on this journey he'd be accompanied by not only a good friend but a budding leader. He imagined his Lord Leuthe and Lady Laehna being pleased at this development. He imagined Halas would have approved as well, and that encouraged him. But he was brought back to the moment when Emily asked him about the high ranking soldier.

"Why the interest?"
　　She asked.

"I also met
　　a high ranking soldier
　　in a dream once,"
　　Valéon admitted.

"I gave him the peace treaty draft
　　that I had kept safe while captive in the Ribbon Fortress."

"Wait, what?"
　　Emily leaned forward
　　in complete interest.
　　"How did it happen?"

So Valéon described the dream that he had at the lowest point of his life, when he had nearly despaired and given up on trying to survive in the nightmare-ridden Ribbon Fortress.

"I stood on a mountain top on the clearest day.
　　I guarded the entrance of a temple made from white stone
　　in the center of a grove of trees, and I waited for
　　the right person to come.

In my dream, my wings were still with me,

as if they had never been torn off,
and I wore a robe of bright colors.

I waited until the right person came –
a high ranking soldier.

He held the peace treaty draft in his hand
and said they hadn't forgotten
and would find a way to reach me.

I asked him to vow
to defend the legacy of peace
that remains
the key to the future."

Valéon paused to see how Emily was taking it all in.

All of her attention was on him,
and when she realized that he had stopped,
Emily practically demanded, "Yes, and?"

Valéon went on.

"The soldier said,
'I vow to defend the legacy of peace
that remains our key to the future.
I vow to defend the King's Heart.'

So I gave the peace treaty draft to him and said,
'The King's Heart is yours.
May you be the final stone to tip the scale,
the final drop to make the cup overflow.
Guard it well. Keep it safe.'"

Valéon then described
    the golden gash that had appeared in the sky above their heads,
    like it had been sliced open by an invisible sword.

"It was his way out,
    and since I could fly him there,
    I offered him a lift. He thanked me for that."

There was actually more to the dream,
    but Valéon found that
    he got choked up by emotion
    and couldn't continue.

He was glad Emily didn't press him to go on this time.

When he had composed himself,
    Valéon did tell Emily,
    "I met you sometime after that dream.
    It was that dream that sustained me,
    kept me going until then."

"But that means you know
    who has the original peace treaty draft now, right?"
    Emily asked, still excited.
    "If we find that person,
    then we could start somewhere."

Valéon shook his head.
    "You don't know who the high ranking soldier was in your dream.
    How would we know that it's the same one from mine?
    Also, mine didn't turn into a white wolf,
    and he didn't carry a deck of cards.
    He carried a golden, flaming sword and a square mirror.

Plus, even if we were to say it was the same person in the dream realm, we have no clue as to who that would be in the waking world."

He wondered why Emily grew increasingly eager across from him.

"Maybe we don't need to know who the person is," Emily suggested.

"Maybe all we need to know is...hang on, I'll be right back."

Emily placed the cards back on the table between them and then dashed off to her bedroom.

Valéon dared to peek at the top card on the deck and was surprised to see the word, UNDERSTANDING gleam at him in gold. He looked at the card under that, and it read, CONFIDENCE The one beneath that read, DETERMINATION.

It was so curious, how the cards that came up seemed to reflect Emily's current state. Valéon wondered how this would develop as time progressed. For now, he took comfort in working with someone who had never been to the first peace treaty attempt and therefore didn't carry any emotional baggage from its failure.

Emily rushed back to the table with a small mirror in her hands. It was a plain, square mirror with no elaborate designs etched into it, and Valéon recognized it immediately as the door or way maker they had used the last time Emily had visited.

Then she picked up the deck of cards

and addressed the mirror,

"Show us the person who gave me this in my dream."

Valéon watched as Emily looked at the mirror's changing image with a bemused frown.

"What is it?" Valéon asked.

Emily handed the mirror to him.

"Do you recognize this person? I don't."

Valéon took the mirror and nearly dropped it. The image shown by the little square mirror was of a man in his fifties, dark skinned and dark haired, in a blue military uniform that boasted of Silkairen's handiwork, but with the insignia of the palace of Eld Mané embroidered upon its back.

"Ionthann?" Valéon exclaimed.

"Who's Ionthann?" Emily asked.

"He's the captain of the guard
    at the palace of Eld Mané…"
Valéon finally answered.
"He's a good friend."

"Well then what are we waiting for?"
    Emily took the mirror back from him
    and set it in place into the air
    by pushing it with both her thumbs and forefingers.
"Let's say 'hello.' And 'thank you.'"

With that, she pushed the mirror,
    and an invisible door opened into a completely different place,
    one that Emily did not recognize, but Valéon did:
    to the royal gardens in the palace of Eld Mané.

It had been quite some time since Valéon had been at the royal gardens in the palace of Eld Mané. He had come to visit the royal library on the third floor to do occasional research and ask Duke Vandek a reference question or two, but unless he was on his way to the throne room to speak with Avorne, who still hated being referred to as "majesty" or "King Ehrthann," Valéon had little reason to come by the gardens. But now, as he looked into the gardens that were lush and green, thanks to the work of the royal gardener, Iris, he wondered why he hadn't come by more often. It was quiet, calm, and beautiful, amid the pathway lined with trees and shrubs. It was a perfect place to rest or meditate.

Valéon watched Ionthann jerk back as the invisible doorway opened. The captain of the guard sat on a wooden bench with a stack of papers beside him. They looked vaguely like work orders. Beside the captain of the guard, Iris was tending a young sapling. Upon seeing Valéon across the open doorway, Ionthann said,

"Valéon? What brings you here?"

Iris looked up in surprise as well.

"Vandek was just asking about you."

"Who's Vandek?"

Emily asked Valéon.

"Another friend?"

Both Ionthann and Iris glanced at Emily and then back at Valéon for an explanation.

Valéon cleared his throat, at a momentary loss for words. His interactions with Emily in her domain were so different than his with those in the palace of Eld Mané, he wasn't sure how to proceed. He decided to start with Emily's question, because it was the easiest to explain.

"Vandek is the royal advisor to the King of Eld Mané."

He didn't bother trying to explain to her that

once, years ago,

Vandek had been his worst enemy,

who had beaten him

and broken his wings,

accusing him of northern treachery.

All of which had happened

at the first peace treaty attempt

that had utterly failed.

Valéon just told Emily

the current state of things as of now.

"I consider Vandek a friend."

Emily didn't seem to notice any of the weight of his unspoken knowledge. Instead, she mused,

"Royal advisor? Never thought that Avorne would have one, but then again, I also wouldn't have thought of a captain of the guard or a..." she looked at Iris with curiosity.

"Royal gardener and tutor," Iris offered with a smile.

To Valéon, Iris said,
"Vandek would appreciate
a visit at your earliest convenience.
He didn't say what for, but it seemed urgent."

Valéon asked Emily.
"Would it be all right if I stepped out for a bit?"

Emily looked at him as if he'd lost his mind.
"What are you asking me for?
I'm not stopping you."

She waved him on.
"Just come and find me after you're done. Or I'll find you."

Emily pointed to the mirror that still hung in the air,
keeping their doorway between places open.

Valéon nodded.
"Right. Well, I'll do the introductions.
Ionthann, Iris, meet Emily,"
he made a motion to present Emily.
"Ribbon Princess by title, but like Avorne,
she prefers her name over titles."

Then he said,
"Emily, this is Ionthann and Iris.
They may know the use of your cards

in the dream realm or waking realm."

With that, Valéon stepped from Emily's kitchen into the royal gardens and made his way to the palace library on the third floor. He had rarely been called upon by Vandek directly, so Valéon wondered about the reason why and the timing of things.

What did Vandek want?

Was it related to the peace efforts?

His heartbeat wouldn't slow down,

even as he tried to steady his breathing and his steps.

His legs willed him to walk faster anyhow,

and Valéon soon took wing and flew up the three levels of the palace,

following the spiraling staircases from one floor to the next.

He landed once he had come to the third floor

and entered the massive library with its stacks

and stacks of shelves and books and archived material.

He found himself being tugged towards the left side of the library with a very gentle suggestion in his mind. It was nothing like what had once compelled his legs to walk into the light to force him to confront a duke under the heavy influence of a nightmare. But Vandek's influence still directed him, cordially but firmly to the meeting area. Valéon wondered at how different things had become from their first unfortunate confrontation, deep in the dark waterways of the palace that led into the peace treaty chamber.

"Vandek?" Valéon spoke at last.

He rounded the corner around a book shelf and found the royal advisor seated at a long wooden table filled with books. He found an amused smile coming to his lips as he said,

"Here you are, surrounded by books. What did you want?"

The older man looked up
  with a smile of his own,
  but then it wavered,

as if Valéon's presence
couldn't quite chase away
whatever shadow
haunted his thoughts.

The hair upon his head was gray, and the lines that wore themselves into his face deep, but his blue eyes were ever sharp and keen as he studied Valéon from head to toe. His robes were of a royal blue and white, patterned with elaborate designs of mythical creatures of the land, sea, and sky. But he seemed oblivious to the grandeur that he wore and seemed almost guilty to see the bright array of colors that Valéon boasted across his waist, chest, and shoulders.

"I see our Ribbon Princess's silk enchantment holds strong as ever,"
  Duke Vandek murmured. "Your wings are well?"

"Vandek, they're fine,"
  Valéon felt a deep discomfort in his stomach.
  "I'm fine.
  I keep telling Sylasienne I'm fine,
  and she doesn't believe me."

"That's because it's a half truth," Vandek said.
  "Your wings are fine, and your heart on the mend,
  but your mind is not. Isn't that so?"

It was as if the silence told Vandek
  more about the situation than anything else,
  and the older man sighed,
  "Have a seat, Valéon. Have a seat."

"You perceived all of that?"
  Valéon murmured as he sat on the bench next to Vandek.

"I perceived more than that," the royal advisor admitted.
  "But I try not to overwhelm everyone
  who comes to speak with me
  with everything all at once."

"I appreciate that," a shiver ran through Valéon's body,
  traveled through his wings. "So, why am I here?"

Valéon watched the royal advisor swallow
  and try to find words to express himself.
  He expected to hear some sort of request,
  but he didn't expect what he actually heard.

"I wish to ask for your assistance.
  Would you accompany me into the peace treaty chamber?
  I haven't stepped into it for twenty years,
  and I'm afraid to enter it myself."

11

Meeting the Princess of Vinduren

Darkon felt strange
    flying to Vinduren with Tal, a native of Inkaien,
    sitting beside him on a fireproof kite with a letter from Eld
Mané.

They flew over the Inkstone Mountains,
    since it was an easy path to follow towards the east,
    and would lead them directly to Vinduren and Kalos Fyrian.

Granted, the King of Kites was a lover of exceptions;
    in fact, he often boasted that his entire life was one.

But as he considered this strange situation,
    he couldn't help but wonder about the involvement
    of three northern countries and two southern ones.

Asking five countries to try to solve one problem seemed a bit excessive.

When he expressed this sentiment to Tal,
    the other shrugged and pointed out
    that it was more like five countries

trying to solve five problems.

The Kite Kingdom had a kite failure issue.

Inkaien, or Ink Country,
    had a "no ink" requirement
    for the next peace treaty attempt.

Kalos Fyrian, the Land of Fire,
    was supposedly calling for aid,
    but only heard by
    their southern neighbor,
    Vinduren.

Vinduren wanted to support the peace efforts,
    but was preoccupied with all the fires
    coming from Kalos Fyrian.

Meanwhile, Eld Mané was trying to figure out
    how to begin the second peace treaty attempt under Avorne.

"If you think about it," Tal said,
    "Every country needs a miracle it can't afford.
    But it may be that we may each be the miracle
    someone else is looking for and desperately needs."

"That's rather optimistic," Darkon said to his younger friend.
    When Tal pointed out that his wife, Raehn, thought so too, Darkon smiled.
    "Ah, our beloved Singer of the City."
    Darkon had to remember that Tal was closer in age to Avorne and Raehn,
so their reasoning and lines of thought were similar.
    "How is she? Has she decided on the next Singer to be?"
    "She's still listening for the right candidate," Tal answered.

"Raehn's still torn about choosing a successor from our son or daughter or looking outside the family. She remembers what Saheun did for her. I think part of her wants to honor him with the decision to bring up a successor from outside of her bloodline."

"And what are your thoughts on the matter?"
    Darkon prodded Tal gently.
    "The spouse of any ruler should have a say in that,
    even in a country as liberal as Cantabelle."

"My thoughts?" Tal laughed.

"I can hear the songs they sing into things,
    but not before, and singing isn't my forte,
    so I'll let a native of Cantabelle
    decide what's best.

But the kids do have a leaning
    towards the musical,
        as opposed to ink, like me.

It's their greatest lament.
    They want to be able to listen and sing
    and be a master ink enchanter or enchantress.

I'm not sure how Renadé's ambition ended up in both of them.
    Their demands are exhausting.
    Lately, they've been begging me for musical ink enchantments."

"Oh?" Darkon was intrigued. "How so?"

"They compose the songs they hear
    like a musical score on paper,

136

and then they ask me to recreate it
using my ink to turn it into
an enchantment
they can wear on their skin,"
Tal explained.

"What they like about it is
if they give it to anyone from a different country,
that person can sing that song
or play it on an instrument
and give it life outside of Cantabelle."

"What a novel idea,"
Darkon was rather delighted with this new discovery.
"Have you got one to show as an example?"

Tal grinned.
"As a matter of fact, I do."

He pulled back the sleeve to the robe he wore, and on his right forearm was what looked like a stream of notes. It was as if a page of music had been connected into one continuous line from beginning to end, and it wrapped around Tal's wrist and continued up his forearm.

Darkon bent down closer to examine it, and then frowned. He thought he could hear a faint melody rising from the notes that rested upon Tal's skin. He asked,

"Is it just me, or can I hear the song being sung?"

"You're hearing it correctly," Tal confirmed.

"The kids wanted to make sure there were two ways to access the song. The first is by reading the notes. But for those who don't know how to read music, there's an alternative, which is to listen by ear and learn the song that way. And if you follow the recording as you read the notes, you may learn how to read music better as well."

"How did you manage to do that?" Darkon asked, impressed.

"They sang the song into the ink I used before I spun it into an enchantment," Tal explained. "I think they just like seeing the tangible result of their work."

"Who doesn't?" Darkon laughed. "They wrote this?"

"Actually, Raehn sang this one, the kids transcribed it, and I spun the ink enchantment. Raehn thought that I should wear one of the more sophisticated works if I'm traveling between countries. Might as well showcase our best while we're out and about, right?"

"I suppose so," Darkon mused.

He had long been of that opinion, but he wasn't sure when he had lost his energy and enthusiasm. Maybe sometime in the last year or so, after helping one too many people in need and not being able to rest. And then his own country's crisis had been the tipping point. A wave of discouragement bore down upon him without warning, and Darkon fought to keep his face straight. He wrestled with the bout of depression that threatened to take over momentarily. But it was lessened all of a sudden, and it startled Darkon so much, he looked around to see what could chase away the discouragement and depression so easily.

It was Tal's musical ink enchantment, which had unwrapped itself from Tal's arm and began to wrap around Darkon's left wrist. The score of music worked its way up his arm and shoulder, curling up his neck and chin, resting just upon his cheek and around his eye and beneath his ear. And there, the entire song played softly in Darkon's ears. It was Raehn's voice that sang the song with its melodies and intertwining harmonies, and Darkon could even hear her hands that clapped or drummed the underlying beat. Hearing her sing made the depression dissipate. It was as if he'd been given a helmet or suit of armor of live ink and music.

Darkon looked to Tal for an explanation.

Tal just said,

"You looked like you could use it.

At least until you get your cheer back."

Darkon smiled meekly.
"Thank you."

"Anytime," Tal shrugged.
"We'll get your kites up and running again soon enough."

Then he leaned forward and pointed to something in the distance.
"Is that Kalos Fyrian?"

Up ahead to their left,
was a blazing wall of fire
that traced the perimeter
of Kalos Fyrian.

Darkon swallowed
when he saw
the towering flames.
"Looks like it."

He already felt the heat building up in the winter air. Had he not been aware of the source of that heat, Darkon would have welcomed the increase in temperature. The warmth and feeling that had been stolen by the cold now trickled back into his fingers and his face.

And he had thought the kite failure in his kingdom was an issue.

What had kept this firewall up for so long? Darkon had only seen the blazing borders of the land of fire from a distance and never ventured close by. Even with his fireproof kites, he had interpreted the wall of fire as everyone outside the borders had:

Keep out.
Stay away.

But as they flew closer and closer
to the border of Kalos Fyrian,

it seemed like there was one person
who did not heed the fiery warning
and was approaching the flames.

"Is that…?" Darkon began,
   as his mind registered
   the sight of a young woman
   obscured by heat waves,
   whose gown of royal purple and gold
   glittered fiercely in the light of the flame.
   "Princess Featherfall?"

"Falleyne," Tal murmured.
   Without asking for Darkon's permission,
   he spoke a word of urgency
   to the kite they rode on.

The kite leapt forward at a speed
   that made Darkon grip the edge to steady himself.

And it was not him, but Tal,
   who reached out
   as they passed the princess,
   and intercepted her
   as she reached out her hand
   towards the massive flames.

"Whoa there," Darkon said as they rounded to a halt and placed the princess
down at a safer spot, some ways back from the fire.

To the young woman
   who had been unable to speak
   due to her surprise,

he said,
"My apologies, dear Princess.
Tal feared for your safety.
As did our kite."

To Tal, he gave an amused look and said,
"Next time, a warning would be appreciated."

The young woman looked first at Darkon and then at Tal. Her light brown hair was pinned back in gold and silver, and she stared at them with curious green eyes. Then recognition lit up in them as she registered what Darkon had just said.
"Tal!" She leapt up
and practically tackled him
out of the kite in an enthusiastic hug.

"I thought I heard
a different melody
coming my way!
I was right!"

She greeted Tal and peppered him with question after question.
She asked how he was,
what he was doing here,
how was Raehn,
how were his children,
and how was the Ink Prince
now that Tal was investing more time
in being a father closer to home
than a royal advisor across the mountains?
Darkon was amused at the bashful fondness that came over Tal. It seemed as if Princess Featherfall was quite the charmer. It made Darkon wonder about the history between these two, but he decided to wait before

interrupting this rather joyful reunion. Instead, Darkon studied the current
ruler of Vinduren with great interest.

It was said
that of all of the six southern countries –
the six being
Eld Mané,
Cantabelle,
Aequaré,
Vinduren,
Ohngara,
and Pent –
it was Vinduren who was the most
traditional and conservative of the mix.

Cantabelle was the forerunner
to integrating northern culture into the south,
and Eld Mané was the second country
to follow with much more influence.

Aequaré was neutral for the most part,
and Ohngara and Pent were so far down south,
they had little against the north,
having the fewest interactions with them.

But Vinduren was a bastion of tradition and culture,
proud of its roots, its history, its heritage.

Vinduren did not believe in the integration of northern culture
into their way of living, but it had the most favorable relations
with the north – specifically Kalos Fyrian – for centuries.

Perhaps it was because in the oldest annals of dream lore,
it was documented that the first King of the Dream Realm

originated from the north in Kalos Fyrian,
and the first Queen of the Dream Realm
came from the south in Vinduren.
They were the first known alliance
forged between the north and south,
and somehow, they became
and remained the strongest.

Darkon wondered if that was what kept the princess so determined to maintain peace with the land of fire that threatened to burn all of its neighbors. He would have to ask. But until then, he found himself utterly intrigued by his southern counterpart and all that she stood for.

It seemed the traditional garb of royalty in Vinduren reflected the family surname of Featherfall in rather literal terms. The princess appeared to be adorned in a waterfall of feathers. Everything from the belted outer garment of golden feathers to the ridged long-sleeve dress that she wore underneath rippled and cascaded like water. The bright blue feather pinned to her hair gave a nice accent of color as well.

As the non-stop questions continued, Tal was unable to keep up with the eager one-sided interview, so he just pointed to Darkon as if to suggest that the Kite King, with the kite he rode and the letter he carried, would answer everything.

"Oh!" Falleyne said as if just remembering the situation and looked slightly miffed at herself for missing a tradition she was very familiar with.

"I'm sorry. Where are my manners?" She bowed and made a slight hand motion of high respect to Darkon and gave the formal greeting.

"In the name of Eladan, I welcome you to the borders of Vinduren. May He guide your way with songs fit for this time and age. It's an honor to meet you, Majesty."

"The honor is all mine," Darkon stood atop the kite and swept a bow.

He heard the musical ink enchantment that Tal had bestowed upon him sing sweeter and louder in response to the princess's greeting, and it made him wonder at how easy it was for him to recall his long-lost cheer and

bright outlook. His smile came back to him naturally, and he felt some of
the tension leave his body.

"I, Darkon, King of Kites,
greet you, Princess Featherfall
with all due respect and honor.
I come bearing the reply
of Avorne Ehrthann,
King of Eld Mané.
He requested that I bring the letter to you
to start what we hope will be
an alliance between our countries."

Darkon took out the letter
from inside his coat pocket
and handed it to the princess.

She reached out,
opened the letter,
and read with breathless wonder,

"I,
Avorne Ehrthann,
King of Eld Mané,
do send my regards and aid
through these three fireproof kites;
the willing assistance and guidance of
Darkon, King of Kites;
and Inkaien's former royal advisor,
Tal Roethal, master ink enchanter.

While I regret not being able to
deliver this message in person,
I am currently undertaking the efforts

to realize the second peace treaty attempt
and unable to come.

I pray that you will understand and accept the little I offer.
Know my heart is with you in this matter.
My only request is that you aid those who help you as well.

May your newfound allies help you to reach
Prince Elias Blazewick and his people.

May Eladan keep you through the flame
and forge you into an unbreakable blade in the fires of this trial."

The expression that came upon Princess Featherfall's face was something
to behold. Darkon marveled at the excitement that emanated from the
young ruler.

"This is so much more than what I expected!" She gushed.
"I thought I'd get one kite, not three!
And I get to work with the King of Kites *and* a master ink enchanter..."
she looked to both of them, put her hands together and bowed again.
"Thank you for coming! I'll do my best to not waste your time."

"Falleyne," Tal gave her a gentle reminder.
"You don't say things like that as royalty."

"I know..." Falleyne let out a small huff.
"When I'm with you, I forget.
I feel like I'm back at Matai's place
with his garden and the woods..."

"Pardon my intrusiveness," Darkon interrupted.
"But may I ask how you two know each other so well?

145

I've known Tal for some time,
but I never met you in person before, Princess."

"You can call me Falleyne,"
the younger ruler hurried.
Then she tilted her head in curiosity and asked,
"Would you prefer being called
by title or by name, Majesty?"

"Darkon is fine," he laughed.
"I prefer my name over my title too.
So what's the story?"

Falleyne beamed.
"How about I take you around
this side of the fire wall
while I tell you?"

12

New Friendship

Emily wasn't sure what to think
about being left alone with two people she had just met
as she watched Valéon leave her side of the apartment
and walk out of sight in the palace gardens.

She stood rooted to her kitchen floor,
not sure how to begin her conversation with Iris or Ionthann,
who seemed nice enough and politely waited for her to make the first
move.

For one moment,
she wished to still be
with Valéon,
Darkon,
or even Avorne.

It wasn't that she was in desperate need of their guidance.
It was that she craved to have someone to lean upon.

It was the realization that
contrary to the role she had taken on in her relationships,

she did not want to be the strongest and most steady one all the time.

Emily wanted to be an equal,
    to have a relationship that was
    desired and not imposed,
    that was truly fifty-fifty,
    give and take.

It occurred to her that the reason she so strongly wanted to be with Valéon, Darkon, and Avorne, was because their relationships were the only examples of balanced and healthy ones that Emily had experienced for most of her life. Perhaps it was time to learn how to pursue new friendships, healthier ones.

Emily walked to the edge of the invisible doorway
    towards Iris and Ionthann,
    and held out the deck of cards in her hand.

She decided to address Ionthann first,
    since that was the reason why the mirror
    had opened a doorway to the gardens of Eld Mané's palace.

"I got these cards from a high ranking soldier in my dream last night,
    and when I asked the mirror who gave them to me,
    it showed me you. Was the mirror right?"

"So *you* were the disillusioned leader at the crossroads!"
    Ionthann exclaimed in sudden recognition.
    "The one who almost gave in to the pressure
    but chose the path of leadership at the last minute?"

Emily blinked.
    "Well, I never would have thought

148

to consider myself as a disillusioned leader,
but I suppose that's pretty accurate."

She wryly added,
  "Could we add 'mentally harrowed'
  and 'emotionally thread-bare' to that?
  If I didn't have that dream or get these cards,
  I don't know what I would have done."

"I'd say," Ionthann shook his head.
  "Funny you came when you did.

I was telling Iris about that dream,
  and all those cards that revealed your current struggles.

In a strange way, it encouraged me to see that list of challenges,
  because I thought we were the only ones dealing with insurmountable
problems.

It was nice to know one leader found a clear path forward
  in the middle of the tension and demand of expectation.

I'd like to share that dream with Avorne, but I don't know where he is.
  He's been wandering the mountains behind the palace a lot as of late."

"You'll find him sooner or later," Iris didn't sound worried.

She seemed to be curious about the pattern
  the cards had taken under Emily's ownership.
  "You changed all thirty of your challenges into alternative solutions?"

"I suppose," Emily shrugged.
  "Can't say I know what use they have though,

except to lift my spirits and remind me not to give up."

"In the Dream Realm,
   a hand that is dealt to you
   is your current circumstance,"
   Iris said thoughtfully.

"A deck of those cards can represent your life.
   So in your case, the current situation
   that was originally dealt to you
   made you feel like the problems surrounding you
   defined your identity and would last your entire life.

But when you took your life in your own hands,
   you discovered the truth.

As a leader, you will face hardship,
   but if you take the paths of
   strength, honor, wisdom, and kindness,
   you will not only find allies to help you along the way,
   but your life will be defined by the qualities of a true leader."

Emily was speechless.
   She had been encouraged
   when Valéon had told her his take on her dream,
   so she didn't think anything else would come of it.

But hearing this objective presentation of her dream
   revealing yet another layer for her to ponder, Emily wondered.

Maybe there was something meaningful and valuable
   to her unseen service of being a good listener and supporter.

Maybe if she took this time to pursue her calling,
    she would find a way to convert every
    harrowing experience in real life
    into something beautiful.

But Iris wasn't finished yet.

She took the cards,
    shuffled them gently,
    and held them out
    stacked face down
    towards Emily.

"Pick a card."

Emily had to smile.
    "Are you a magician as well as a gardener, Iris?"

Iris laughed.
    "No. I know my dream lore,
    and it is truer and deeper than magic.
    Have you picked a card?"

Emily took one
    about three quarters
    of the way down.
    "Now I have."

"Without showing me, take a look at it
    and then give it to Ionthann,"
    Iris directed her.

"Can I look at it?"

Ionthann asked as he glanced at Iris curiously.

"You've never done this?" Emily asked.

"Done this?" Ionthann shook his head.
   "I've never seen this.
   My wife is full of surprises,
   even after all these years.
   She's quite the master of dream lore, though."

He seemed especially pleased
   when Iris gave him permission to look.

Holding the card in her left hand
   and shielding it with her right,
   Emily glanced
   at the card she had picked
   and silently read,
   HOPE

Then, she passed it along to Ionthann.

She wasn't sure what accounted for his expression
   when he read it and had a double take,
   staring at Emily in shock.

But without saying a word,
   he waited for Iris's next direction.

"Now, Ionthann," Iris said.
   "Hold onto that card.
   Don't show me what it is."

To Emily, Iris held up the cards and fanned them out
 so only Emily and Ionthann could see the bottom side of the cards.

"Emily, is your card in the rest of this deck I'm holding?"

"No,"
 Emily wondered if this was a trick question.
 "Ionthann still has it."

"Ionthann, show the card to Emily
 to confirm you still have her card." Iris said.

Ionthann did.
 The card was still the one
 that Emily had given to him,
 with the word HOPE on it.

Iris asked,
 "Can you confirm that the card you're holding
 is not in the cards I have in my hand?"

Ionthann confirmed it.

"Good."
 Iris closed the fan of cards
 back into its rectangular stack.

"Touch the card you have face down
 on the top of the stack."

Ionthann did.

Iris showed Emily and Ionthann the cards she held.

They were still the same.
And Ionthann held the card
that read HOPE in his hands.

Iris asked Ionthann to give the card back to Emily.

To Emily, Iris asked her to slide her card face down
　　somewhere in the middle of the stack.

"Anywhere?" Emily checked before following through.

"Anywhere but the top or bottom," Iris clarified patiently.

So Emily did, sliding her card somewhere close to the middle.

After this, Iris sat on the ground as she shuffled the cards once more.

She asked the two of them to sit down as well,
　　and began to take the cards
　　starting from the top of the deck
　　and laid them out on the ground
　　face down between the three of them.

As she did this, she explained to Emily,
　　"In ancient dream lore,
　　this is a means of gauging
　　the significance of a person or thing
　　in relation to the current circumstance."

"So it's like fortune telling?" Emily asked.

Iris shook her head.
　　"No. Fortune telling

came out as a counterfeit
of the original dream lore.

This is a measure of the present;
   it doesn't dictate what you should do.
   It leaves everyone the freedom to choose
   how to act in light of the measurement.

In our case, Ionthann and I can see
   your significance in relation to us here.

Well, provided I did it correctly.
   We'll find out."

By now, Iris had laid each card
   face down on the ground between them.

Iris asked Ionthann to flip them all over, one by one.

As she watched Ionthann do just that, Emily started.

The first card Ionthann flipped over,
   the one that had been at the top of the deck read, HOPE.
   But that wasn't the end.
   The second card read HOPE.
   As did the third.
   And the fourth.
   And the fifth…
   all the way to the thirtieth.

Each and every card
   that the captain of the guard
   flipped over face up read HOPE.

"But how is that possible?" Emily asked first.
  "Hope was only one of the thirty cards.
  All the others had different words on them,
  like COURAGE or PATIENCE or JUSTICE.
  There were thirty different qualities altogether."

Iris and Ionthann were just as floored as Emily.
  They only exchanged a knowing look
  that explained nothing to Emily.

Iris frowned as she picked one of the cards in her hands.
  "If I recall correctly,
  the card that you drew is the quality you bring to us,
  and the number of cards that carry the same word,
  in this case, HOPE, gives us the percentage of certainty."

"So, if all of the cards say HOPE,"
  Emily tried to make sense of this.
  "Then it's a hundred percent that I signify hope to you two?
  But why? I don't know either of you. We've only just met.
  How could I be hope for your current circumstance?"

Ionthann, who had said nothing
  up until this point, cleared his throat.
  "I think I have the answer to that."

He reached into the inside coat pocket of his blue uniform
  and pulled out a battered piece of folded parchment.
  Very carefully, he unfolded the paper
  and pondered it for a moment,
  glancing at Emily as if he were
  assessing her worthiness
  for some unknown honor.

"What's that?" Emily asked,
    still lost as to what this bizarre result
    and turnout of cards meant.

It really was like getting to the end of a magic trick,
    only instead of thinking,
    "wow! How did that just happen?"
    Emily thought,
    "What just happened
    and what does it mean?"

But she didn't have to wonder for long.

Ionthann answered,
    "This is the first peace treaty draft.
    It was bestowed upon me by Valéon years ago during a dream.
    And now I believe it's time for me to bestow it upon you."

"What?" Emily held up her hands in protest.
    "Wait a minute. That's a very important document you've got there.
    Valéon said he entrusted it to a high-ranking soldier –
    well, I guess we know for sure that's you now...
    but Valéon gave that legacy to you to guard and keep it safe."

"Which I have done," Ionthann agreed.
    "But his final direction was
    'seek a new heart and mind
    who will give it new life.'"

It finally clicked in Emily's mind.

"You mean me.
    You mean to give it to me."

"Yes," Ionthann nodded.
  "If it would help you to know,
  I can see auras around people among other things,
  and the one emanating from you matches
  that of the cards that read HOPE,
  this peace treaty draft,
  and the one that Valéon had in that dream
  years ago when he passed the legacy on to me."

A shiver passed through Emily as she heard that statement.
  What could she even say to that?
  She knew Ionthann was telling the truth.
  For a reason she could not name,
  Emily felt words rise within her that led her to ask,

"What does the defender of this legacy desire?
  What does the keeper of the future say?"

Ionthann asked,
  "Do you vow to give new life to this legacy of peace?
  Will you revive the King's Heart?"

Emily replied without hesitation,
  "I vow to give new life to this legacy of peace.
  I will revive the King's Heart by traveling the path of leadership,
  the directions of which are strength, honor, wisdom, and kindness."

The first question came.
  "What will you do with the strength you gain?"

She replied,
  "Strengthen the hands of all who rebuild."

The second question came.
  "What of the honor you will receive?"

She answered,
  "Honor the memory of those who first came."

The third question came.
  "What of the wisdom you will find?"

She said,
  "Wisdom will speak to those who would hear."

The fourth question came,
  "What of the kindness you will claim?"

"Kindness will bind what is broken and mend every hurt."
  She spoke loud and clear.

"Then by choice and right, the King's Heart is yours.
  May the breath you breathe bring new life,
  and may the words you speak bring hope and healing,"
  Ionthann concluded as he gave the first peace treaty draft to Emily.

"May the King's Heart no longer be a dream, but become reality."

"Just so," Emily replied as she received the legacy
  with a slight bow and nod. "Just so."

Emily was smiling. She couldn't help herself.
  Confidence she didn't know she had filled her chest, making her stand straighter and taller. She looked at Ionthann and then Iris, and they shared her bright countenance. It really was as if they had found hope again.
  "Thank you," Iris murmured beside Ionthann.

"Don't thank me yet," Emily glanced down at the peace treaty draft, and the significance of what had just happened began to sink in.

"We've got a lot of work to do."

13

Requesting the Impossible

Whenever he looked at Mirae,
    Avorne was reminded of an amalgamation
    of people he had met in previous years.

More specifically, he thought the young architect
    from the Invisible Lands reminded him of three friends
    he originally met at an enchanted mail shop
    called the Hourglass in Honoraire,
    the city just south of the palace.

Mirae's passion for her leaders
    reminded him of Haliien,
    the owner of the Hourglass,
    who held a fierce dedication to Avorne as king,
    even before she unknowingly hired him
    when he had arrived at her mail shop looking for his crown.

Mirae's need for an outlet
    to test her limits in a safe and productive way
    reminded Avorne of Cassan,
    an employee at the Hourglass and a former thief,

who stole Avorne's crown after falling back into old habits.

And Mirae's pent up frustration due to her talents
    reminded Avorne of his dear wife
    and ink enchantress, Renadé,
    whose skill with ink was formidable.

It was like looking into a window of the past, Avorne thought as he leaned forward to study the rose-colored crystal tile that Mirae held out towards him. She showed him how she could shape it into whatever she desired, like a small figurine of a whale. When he requested a shark, it morphed into what he asked for. Then as a playful compromise between the two sea creatures, Mirae transformed it into a whale shark and offered it to Avorne as a gift. Avorne was flattered and graciously accepted it with a "thank you."

What he did not say was how shocked he was at seeing the enormity of her handiwork. Avorne was floored to think that Mirae had come to design this King's Heart that they were in.

How much time had gone into this?

She had said her whole life?

Since she was ten? Avorne thought that even if someone had told him to design something akin to a palace that was ever-changing, he would have failed miserably. He wouldn't have known where to start. But Mirae worked with the ease and natural talent of someone who had been born for her occupation.

When he mentioned this, he was surprised to hear Mirae laugh.

"What?" He asked.

"I failed so many classes,"
    she said, running her hand
    through her silvery-white hair
    before tying it back into a ponytail.

"All the kids in my class were naturals.
I just had a double work ethic, that's all."

"What sort of classes did you take?" Avorne asked, wondering how different
it was from history or math or even southern architecture.
She listed names he had never even heard about:
Shaping,
forming,
molding,
crystallizing,
refracting,
reflecting,
visualizing.

"Visualizing was the worst,"
Mirae shuddered.
"I hated that class.
You know the comment I got the most
from my instructors?
'Visualize more.'
I did!
There was nothing more to see
on the models they presented me.
They said I lacked vision."

"I would say that your vision is fine,"
Avorne looked around at the stained-glass cathedral they stood in.
"It's certainly functional."

"No one could see my work when I started," Mirae shrugged.
"I was too self-conscious
and the pressure made me do worse.
I barely passed that class.

After that, I worked on visualizing every chance I got outside of school,
and I finally turned my greatest weakness into my greatest strength.

Deep down, I always had this vision,"
    Mirae motioned to the King's Heart.

"And what is your vision?"
    Avorne asked, curiously.

"To provide my leaders with a means to fulfill their heart's desire,"
    Mirae said without hesitation.

Then looking straight at Avorne,
    she said, "Name one of yours."

"What?" Avorne asked.

"Say it out loud," Mirae explained.
    "It's like what I did with the crystal tile
    and the animal figurines, only bigger.
    If you speak it,
    I'll show you what I mean.
    So name one."

Avorne thought about this, and said,
    "How about a library?"

When Mirae looked at him in bemusement, he qualified,
    "Halas, my brother, really loved books and libraries.
    He passed away some years ago, but if he were here,
    I'd want to have a library to show him and let him explore it.
    I'd want the books to be of the north and south,
    but ones that no one has ever read before.

Like books on lost dream lore;
books on the true nature of every country,
its makeup and its people;
books on Eladan, who we almost never mention,
though most of us still share a belief in Him."

And then it occurred to Avorne
that he had asked this young architect
to do the impossible.

He sighed,
"You know what,
why don't we start with a book,
instead of a library?"

But Mirae's face lit up in a brilliant smile. It was as if she couldn't contain the delight that bubbled up within her, and she clasped her hands together in excitement.

"No, that's perfect. I've never done anything quite that specific before, but...give me a minute. I can figure this out."

She made a motion with her right arm, as if she were lifting something invisible up above her head. From out of the floor, an enormous storage room emerged.

Avorne had to take a step back, because a set of cabinets and shelves and drawers rose just in front of him. A work table with two chairs rose as well, which Avorne discovered by backing into one and sitting down. He looked down at the table, and on it was a large sheet of paper that unrolled itself. Upon it, an invisible hand wrote in neat handwriting the dimensions he had just asked for:

Request to be fulfilled:
·*1 library filled with books*
·*Nature of books: dream lore, forgotten truths revealed, Eladan inspired*

Avorne's jaw nearly dropped open. He stared at the words on the page before him and tried to wrap his mind around what he had just witnessed. Mirae was still bringing up what started out as a storage room but now looked more like a warehouse of materials. There were crystal tiles everywhere in crates and bins, boxes and glass jars. Everything was neatly labeled in the same handwriting.

"You have your own warehouse?"

Avorne asked when he could speak again.

"Where did all of this come from?"

"Oh, these are scraps," Mirae said as she went from crate to crate, taking an assortment of raw materials from them and dropping them into a box she carried.

"Most of our builders throw away the waste material because they can't use it for anything. But I can't afford most of the materials, so I settle with the left overs no one wants. It's amazing what I've managed to collect."

Then she said,

"Take a seat, Majesty. I'll be there in a minute. Are you comfortable?"

"It's Avorne," he had to remind the young architect, to which he received a torrent of profuse apologies. He stopped her from going overboard by saying the chairs might be more comfortable with cushions on them.

"Oh, right." She rushed over, tipped half of the box's contents on the empty blueprint and placed the box with whatever remained on the table's corner.

Mirae plopped herself down in the chair beside him and studied the many multi-colored crystal tiles piled before her, and then pursed her lips. In the middle of this, she took a deep scarlet tile in her hand and closed her eyes. It became two scarlet cushions of silk with golden tassels around the edges. She opened her eyes and then handed one to Avorne and took one for herself. "Will this do?"

Avorne said it would as he took it and put it on his seat and sat down again. He still had no idea how invisible land architects did what they did with their mysterious building properties. He wondered how the design of this cushion mirrored the cushions that were in Renadé's study on the third floor of the palace of Eld Mané. The study had been his mother's, the late queen Annette, and just before passing away, she had expressed her desire to hand it down to the next queen, which was Renadé. The cushions were scarlet and gold, but how would Mirae know?

While Mirae shuffled tiles in one formation and then another, Avorne ventured to ask, "Have you ever been in the palace of Eld Mané?"

"No," Mirae shook her head, not looking up from her work. "Why?"

"No reason," Avorne said, not even sure what to think of this development. "Are you sure you don't want to just start with a book?"

He knew it was a silly question even as it left his lips.

He thought about the beauty of this place when he had mistaken it to be a mysterious ink sign that only he could see. He thought about the doors that had appeared at his wish, and the keyhole that had been made for his crown alone to allow him to enter in. And he thought about the elaborate art on the floor that still boasted the design of his golden crown with its bold statement: A KING IS NOTHING WITHOUT HIS PEOPLE.

For Mirae, this was a challenge. It was a chance to try her hand at a skill that had until now, remained untested. Avorne had often witnessed this same intrigue, enthusiasm, and determination from Renadé while working on a new ink enchantment. He was brought back to the current situation when he felt a light tap on his shoulder.

"I need a little more. Can you tell me about Halas?" Mirae asked.

Avorne swallowed and tried to blink the sudden tears that came to his eyes. To hear someone ask about Halas as if he were still alive moved him.

"Halas was…"

Mirae stopped him.

"Is. Not was."

"He's got a double affinity of perception and influence.
    He's my half-brother from the sky,
    who was saved by the Sky Maiden
    and brought up at the Pondragai Estate

by its Lord and Lady and attendant Valéon,"
Avorne tried.

"Okay," Mirae frowned.
  "But that doesn't tell me what he's like."
She handed Avorne a lavender tile that looked blue at certain angles,
which made Avorne realize matched the color of Mirae's eyes.
  "What does everyone know him for?"

"Being a chronic worrier," Avorne said.

Mirae smiled and suggested,
  "Something positive."

Avorne took the tile
  and flipped it in his hands.
  "He's a peace maker."

"That's better," Mirae nodded.
  "How does he make peace?"

"By perceiving a need and influencing the situation to meet it.
  By letting everyone keep their dignity and pride.
  By being gentle and kind and considerate.
  By protecting people with his own life."
  Avorne found it hard to continue, but he had no need to.

"I can work with that,"
  Mirae gently took the lavender tile back.
  "Thanks, Avorne."

She swept the rest of her pile of crystal tiles back into the box, and then set
her lavender tile squarely in the middle of her blank blueprint. She placed

her hand on the tile and then closed her eyes once more. Avorne kept his eyes open, and watched as the lavender tile melted and seeped into the paper, bleeding out from under Mirae's hand and fingers.

Lines of lavender outlined a room filled with shelves and tables and chairs, benches and light fixtures and tall, arched windows. It extrapolated and provided multiple views from different angles.

To his actual left, Avorne realized that a large set of glass, double doors had appeared in the wall. The doors were closed. Above them was a sign that read: *Welcome to the Library.*

Had Mirae just transferred the design on her blueprint into this place? Avorne couldn't help himself. He stood up and walked towards the double doors. He could see rows of shelves inside, each one filled with books.

"Mirae, is this...could I...?" He wasn't sure how to phrase his question.

Mirae finally opened her eyes, took her hand off of her blueprint, and glanced at it with a nervous eagerness.

"I don't know how that turned out. I guess we should take a look and see." She rolled up the blueprint and then hurried to Avorne's side. But when she looked at the glass doors before them, she paused.

"Do you want to go first? It's your library."

Avorne didn't even need to worry about an answer. The doors opened for him. They were opened by a person, who was in princely attire of cerulean and white. Avorne felt his knees buckle, but he stood fast, making himself look upon the dark-haired man who seemed equally surprised as himself.

Avorne found his voice first.
  "Halas?"

Mirae was beside herself.
  "It worked!"

Halas, because it really was Halas,
  looked in bewilderment from Avorne to Mirae
  and then pointed to the young architect.

"Who's she?"

"I'm Mirae Hope," Mirae bowed her head respectfully.
    "Are you Avorne's brother? It's nice to meet you."

"Yes, I'm Halas Endronil, fifth prince of Eld Mané."
    Halas bowed in return.

"But I'm afraid you have a lot of explaining to do.
    Is this the King's Heart?"

He didn't hide the astounded expression on his face
    as he looked from the library
    to the rest of the King's Heart outside.
    "This is enormous."

"How did you know I named this place the King's Heart?" Mirae asked.

"I didn't," Halas admitted.
    "But this is the King's Heart all right;
    I've been here before. Twice, actually.
    But it's never been on a scale like this
    with this sort of form and function."

He frowned, and then his gaze fell onto Avorne with slight suspicion.
    "Did you give up your heartbeats again?
    Are you fighting another nightmare?"

"No," Avorne said.

He was still struggling with the fact
    that he was talking with Halas,
    who had died years ago,

and whom he had dreamed about
speaking with many times.

He decided to stick with something he knew for certain.
    He pointed to the architect from the Invisible Lands
    who stood beside him and said, "Mirae designed this place."

"She what?" Halas was stunned.
    "But how is that possible?"

"I've been working on this since I was ten?"
    Mirae offered, just as bewildered.

"I'm from the Invisible Lands,
    and this is what we do for a living.
    It's just that my project is…well,
    different from the accepted standards.
    I've got a heart for leaders,
    but no one's understood my vision yet.
    So I'm building it here
    in the Inkstone Mountains
    by Eld Mané's palace,
    because Avorne said it was okay
    after seeing it when no one else was supposed to.
    He's the one who gave me the idea to name it the King's Heart."

A light of understanding came into Halas's eyes then,
    and he turned to his older brother.
    "Avorne, what are you working on right now?"

"The second peace treaty efforts," Avorne answered.
    "Everyone expects me to start it, and I've been stuck,
    until I saw Mirae's work behind the palace.

It's the first time I can see what my vision for all of this looks like.
But I still don't understand how you know about the King's Heart.
What do you mean you've been here before?
What do you know about it?"

That was when Avorne first learned
   about what his sacrifice of heartbeats had created
   when he first sought to free Uncle Vandek and the palace
   from a nightmare that had plunged the first peace treaty
   into such a messy failure twenty years ago.

Apparently, in that desperate fight
   to save Vandek from the nightmare,
   Halas had ended up in a state between reality and dreams,
   where he had come across a place with their tutor Iris.

The sacrificed heartbeats, Halas explained,
   brought the King's Heart into being,
   which generally appeared in times of great need.
   It was a suspended time and place to let those in it
   have time to think and get their bearings
   before they returned to their current situation.

Halas's theory was that Avorne's desire to sort out the second peace treaty
efforts had allowed him to see Mirae's invisible architecture because her
heart was for her leaders. And he also suspected that Mirae's heart for her
leaders was also the King's Heart, or the heart that Eladan had for all of his
people. It wasn't that Mirae was the only one who had this sort of vision
or heart, but she was the first who had brought it into a tangible reality
through her abilities.

"You must have a very big heart for your leaders," Halas said to Mirae
when he had finished sharing his idea with them.

Mirae blushed at that compliment. Avorne chuckled as he watched her try to hide her face behind the blueprint of the library that she still carried. He wondered about how natural it was to speak to Halas even though they hadn't even been able to say goodbye to each other before Avorne had learned about Halas's death from Tal years ago.

"Say, Halas," Avorne felt a lump in his throat as he tried to swallow. He noticed that Halas still looked like he was in his late thirties, the age he had been when he had died in the Inkstone Mountains. But somehow his brother seemed to have gained a youthfulness and wisdom that Avorne wished he could have.

"Will you stay for a while?
   I've missed you."

Avorne was overtaken by a tight embrace as a response,
   and he realized that he wasn't the only one
   who wanted to make up for lost time.

"As long as you need me to," Halas replied after letting go.
   "I can't step out of the King's Heart;
   that's as far as I can come from the other side.
   But so long as we're here, we'll be fine."

Avorne nodded.
   He was glad to have this chance
   to see Halas,
   talk with him,
   spend time with him.
   It felt good to be with his brother again.

He grinned.
   "Want to help me with the second peace treaty attempts?
   If Mirae pulled off my impossible request
   and managed to bring you here on top of that,

then she definitely got the library part right.
I'll need your brains to help out."

Halas glanced at Mirae for an explanation.

She offered,
    "Avorne asked for books on dream lore,
    the northern and southern countries
    as they should have been or could be,
    and anything on Eladan."

Halas turned back to Avorne, amused.
    "Since when did you get an interest in studying?"

"I thought about what I'd want to show you
    if you were still here," Avorne paused.
    "It also made me think that it would
    make other people feel at home if they came, like…"

"Valéon," Halas said.

Avorne nodded.
    He was comforted by Halas's perception and influence
    that worked in tandem to intuitively sense
    and address Avorne's unspoken sentiments.

"Who's Valéon?"
    Mirae asked,
    but her question
    remained unanswered
    for the time being.

"We've got to get him here," Avorne said.

"We'll never have the second peace treaty if he doesn't come."

14

Confronting the Past

It was an understatement to say
    that Valéon was surprised to hear
    that Vandek hadn't entered
the treaty chamber for twenty years.

He didn't know what to think about it,
    so naturally, he didn't know what to say either.

But perhaps words were not needed.

Valéon stood in the treaty chamber with Vandek
    and stood side by side with the royal advisor,
    who trembled uncontrollably.

There was nothing in the room that would have hinted that anything terrible had happened. The damage done from the ink explosion all those years ago had been repaired. The large meeting room table had been replaced with a new one, as were the chairs. The water system that flowed around the perimeter of the room was clean as well.

But still, Valéon could feel

where the ink had struck him
and eaten away at his flesh.
Remembered the screams
and the cries of pain
from the ink that
Duke Vandek had poured
into the waterway.
Remembered his Lord and Lady
tossing the peace treaty draft to him
and telling him to "Read, Valéon.
Read, and do not forget."

For a brief moment, Valéon came back to the present and was able to look
at the room without any negative side effects. Right now, today, this room
was nightmare free and ink free, as was Vandek.

"Vandek," Valéon started,
    trying to get his breathing back to normal.

"We have to stay in the present.
    Stay in the present.
    Avorne needs our help."

Even as he tried to speak those words with conviction,
    Valéon's wings ached in the places they had been broken.
    He fought the pain – the memory of pain, rather –
    and reminded himself that his wings were mended.
    He mastered his fears regarding that,
    no longer fought the memory of the failed peace treaty attempt.
    But the first memory of pain
    triggered the other memories of pain
    from his captivity that had followed.

Valéon knew the ribbons and needle were no longer
    embedded into his body as they had been while he was captive,
    but he felt the jabs pierce his skin
    and searing pain burn through his limbs.
    He felt the way they had punctured his throat,
    found a way to reach his voice and extract it from him.
    His breaths came in shallow gasps, and he tried to steady himself,
    bring himself back. He had his voice now.

Emily and Darkon had helped him to regain it.
    He could speak now.
    Valéon fought with all his mind to come back to the present.
    He had passed on the first peace treaty draft to the next keeper in a dream.
    He had been rescued from the Ribbon Fortress by Emily,
    been freed of all of those needles and ribbons
    that embedded themselves into him.
    Not a single needle or ribbon remained in his body.
    The silks and scarves he wore were just Emily's silk enchantment
    that kept his wings attached to his back, enabling him to fly.
    He was free of the needles and ribbon.
    Sylasienne, the Ribbon Queen restored,
    was currently his most fierce protector.
    He wasn't a victim anymore.
    He was free.

It was Vandek's influence that saved him in the end.
    It came first as gentle vibrations,
    then strong waves.
    Soon, it was a battery of constant pulsing
    that kept Valéon strictly in the moment.
    It kept the memories and the pain out,
    and it served as a temporary reprieve
    from unnecessary suffering.

Valéon had never experienced the full extent
  of Duke Vandek's influence used for good.
  He had heard plenty of what Vandek could do,
  but he had never felt it for himself until now.

"Are you with me?" Vandek was asking him in concern, breathing deeply himself.

Valéon swallowed and gave a small nod. He didn't know why it comforted him so to feel this enormous influence engulf him, steady his trembling, clear his thinking. Now that he had his mental fortitude back, Valéon was grateful to find that he wasn't the only one who struggled to keep the past in the past. He also drew strength from the fact that he was working through his troubles with a friend.

"Thank you, Vandek."
  He said as he finally felt
  his wings again and found his voice.

"If we have the second peace treaty attempt,
  you could help us with your influence."

Vandek shook his head.
  "If those of Inkaien say 'no ink,'
  then I say, 'no influence.'"

"But we need your influence," Valéon tried to argue.
  "Look at what you're doing for us now. I need this.
  I'm not sure I'll be able to function without it if we stay here."

Vandek confessed.
  "Valéon. It's hard enough for me to function with my own influence.

Every day, my double affinity reminds me

179

of all the terrible things I did
with my perception
and my influence.

Every time I speak with you,
   I remember how I perceived
   your voice of power all those years ago,
   and how I considered it the biggest threat to my ambition.

Every time I am reminded
  of how I used my influence
  to deal with you,
  how I dealt with everyone else
  who stood up against me.

I am so sorry."

Valéon felt an acute embarrassment settle over him
   and tried to shake it out of his wings.

"I forgave you years ago, Vandek.
  Did you forgive yourself?
  And have you forgotten that
  for eighteen years you sought to free me
  from the Ribbon Fortress up north in Silkairen?
  Everyone told me how much you did
  since you were freed from the nightmare.
  That's more than enough."

Vandek only seemed half convinced.
  He avoided addressing that and said,
  "We need your voice of power.
  It was what brought me out of my panic.

We need you to speak, now more than ever.
Plus, as living legacy of the first peace treaty,
your word has more weight than ours."

Valéon felt his heart beat slightly faster at that.
"I can't promise anything, but I'll at least consider it."
He was distracted by the sound of approaching footsteps and voices.

"This is where
the first peace treaty attempt took place,"
the first voice explained.
It was Ionthann.

Apparently, the captain of the guard
was giving someone a tour of the place.

Valéon almost cringed at the timing of things.
Why now?

But then he heard
the familiar voice of Emily.

"How long ago was this?"
She was asking.
"Twenty years?"

"Just about," Ionthann replied.

What was Ionthann doing, bringing Emily down here?
Valéon could see Emily sporting her silk robe and blue-gold scarf while hugging her *Gold: Leadership at Heart* book to her chest as she walked beside the captain of the guard. Valéon was about to speak up to get their attention, but just then, he felt Vandek reach out and pull him back away

from the doorway, motioning him to be silent.

Valéon felt a strange sensation trickle down over him from head to toe. Was Vandek's influence at work again? Apparently it was, because when Ionthann and Emily walked into the chamber, they looked straight through the spot where Valéon and Vandek stood. Valéon didn't know that influence could be used to cloak one's presence from the knowledge or awareness of others. He was impressed that Vandek could do it so easily, and then wondered why it was necessary to hide themselves from Ionthann and Emily.

"It's a nice room," Emily was saying.

"Yes, very fine," Ionthann agreed.

"The problem is that most who survived the disaster
   have no desire to come back here
   because of the memory of what happened."

"Was it that bad?" Emily asked.
   She pulled out a folded parchment
   that had been stowed inside of her book,
   and Valéon felt his breath catch in his throat.

He would know that paper anywhere,
   even without seeing its contents.

He heard the sharp intake of breath
   from Vandek beside him as well.

It was the peace treaty draft.
   Valéon knew for certain that he had given that to the high ranking soldier in his dreams. So if the treaty draft was now in Emily's possession, that meant...Valéon looked then to the captain of the guard.

That meant Ionthann was

the high ranking soldier
who had come to him,
and had been true to his word
to keep the peace treaty draft safe.

It also meant that Ionthann
must have deemed Emily the individual
with the new heart and mind needed to give the legacy life.

"Yes," Ionthann said with a shiver.
"It's better that you don't know the specifics.
We would erase the memory from our minds
to ease the pain if we could."

"Don't do that," Emily said.
"There's another way."

She pulled out
the deck of cards
from her pocket
and placed it on the table.

"Keep the memory, because it's important.
We can do something for the pain instead."

Then she said,
"Can you bring the memory to the forefront of your mind?
You don't need to tell me,
just think of it and put your hand on the deck."

Valéon watched Ionthann place
his right hand on Emily's deck of blue-gold cards.

He studied the way Emily
   took those cards,
   shuffled them,
   and laid them out face down
   on the large meeting room table
   in three rows of ten.

The first row of cards remained blue and gold.

But in the second row,
   second card in,
   one blue-gold card
   turned black.

The third card also turned black.
   As did the fourth, fifth, and sixth,
   continuing into the seventh, eighth, and ninth.

All the remaining cards she laid out
   kept their blue and gold design.

Emily didn't react,
   though Ionthann, Valéon, and Vandek recoiled.

To those who had been present at the first peace treaty attempt,
   the layout of the cards resembled something more.

The eight black cards in the center
   looked like the meeting room table,
   and the surrounding blue cards
   looked like the seats of those who sat around it.

But Emily considered this development

184

with nothing more than a curious glance.

She reached to turn over the first black card
 starting from the left, second row, second card.
 She flipped it over,
 and in a blood red hand
 was written the word FEAR.

Valéon and Vandek both bent over slightly to get a better look.
 They watched as Emily flipped over the next card,
 it read
 GUILT.
 Then came
 SHAME,
 ANXIETY,
 DESPAIR,
 and REJECTION.
 The last two were
 PAIN and LOSS.

Valéon watched as Emily picked up the one that said FEAR on it, and tried to shake it,
 as if she could get it to change back into the blue and gold card it had been.
 It remained black and red.

"I can see why no one wants to come back,"
 Emily said softly.
 "Why not just have the next peace treaty somewhere different?"

"Where would we have it?" Ionthann asked.
 "Everyone expects it to be in Eld Mané.
 They believe Avorne is the best shot we've got

at accomplishing the second peace treaty,
and our poor king is beside himself
trying to figure out how to make it happen."

"Well if you ask me,"
Emily looked around the room,
"it's too small."

Valéon's eyebrow shot up at that matter-of-fact assessment from his friend.

"Too small?" Ionthann voiced the question that Valéon knew he and Vandek also shared collectively.

The treaty chamber was the largest meeting room in the palace. It had a rather large holding capacity as well. Surely Emily hadn't missed all the chairs around the giant meeting room table and along the walls?

"That's right," Emily said with a nod.

"We need someplace bigger.

Someplace different.

Outside the palace.

There may be people who still have wounds that haven't fully healed.

There's no need to torment them by forcing them to come here.

Sometimes it's easier to start over in a completely new place that's has no resemblance to where you began."

For some reason, Valéon felt a tight knot deep within him loosen at that comment. Beside him, he heard Vandek let out a low sigh of relief.

"What sort of a place?" Ionthann asked.

"We've got a limited set of choices here."

"Well," Emily looked down at her card configuration.

She swept the blue-gold cards back in a neat pile. She then collected the black cards in her hand and tapped the pile of eight cards to her forehead in thought.

"Do you remember our dream?"
Emily asked Ionthann at last.

186

"Where we met at the crossroads?
Well, the way of leadership had four directions."

Valéon watched Emily lay down the cards again.

This time, Valéon thought the layout looked like a simplified compass rose.

Two cards pointed north,

two cards pointed west,

two cards pointed east,

and two cards pointed south.

Emily pointed to each direction and recited,

"STRENGTH,

HONOR,

WISDOM,

KINDNESS."

Then she paused.

"Something's missing."

"What?" Ionthann asked.

"My allies," Emily said.

"Ionthann, if you were the high ranking soldier in my dream,

do you know why you turned into a white wolf at the end

to lead me down the first path?"

"I did?" Ionthann looked taken aback.

"I thought I was just showing you the way."

"You were," Emily agreed. "But you were also a white wolf at the end.

And it was the most brilliant white I've seen, like sunlight on snow."

Ionthann made a thoughtful noise, and then reached over to fish something out of a leather pouch that he wore around his waist on his belt. He brought out something that glimmered even as it caught the light from the northern lights of the treaty chamber and reflected it. Ionthann held it out for Emily to see.

"You mean like this?"

Emily's eyes grew wide.

"Exactly like this. Ionthann, what are you doing with a crystal wolf? You know what, tell me later. Do you mind if I borrow it?"

Ionthann handed the small crystal wolf over to her.

Everyone watched as Emily placed it in the center of the black cards as if she were playing a game of chess and moving her piece to a new square. As soon as she did, the cards turned from black to their original blue-gold. Emily stared at that, and then looked at Ionthann.

"I don't know what that means,

but I'm pretty sure you're the one who's going to help us

get to the place we need to be for the second peace treaty.

And I have no idea what that wolf is supposed to mean either."

"I might," Vandek spoke at last, and everyone, Valéon included jumped. The influence that had kept them invisible all this time had been released.

"Okay," Emily put a hand to her chest.

"Next time, I need a warning."

Ionthann recovered first.

"Vandek, you almost gave Emily a heart attack.

Also...private conversation?

What are you and Valéon doing here?"

"We were having our own private conversation before you came,"

Valéon tried to explain. "We didn't want to interrupt."

"We thought you'd come and go," Vandek nodded.

"I thought I saw your aura close by,"

Ionthann said then.

"I thought it was just me."

"I hate to interrupt all of you," Emily cleared her throat.
  "But if we're going to figure out where to go next,
  I'd rather not do it in the place where you're all fighting bad memories."

"We can move to the gardens," Ionthann suggested.
  "Plenty of light and room. Iris could chip in if she wants,
  and if Avorne happens to come back, we may be able to call him over."

Valéon turned to look at Vandek.
  "Why don't you join us?"

Vandek looked hesitant.
  "Well…"

"You just said you might know what this means, right?"
  Emily motioned to the card formation
  with Ionthann's crystal wolf still seated in the middle.
  "I'll take all the help I can get."

Valéon smiled.
  "Exactly.
  Plus, it might make a good memory for all of us.
  We could use some good new ones."

He was more than glad when Vandek agreed at last.

15

The Blade Pass

As he followed Falleyne along the mountainside, Darkon kept noticing the rocks and stones that were lined up along the barrier of the firewall. There were large ones and small ones, almost as if they marked intervals of some sort, and it was interesting enough for him to interrupt Falleyne in the middle of her storytelling to ask her what it was.

"Oh, all those stones sing of protection," Falleyne casually explained.

"I replace them from time to time with others if I hear stronger songs from them, but so far, they've done their job and kept the fire from jumping over to our side. I just wish I'd thought of the solution sooner. It would have saved so many crops in the years past."

Now that his curiosity in this matter had been satisfied, Darkon contented himself to listen to the rest of Falleyne's tale of how she and Tal had met. Apparently, Vinduren had undergone several periods of upheaval, and when Falleyne was a child, the instability was at its worst.

While the royal princes plotted against each other,
Falleyne's older sister had snuck her out of the bloodbath
that had begun to ensue and smuggled her to safety to Eld Mané,
just by a wood called Drehnfall.

For years, Falleyne was raised as a refugee under the care of a gardener named Matai, his wife Elle, and son Garin. The strange thing was that they never once realized that they were in fact raising the royal princess of Vinduren. That was when she had first met Tal, who had come to Matai's place for safe haven before returning to Eles Teare to hide Raehn's jewel from the Ink Prince who sought to take it for his tower in Ink Country.

"Wait," Darkon raised his hand.
"How did no one know you were the royal princess?"

Falleyne only asked,
"How did no one know that Eles Teare suffered an attack
from the Ink Prince taken over by a nightmare?
How did no one know what happened to the King of Eld Mané
the six weeks following his coronation?"

Darkon frowned and gave voice to his disbelief.
"Vandek? But how would you know?"

"History," the princess of Vinduren stated.
As Darkon learned very quickly, Falleyne was keen on history. She was fully aware that if Avorne had killed Vandek all those years ago during the first nightmare outbreak at the palace of Eld Mané, then Vandek wouldn't have repented and become an ally, because he'd be dead. And if not for Vandek, then most likely, she wouldn't be alive or restored to her throne either.
"I owe my life to Vandek and Avorne," Falleyne admitted.
"And so we discover that Vandek has kept yet another secret well hidden in all these years after his release from the nightmare," Darkon quipped wryly, making Tal laugh.
"Well," Tal said, "If Vandek hadn't hidden Falleyne so well in Eld Mané, I might not have met her, and she might not have given me a gift that saved my life."
More information that Darkon hadn't known about. Darkon had always tried his best to stay in the loop, seeing as his country was so up north

that he wanted to stay connected with the current events in the rest of the world. But today, he felt as if he knew nothing and had just moved to the area. How had Falleyne saved Tal's life? What was the gift? The answer surprised him. A pebble. Falleyne had given Tal a pebble that sang of life, and it had preserved his life from the ink enchantments that the Ink Prince had bound him with after failing to take Raehn's jewel and sign of authority.

Tal took out a small grey pebble from his pocket and held it out for them to see.

"So this pebble sings of life like those stones sing of protection?" Darkon asked.

"Yes," Falleyne answered.

She then told him how she began her practice of listening to the stones around the time that she came to Eld Mané, because back then, she was terrified of the fires that ravaged Vinduren. As a girl, she wanted to find a way to protect her new family from the fire, so she collected stones that sang of protection and set them all around the house and in the gardens and down the front path to the street. It had alarmed Matai and Elle, since they couldn't hear the songs, and though they tried with all their might to get Falleyne to stop, it only made her redouble her efforts.

"They even called a physician to examine me," Falleyne laughed.

"That might have been the best worst thing that happened to me."

"Best worst thing?" Darkon asked.

"It was the worst
　　because I was afraid that he would find out
　　that I was the princess of Vinduren
　　more than I was afraid he would tell my guardians
　　that I was mentally unstable," Falleyne said.

"It was the best,
　　because that was how I met the person
　　who would become the royal family's physician

192

and my most trusted advisor.

It was also the best,
  because Sephalon helped Tal to speak again
  and bring him out of his condition."

"What condition?"
  Darkon demanded to Tal.
  "You had a condition? Since when?"

Tal gave an accusing look at Falleyne.
  "Are you going to tell him all my secrets?"

"Why are you embarrassed?" Falleyne asked.
  "I just want Darkon to understand our history
  before he risks being burned to a crisp
  with us trying to get into Kalos Fyrian."

Tal sighed. To Darkon, he said,
  "I was fighting a severe case of being sun-lit and shadow-bound.
  I had to go against the Ink Prince and keep Raehn's jewel out of his grasp,
  but if I were to unweave Raehn's jewel,
  I was in essence unravelling her ability to function as Singer of the City.
  I knew what I had to do; I just couldn't bring myself to do it."

"You never said a word," Darkon said, concerned that Tal hadn't told anyone
this until now, years after the incident had passed.
  "Who would I have gone to?" Tal asked.
  "I just took my dilemma to the most secluded place I knew, completely
separate from the insanity surrounding me. Fortunately, help came to me
in the form of a kind gardener and his wife and hardworking son, their
adopted niece, and a traveling physician from Aequaré."
  "Had I known," Darkon said with some regret, "I would have offered

help."

He was glad to see Tal relax at that, even though the offer was years too late and Tal had long recovered from that ordeal. But all of this mention of history made Darkon wonder.

"Falleyne," he said, as she continued to lead them along the firewall.

"Would you like me to share my history with you?"

Falleyne waved away the offer with her hand and said, "There's no need to."

This was when Darkon learned that Falleyne really did know her history.

It was strange hearing her talk about his achievements and accomplishments of the last twenty years like she was retelling a hero's tale. She knew that Darkon was the first northern ruler to openly display their alliance with the south by working with Queen Annette. The Queen of Eld Mané had asked the King of Kites to intercept the corpses of the representatives from the first failed treaty attempt. By intercepting Vinduren's dead representative, Darkon had saved Vinduren from falling into a worse state.

"But what I admired most," Falleyne declared unabashedly, "Is how you maintained peaceful relations with Silkairen even while the Ribbon Fortress was entrenched in a nightmare. It made an impression on me, the way you didn't try to just kill the Ribbon Queen, but save her with the help of the Ribbon Princess. It inspired me to keep my stance regarding Kalos Fyrian."

Darkon was impressed and amazed. "How do you know all of this?"

"History is what saved me," Falleyne answered. "I'd be a fool to forget."

But the Princess of Vinduren deemed that lengthy history lesson to be enough, because she stopped and pointed to a place where there was a break in the line of stones and rocks that sang of protection.

The fire emanating through the pass was twice as hot as the firewall they had been walking beside. Falleyne said it was because there were no stones for protection here. This was one of two passes that led into Kalos Fyrian. One was the Paper Lantern Pass, which had flames too hot and intense to even approach the entrance. The second was this one, the Blade Pass, and for some reason, it had less flames in it overall. Falleyne didn't know why.

Darkon peered into what felt like an unbearably hot, flaming furnace. He saw certain shapes wavering in the blaze and asked,

"Are those swords embedded in the mountainside?"

"That's why it's called the Blade Pass," Tal surmised.

"But I don't think we can go in even with our fireproof kites.

There's too much fire here. We'll be burned before we know it."

Darkon silently agreed. But he also wondered about why there was less fire here than in the other pass, when it seemed like the firewall around the border was equally strong everywhere. Could it have something to do with the swords themselves?

With his left hand, Darkon reached out towards the flames,

and Tal and Falleyne both cried out in alarm at his seemingly foolish action.

Darkon held up his right hand and said,

"Wait. It's all right."

The flame was uncomfortably hot, but it didn't burn his hand.

Darkon attributed it to Tal's musical ink enchantment, which had loosened from his left side and kept the fire at bay, much like the stones Falleyne had lined up along the border did. The song in his ears increased in volume, and Darkon knew this was his chance.

He gripped the hilt of the sword closest to him,

winced from the burning sensation

that immediately met the palm of his hand and fingers,

and pulled with all of his might.

The sword came out of the mountainside as if it were being pulled out from its sheath. He dropped it as soon as he pulled it out, because it was so hot. Darkon tried not to wring his hand from the pain, but his discomfort left relatively quickly. He was miraculously not burned.

Once the musical ink enchantment had settled back on his skin, Darkon bent down to pick up the new sword. It was cool to the touch.

He offered it to the others.

"Sword anyone?"

"If you pulled it out," Tal said,
  "then it's probably meant to be yours."

Darkon didn't want it.
  The blade made him feel awkward,
  and the sight of the firewall
  reflected in its shiny reflection
  made him uncomfortable.
  Darkon thought the gem at the sword's pommel looked like a live ember
smoldering and gleaming in bright intervals. As a general rule, the Kite
King disliked weapons of any sort.

"I don't believe in violence or bloodshed."
  Darkon took up the sword and held it out before him,
  as if he were presenting it to another with both palms face up.
  He wished Falleyne would take the sword off of his hands.

She didn't.
  Instead, Falleyne ran her fingers along the blade
  and bent her ear towards it.
  "Don't worry.
  It doesn't sing of war.
  It doesn't even have a whisper of violence or bloodshed."

"Well, it is a new sword," Tal pointed out.
  "It might be different after it's seen a battle."

"It's not a new sword," Falleyne disagreed.
  "It's seen lots of battles.
  It's got one of the oldest songs
  and has been around
  as long as the mountains.
  It sings of a different sort of valor."

"Does it?" Darkon asked.

Falleyne nodded, quite intrigued.
  "It sings of the valor to set things right.
  This is a sword of peace.
  It can't be drawn for battle.
  You should hold onto it.
  It's not every day someone can pull a blade from this pass.
  The sword responded because your belief resonated with its core."

"She's got a good point," Tal agreed.
  He put a hand on Darkon's shoulder.
  "Keep it and give it a name, Darkon.
  It may prove to be the key you need
  to help your kingdom and people."

"Name it?"
  Darkon looked down at the sword.
  He noted the way their fireproof kite flew around him and the sword with a new vigor and approached the sword and bumped it gently with its nose.

"All right."
  He spoke to the sword as he said,
  "I'll name you Valor."

At that, the gem embedded at the pommel glowed bright, and before Darkon realized what was happening, the flames from the pass began to be sucked into the sword through it.
  Tal and Falleyne jumped back, but Darkon didn't move.
  He just held the sword with his two palms open, and let the torrents of fire enter it.
  The sword absorbed the flames and the fire from the pass. Strangely,

though more and more heat entered his sword, the metal remained cool to the touch. Darkon felt the distinct feeling with his hands, and wondered how he wasn't getting burned. The streams of fire kept coming, torrents of blazing flame, and all of it was absorbed into the sword.

When the flow of fire stopped,

there was a mountain pass devoid of fire,

and a clear path into Kalos Fyrian.

"Well then," Darkon said at last.

"Looks like we've found a way in."

16

From Strength to Honor

I n the royal gardens, Emily thoroughly enjoyed getting to know her new group of allies. She liked seeing how they all got along with Valéon and each other. Emily could see how in love Iris and Ionthann were in the way that they'd steal glances at each other when they thought the others weren't looking. She took pleasure in seeing Valéon take flight to locate and bring a book from the library on the third floor, while Vandek, the newest addition to the group presented his knowledge and theories about Emily's cards and Ionthann's crystal wolf.

Half of the time, Emily was distracted and unable to focus because she was happy simply to be there. Even the mundane act of sitting and listening to a group of individuals who were focused on solving the problem at hand together was exhilarating. Emily didn't know how this was possible when the conversation was so technical and full of jargon she didn't understand. Iris, Ionthann, Vandek, and Valéon exchanged ideas and points with the ease of experts.

Yet, something about it helped her to regain her joy. Not only that, Emily realized that she didn't feel tired anymore. She got her energy back, and it made her wonder. Was this the first direction of the path of leadership she had dreamed about? The one called STRENGTH? Because she certainly felt stronger now, though she had fought no battles. It was like her inner reserves, which had gotten severely depleted in the last year, were finally being filled to the max.

Emily didn't interrupt the conversation that was going on around her. There was talk about places she had never heard about, like the Invisible Lands, which supposedly could build entire cities with the crystal material that Ionthann's wolf was made out of. They also mentioned another place called the Changing Lands, which was about as far north as the Kite Kingdom, where a certain traveling merchant had come from who had given the crystal wolf to Ionthann as a gift when he was just a boy. There was also a possibility that the cards Emily carried had qualities linked to the affinity of the inhabitants of the Changing Lands, which was foresight.

Convinced that she had nothing of value to add, Emily temporarily excused herself, saying she needed to stretch her legs and would keep an eye out for Avorne if she saw him. No one objected, so Emily left her little square mirror with Ionthann after learning that he also knew how to use it, along with her cards for the others to speculate over. She picked up her book, left the gardens, and took a walk outside the palace. She meandered through the four courtyards that surrounded the palace itself, and then, because she was curious, took a step onto the mountains.

As soon as her foot touched the mountainside, her scarf came to life. Emily had nearly forgotten her title of Ribbon Princess until this point. It was like finding an old, unpracticed talent coming back into use again.

"Hello, friend,"

Emily greeted her new scarf with some amusement.

"I have no use for a summons today.

But I would like help with a riddle I'm trying to solve.

Would you like to help?"

The blue and gold scarf unwound itself from her neck, circled her once, twice, three times. Then it hovered in silent expectation.

"I take that as a 'yes,'" Emily said.

"I'm on the path of leadership,

and I just regained my strength.

I know the next direction I should take

is called HONOR, but I don't know how to start.

Could you lead me to the next clue?"

The scarf scrunched itself up, as if thinking hard, and then it unwrinkled itself with a sudden 'aha!' sort of movement, with its tassels quivering in excitement. Then, it began to fly, moving forward. The scarf only paused long enough to curve one end towards Emily, as if to ask, "Are you coming or not?"

Emily got the message. She began to follow the scarf. She wondered where in the world the scarf was taking her, as she went up and up, deeper and deeper into the mountainside. And then, strangely, she saw a familiar figure in the distance.

The King of Eld Mané stood in the middle of the mountains behind his palace. What Avorne was doing there all alone, Emily had no idea, but she imagined he had stepped away from his responsibilities to take a brief walk, get some fresh air, and clear his mind.

She watched as her scarf would loop itself around the man and this time slowly circled him. She thought she could hear him laughing as he reached out towards the scarf, and then raised a hand in greeting to Emily.

Emily raised her hand and waved back.

As she got closer, she called out,

"Avorne, did you know people are looking for you at the palace? Ionthann wanted to see you."

"Emily!" The King was absolutely delighted.

"When did you come here?

What brought you here?

Is everything all right?"

It felt so good to see Avorne again. Emily just grinned.

"I came today. Valéon brought me."

Emily took in a deep breath, entertained the idea of hiding her struggles and saying she was fine, and then decided to tell the truth.

"At home, I've hit my limit and am about to burn out. Which is why I'm here. Also, I wanted to know how your second peace treaty went, but Valéon says nothing's happened yet. Did something happen? Is there anything I can do to help?"

But Avorne was not so easily swayed.
  He honed in on Emily's unspoken struggles immediately.
  "Is Crystal in trouble?"

Emily blinked.
  "Crystal? She's fine."

"What about Vincent?"
  Avorne asked next.

"He's fine too," Emily replied.

"And Ryan?" Avorne asked.
  "How is he?"

At the mention of Ryan, Emily's brave front crumbled.
  "Ryan's all right.
  It's his dad who's not.
  It's Scott."
  She had tried so hard
  not to think of the problems
  she had left at her apartment,
  but Emily found that
  this one
  had
  trailed behind her.

"Scott?" Avorne asked.

"He's more or less Darkon's counterpart," Emily said.
  "They're so alike, when I first met Darkon,

I kept calling him Scott by accident."

She saw the understanding on his face and knew that she wasn't the only one who was dealing with struggling loved ones.

"The doctors don't know what's going on.

He's gone to the hospital so many times,

but they can't figure it out.

He's not getting better, either."

And then, because she couldn't help herself, she asked,

"Darkon's not ill, is he?

Valéon said it was just

a kite infrastructure problem,

but..."

Avorne paused.

"Darkon may have hit his limit like you have.

I offered help,

but he just told me

to work on the peace efforts."

The King sighed then.

"I don't know.

Where would you have the second peace treaty

if you could pick any place in the world?"

"That's easy. Right over here," Emily waved her hand in the direction of the mountains all around them. She didn't know why he looked so stunned at her answer.

"Where?" He asked again.

Emily's vague hand wave became a definite finger pointing at the space behind Avorne.

"Right here. It's the midpoint between the North and South, right? It's not anyone's country; it's a border. And there's lots of space."

Why was Avorne looking at her like that?

Emily didn't understand that hopeful look on his face.

"What?"

"Emily, can you see anything behind me?" Avorne asked then.

"Right now?" Emily asked. "You mean aside from the mountains, the sky, and the weird ink formations that look like modern art designs? No, not really."

But she picked up on his disappointment and disliked the crestfallen expression that came over his face.

"Why? What's there that I can't see? Is it important?"

She heard him laugh helplessly,

watched him bite his lip,

take off his crown,

and run one hand through his hair.

"You could say so," Avorne admitted.

"Thing is, it's invisible."

"Yes…" Emily agreed hesitantly.

"That's the nature of things that are invisible.

You can't see them. What should I be looking at?"

"A beautiful castle cathedral

that practically touches the sky

made entirely of crystal glass,"

Avorne said at last.

A pang of yearning gripped Emily's heart just then.

"That…" she stared hard at the space behind Avorne,

trying to see if maybe she had just missed something the first time. She closed her eyes tight, opened them, tried squinting and tilting her head.

She still couldn't see anything, but she said,

"That sounds lovely."

"It *is* lovely." Avorne said. "And I can't for the life of me figure out how I'm going to bring people in if they can't see it."

"Must they?" Emily asked.

"If they want to partake in the second peace treaty," Avorne said.

"I'd like to have it there."
  He paused and said.
  "It's called the King's Heart."

"Oh." Emily found herself deeply moved by this, though she still couldn't see a hint of what Avorne described. A small part of her wondered if maybe she wasn't meant to see this beautiful place, but a larger part of her wished to see this King's Heart and enter it.

"Well, just because I can't see it doesn't mean it's not there, right?" Emily tried.

And feeling like a student who hadn't quite passed the assignment, but desperately wanted to please her teacher, Emily opened her *Gold: Leadership at Heart* book and brought out the first peace treaty draft to show Avorne.

"I'm on the path of leadership," she blurted out, before he could say anything. "There are four directions, and so far, I've gotten STRENGTH. I'm on HONOR now, and soon I'll be on WISDOM and KINDNESS. So when I come back, I might be able to see it. Do you mind waiting for me before I try again?"

Emily rushed on, "Because Ionthann just gave me the first peace treaty draft that he got from Avalon in a dream for safekeeping, and now it's been handed down to me. Right now I feel like I have no say in this, since I wasn't here for the first treaty, but I want to come to the second one. I don't want to miss it, and I'll do whatever I need to do to be able to see this King's Heart and enter in. I just don't know where HONOR is direction-wise."

It was as if Avorne's heart melted at that admission.

His voice grew quiet, and he traced the edges of his crown with his fingers.

"You gave me more honor just now than you know.
  I can point you to the path of wisdom.
  On the parapet of the palace, there's an ink portal.

There's no missing it; you'll know it when you see it.
If you walk through that, you'll end up in the Kingdom of Kites.
Renadé, my wife and queen,
is there helping with the kite situation
while Darkon is out giving aid to another country.
In my years of kingship,
I've found that wisdom
has always graced my queen.
Renadé may help you with wisdom."

Gratitude welled up in Emily as she gave Avorne a warm hug.
    "I'll be sure to go there right away. Thanks for waiting for me."

He returned the hug with a heartfelt,
    "Thank you for believing me.
    I'll be waiting."

17

Finding Family

When he dreamt inside the King's Heart, Avorne felt like he was meeting his family for the first time. Once, he saw his mother, Queen Annette laughing and sharing a close moment with his father, King Ehrthann as they rode on horseback across the foothills before the palace. Another time, he saw his three older brothers – Diurne, Gavin, and Okten – engaged in an extensive strategy game at a long wooden table in his oldest brother's suite. They had all called him over, and argued over who he should help first, and which one of them would get to give him the first insight for the second peace treaty attempt.

Avorne often woke up in the middle of the night wondering if he were delirious. Those dreams were so unlike what his family had actually been like, that Avorne wasn't sure what to make of it. The relationship between his mother and father had always been strained and tense, if not icy. It was perhaps made worse with his father's going off and charming the queen of the sky and their secret relations that had brought about Halas as an illegitimate son. And even as an adult, Avorne could still recall the bullying he received as a boy from his three brothers before Halas had come to the palace. Nothing ever really had taken away the sting of his brothers' collective disdain towards him. But in these dreams, it was like his mother, father, and brothers had finally come into their own and were the best of themselves.

Avorne confessed this to Halas when he had woken up and couldn't go back to sleep. He had wandered into the enormous library Mirae had brought into existence, and found Halas completely immersed in his reading, surrounded by dozens of books. Halas hadn't even looked up from his studies, and said matter-of-factly,

"You're not going crazy.

That's what they're like now.

They've changed. In the best way."

It was still strange, though. So in the morning, Avorne asked Mirae if she dreamed while working in the King's Heart, and if she did, what sorts of dreams she had. He didn't want to pry, but he thought that if he could understand the types of dreams the maker of this place had herself, he'd be able to make sense of his own dreams here.

"Oh, I've dreamed all sorts of things," Mirae nodded.

"I used to dream that my leaders found me while I worked and begged me to come back to the Invisible Lands. They'd offer all sorts of awards and recognition – all the things that I should have received when I worked with them but never got. They'd see my vision and understand my heart for them. Of course, it never happened and still hasn't," Mirae said.

"But it did something for me when I woke up. The hurt went away. I found it easier to let go and forgive people and move on."

Avorne thought about this. Then he asked,

"Did you only dream about your leaders?"

"No," Mirae said. "Usually, I dream about building something no one's ever built before. Or helping someone with their blueprints, or stowing secret plans away on a ship to carry it to safety. Other times, I'm bringing important people to safety. Sometimes I rescue a designer from drowning and throw them a lifeline. Other times, I fight off an enemy while my allies get an engineer back to our base. Once, I helped the Queen of the Dream Realm locate a boy who housed the blueprints of a magnificent lighthouse made of voices and one very special light in the palm of his hand. That's usually the sort of dream I have."

"Is that so?" Avorne asked. "Because I had a dream that my three older brothers were playing a strategy game and invited me to join them to help them craft the best strategy. They argued over who could get my help first. And then they argued about who should give me advice first about starting the second peace treaty attempt."

Mirae looked rather intrigued. "That's amazing."

"Except that my brothers tormented me when they were still alive," Avorne pointed out. "In the dream, they were so kind and funny and loving towards me, it was bizarre. I was waiting for them to turn on me one by one, but they never did."

"Maybe it's what you need to get your breakthrough," Mirae suggested.

"What do you mean?" Avorne asked.

"Well, I don't know much about dream lore," the young architect said. "But when I dreamed about my leaders honoring me, I got a breakthrough. The last time I dreamed that, I woke up and got to the place where I could forgive my leaders for the mistakes they made and what they failed to do. It was the first time I was able to let them go and move on. The day after that, you walked in through the doors, and here we are."

"Are you saying
if I forgive my brothers,
I'll get an insight?"
Avorne asked Mirae.

Mirae shrugged. "Maybe you just need to see that there are people who support you that you never imagined would want to help. Kind of like me," she tossed her silver hair away from her face with a playful smile.

"Would you have ever imagined being helped by an architect from the Invisible Lands? Because I never imagined I'd have a leader from the south walk into my life's work when none of my leaders acknowledged it or me."

"Well, Avorne could possibly pass as one of the leaders from your country," Halas called out to them from the open doors of the library.

"Halas, were you listening to all of that?" Avorne asked as he turned towards Halas.

"Every word," Halas laughed as he walked over to them.

"Voices carry here. Also, it's a heart conversation. My perception picks up on that like it's a frequency or something. It happened after I died. Don't know how that works exactly, so don't ask me to explain it," Halas shrugged.

"What do you mean Avorne could pass as one of my leaders?" Mirae asked with a frown.

"Avorne's nothing like them. He's open minded and nonjudgmental about the way I work and how I build things. He gives me guidelines but gives me free reign to test my limits. Also, he actually talks to me. And he doesn't think my method of communication is inappropriate."

"What's inappropriate about talking face to face?" Halas asked in bewilderment. "Did your leaders have issues with communication over there?"

"They didn't want to expose the corruption and faulty foundations in our buildings and architecture. So I tried to get the information to them secretly with the same mechanisms that make up the King's Heart here." Mirae explained to Halas.

"You couldn't just tell them straight out what issues to address?" Halas asked.

Mirae shook her head.

"The infrastructure for clear communication
wasn't functional.
There was a history of corruption, greed, fear, and lying.
It was so bad, it made me paranoid.
One minute, someone would be saying
toxic things about another,
but when that person came by,
they'd pretend to be best friends.
The change happened like this,"
Mirae snapped her fingers.

"Right in front of me.
All the time,
all over the place.

210

So being me, I tried to fix the system.
I set up my own system
to make sure communication got to the top."

"Did it?" Halas asked.

"Sure," Mirae said.
"It was very effective.
It also broke socially acceptable conventions."

A knowing look came upon Halas's face.
"How many conventions did you break?"

Mirae didn't flinch as she said,
"Pretty much all of them."

Halas shook his head.
"It's no wonder you ended up here.
Next time, have a team to back you up,
instead of going in alone."

"Now I know," Mirae said.
"I'm just glad I took my heart and left.
But I'm pretty sure Avorne is nothing like my leaders from the Invisible Lands. What makes you say he could be?"

"Well," Halas began to smile faintly. His smile grew broader. "Being from the Invisible Lands was Avorne's 'cover identity' for a short span of six weeks once."

"Wait, what?" Mirae's jaw dropped open. "You pretended to be one of us? My people?"

"It worked surprisingly well," Avorne said sheepishly, rubbing the back of his neck. "With the help of Uncle Vandek's wide-reaching influence."

"Hilariously well," Halas corrected.

That started the tale of how once, long ago, when Avorne had just been crowned King, he suffered a mysterious illness that came after his crown had been stolen from him by a reformed thief who had fallen into old habits.

Halas explained how Avorne had accidentally been hired at an enchanted mail shop where the crown had been taken, and how the King of Eld Mané spent six weeks rather ill with a few of his citizens, who came to love him and became his friends. One even married him and became Queen of Eld Mané. But it was the details put into that cover identity of Avorne's that reached Mirae the most.

Avorne saw the way her eyes widened when he and Halas explained the "sight-sickness" that Avorne said he had when in fact his condition was from the distance he was separated from the crown. Avorne added that when he was still the fourth prince of Eld Mané, and journeyed far and wide with many allies, he wondered while staying one night at the Sunshade House, if he had an invisible affinity, the ability to be helped by many.

"So in a way," Halas concluded, "You have a six-week leader from your country here who has found your work. I daresay, we should adopt you into our family as a distant cousin or something. I'm sure it would tickle Renadé to no end."

Mirae was so pleased that she said nothing for a minute. When she finally did speak, she said, "I'd rather have you than the highest leader in my country. This is better than anything anyone could give me. I wouldn't trade this for the world."

Now it was Avorne's turn to be pleased. He thought about how desperately he had needed help to get this second peace treaty underway and was thankful for Mirae's presence, skills, and company. In a way, this was better than anything he could have asked for, and he felt similar about not wanting to trade this time with Mirae and Halas for anything else.

That night, when he fell asleep,

Avorne found himself in his oldest brother's room.

Diurne himself was the one who called Avorne over with a holler, asking him to join them again in their game of strategy. Gavin and Okten were naturally at the table as well, setting up the marble board and the various gold and silver pieces. Avorne noticed that the pieces were sea creatures of different kinds: fish, dolphins, whales, sharks, and giant squids or octopi.

"Do you want to play as an overseeing monarch or the advisor?" Diurne was asking.

"He's got the wits to play the monarch," Okten said. "He's King now, remember?"

"But he's got the natural experience to be the advisor too," Gavin pointed out.

"I think," Avorne said as he pulled a crystal whale shark out of his pocket and set it on the corner of the board outside of the grid,

"I'll just watch for this round.

I'll learn a lot from just seeing how you play."

When he said this, the scene around them changed.

He stood beside Diurne, his oldest brother,
   on the edge of the universe,
   with the stars below their feet like a pathway of light
   leading to the unknown. Diurne said,
   "If you have courage enough to reach for the unattainable,
   you will discover a way forward to lead others."
   He handed the crystal whale shark back to Avorne,
   and the scene changed.

This time, he stood watching Gavin, his second oldest brother,
   who sparred with a much younger looking Ionthann who had only just
become captain of the guard at the palace.
   "If you have endurance enough to discipline yourself,"
   Gavin panted as he dodged and parried Ionthann's sword,
   "you will be prepared for the future, whatever it may bring."
   He tossed the crystal whale shark to Avorne.
   When Avorne caught it, the scene changed once more.

Now Avorne stood next to Okten, his third oldest brother,
   who looked through a glass lens at something in the distance.
Okten handed the lens to Avorne so he could look through it as well.
When Avorne did, a sparkling city came into view, beautiful and elegant,
shining in the sunlight and boasting its magnificence. Without the lens,
there was nothing, but with the lens, there was everything.
   To him, Okten said,
   "If you have patience enough to see what others cannot,
   you will find a treasure beyond compare and comprehension."
   He passed Avorne the crystal whale shark,
   and the scene changed again.

Avorne was at the game table
   with Diurne, Gavin, and Okten again.
   His three brothers looked at him intently
   and with a warmth Avorne never knew
   they were capable of expressing towards him.

"Will you remember our insights?"
   Diurne asked.

"I will," Avorne said.

"Will you teach others our lessons?"
   Gavin asked.

"I will," Avorne answered.

"Will you share our vision?"
   Okten asked.

Avorne smiled and said. "I will."

When he awoke,
    Avorne felt like he had found his family
    for the first time in forty years.

18

A Visit to the Changing Lands

Flying into the Changing Lands to rescue the captain of the guard from plummeting to his death was not something Valéon had been planning to do as he glided down from the library with an armful of books and maps in his arms.

In fact, both aspects of what he did in the course of seconds was so out of the ordinary, Valéon still wasn't sure it had happened for real. But seeing as he was currently in a deep chasm looking up at the doorway that was still open above them at the top of a mountain that grew taller and taller, Valéon reminded himself that he had in fact done those two things.

Ionthann,
who was still catching his breath
on a rocky ledge
where Valéon had landed,
managed to say,
"Thanks,
Valéon.
I
owe you
one."

Valéon shook out the nervous energy that still pulsed through his wings.

"Thank me once we're back. This place is crazy."

"I'd say." Ionthann shook his head.

"I know they didn't name this place

the Changing Lands for nothing,

but the geographical changes here are

pretty drastic."

Valéon had to agree.

This had all resulted from speculation on if the merchant who had given Ionthann his crystal wolf could be found in the Changing Lands. Vandek had asked for a few northern lore books while Ionthann offered to open a doorway to the Changing Lands with Emily's mirror, just to see. Valéon had been flying back when he saw Ionthann step from the gardens to a grassy hill in the Changing Lands.

The moment the captain of the guard's foot met the grass, however,

the entire hill,

gave way and sank down,

while the doorway remained in place.

That was when Valéon had dropped everything he'd been carrying, flown past Iris and Vandek before going through to find Ionthann. Truthfully, Valéon was glad that he even caught Ionthann by the arm and was able to haul him to safety. There was nothing but a rocky gorge beneath that grew deeper and deeper, even now as they took a breather on one ledge.

Valéon was used to the changes of cloud formations in the sky, the rhythm of storms in season, and the pathways of wind above. But he had grown accustomed to the land itself remaining stable. And though he knew in his mind that the Changing Lands was one of the northernmost countries, experiencing it firsthand was jarring and rather disturbing.

Everything moved so quickly, like the snow storm that overtook the top of the mountain where their way back to the gardens was located.

Though Valéon was confident he could fly them both up there without much of a problem, he wasn't about to subject them to an unnecessary battle against the elements. Ionthann maintained an optimistic attitude for the both of them.

"We can wait the storm out.

If we're lucky, it'll be over before we know it

and we can try to make our way back.

Until then, I can help you spot a safe place,"

Ionthann offered.

"My affinity is still functional

even though we're this far up north.

It saved me and Iris once

when we were in the Ribbon Fortress

completely by accident,

so it can save us from here."

"Wait, you actually came to the Ribbon Fortress?" Valéon asked. "When I was a captive there? I thought you just came to me in that dream."

"Oh no," Ionthann laughed.

"I physically went there.

On my own.

Completely by accident.

With Emily's mirror, too, on top of that.

Kind of like how I ended up here.

That's how I got the actual treaty draft.

But that's a long story. Let's find a safe place to rest first."

"Right." Valéon took flight

while gripping Ionthann's arm once more,

and as he went higher and higher,

he said, "Can you see anything?"

All he could see was an ever changing landscape. There were hills that were migrating towards a distant sea in one area. There were valleys opening up and sinking down into the earth as other parts rose up high like the mountain that had risen above them before. There were waterfalls that were beginning to flow out of some of them, and new rivers appeared across the fields, snaking through the wide expanse. Some lakes disappeared completely and lush forests became deserts. Valéon felt his head beginning to ache just watching this. And to think this country was in a perpetual state of change.

"There," Ionthann said suddenly, as he pointed towards what looked like a small house on the edge of a set of woods that was growing up around it even as they spoke.

"I've seen that particular aura before, forty years ago. Unless I'm mistaken, that was the same one as the merchant who gave me that crystal wolf. Let's check it out. It'll only be for a few minutes."

When they landed at the front of the small house on the edge of the woods, they found that it wasn't a house, but a shop. It had on the front door, a sign that read, "The Secret Seller."

The two exchanged unsure glances before Ionthann took a hold of the door and opened it, stepping into the small shop. Valéon followed and folded his wings as tightly as he could to keep them from bumping into anything on the shelves. The shop was narrow, with a counter that ran all along the middle, separating the front of the shop from the back, which had shelves and shelves of bottles filled with all sorts of curiosities. There were a good number of bottles filled with liquid light, and these lit up the entire shop quite well.

An elderly man sat at the counter and cleared his throat.

"May I help you, gentlemen?"

Valéon watched Ionthann study that man at the counter with a frown, open his mouth slightly and then close it. The captain of the guard reached into his pocket, pulled out his crystal wolf and set it on the counter. Then he asked,

"Sir, you wouldn't happen to be the same merchant who gave me this wolf figurine for two copper coins, would you? It was almost forty years ago, but you have the same aura as that man did. I'm looking for a lead on either that man or this wolf. I believe it will lead me on the path to help many if I just find the right key."

Valéon blinked. He wondered if Ionthann's affinity of sight had picked up on something that Valéon couldn't see with his natural vision. But he waited in silence as the old man took the crystal wolf with care, picked it up and turned it over in his hands.

"You paid a price higher than two copper coins, son,"
   the secret seller said, as he appraised the treasure.

"It was two copper coins, sir," Ionthann repeated.
   "It was all I had as an eleven-year-old."

The secret seller just shook his head.
   "You paid the price for this crystal wolf by other means.
   What price did you pay?"

Ionthann looked stumped.

But Valéon spoke up for his friend.
   "He became captain of the guard in the palace of Eld Mané
   and has served two generations of royalty.
   He single-handedly held down a nightmare
   for days and nights in the royal gardens.
   He risked his life to reach a captive in the Ribbon Fortress
   and retrieved and safe-guarded an important document."

"Now that sounds more like it," the secret seller nodded.
   "I see that my judgment and foresight was correct.
   For through your actions, you saved many."

Ionthann leaned forward to rest his elbows on the counter.
   "Sir, please. We're trying to realize the second peace treaty, and I understand this crystal wolf is an integral part in helping it come to pass. Do you hold any knowledge – any secret – on how to move forward?"
   "This is the key," the secret seller smiled and handed the crystal wolf back to him.

"It will unlock the door for you, son. You must discover that path on your own. However, I can give you one additional secret."

The old man handed the crystal wolf back to Ionthann, and then bent down to reach for something behind the counter. He brought up a worn wooden box with a lock, and from a key that hung around his neck, the secret seller opened the box, and took out a small, folded piece of paper. He then handed it to Ionthann.

"Everything you need is contained there."

Ionthann was hesitant to receive it and said,
   "What payment is necessary for this?"

"There is no need to pay," the secret seller said.
   "Someone else has paid for it already."

Somewhat bemused, Ionthann thanked the man for his time and help, and then motioned Valéon to follow him out of the shop.

"We should have asked him for directions,"
   Valéon murmured when they finally got out.

"Even forty years later
   he still talks in the language of riddles,"
   Ionthann shook his head.

"We already know the way back,"
   Ionthann pointed at the top of the mountain, which was now clear.
   "We just have to get there before everything changes again."

Valéon had no objections.
   He was curious about the paper though, so he asked.

Ionthann unfolded the small square of paper,

and on it in neat handwriting
read two words:
Mirae Hope.

"What's Mirae Hope?" Valéon asked.

"No idea," Ionthann said.
"We can figure it out later.
Are you up for the long haul back?"

Valéon eyed that mountain peak
and took in a deep breath.
"I can do it."

It was easier to forget the physical strain he felt while flying Ionthann up towards the top of the mountain peak when he was engaged in conversation, so Valéon asked the questions he had meant to ask, before their strange run in with the secret seller. He asked about how Ionthann had infiltrated the Ribbon Fortress when it was still taken over by the nightmare, and how Ionthann had gotten hold of the actual peace treaty draft in the bedchamber of the Ribbon Queen, Sylasienne. And how was it that he hadn't known about this even after he had been freed?

As he listened to the captain of the guard, Valéon learned of the extent of his friend's loyalty and bravery to rescue him. He hadn't known that Ionthann had evaded immediate capture by entering the Ribbon Fortress while wearing a standard-issue Silkairen uniform. He hadn't known that Ionthann had broken through the chest of nightmare strands to retrieve the peace treaty draft, which was also with Valéon's wings at the time. He hadn't known the leg injuries Ionthann had sustained by the ribbons and needles that had pierced him while fighting to escape the Ribbon Fortress.

"I'm sorry I couldn't reach you," Ionthann confessed.
"It practically killed me to leave you after getting so close.
Iris had a hard time too.

She gave me the idea to find you in the dream realm
so we could let you know we hadn't forgotten you."

"I can't believe you actually came," Valéon said.
"But don't beat yourself up over that.
I'm out now, and Sylasienne is restored as well.
Lucky for us Emily came when she did."

"About that," Ionthann paused.
"Valéon, how did Emily free you?"

"Ask Emily," Valéon said.

"I did." Ionthann said.
"She doesn't know."

Valéon didn't let his surprise affect his wingbeats.
He kept rising steadily as the air around them grew colder and colder.
He could see the doorway getting closer and closer.
They were almost there. But he still asked Ionthann,
"She doesn't know? How is that even possible?"

"You tell me," Ionthann said.
"Right before I brought her down to the treaty chamber, I thanked her
for getting you out. But when I asked her about how she freed you, she
didn't know. She only told me about the scarves she used to put your wings
back in place. She knew nothing about the needles and the ribbon that
were like a parasite."

Valéon flew in silence for some time, thinking about what he had just
heard. He had always thought that Emily knew the terrible state he had
been in while at the Ribbon Fortress. He thought she had seen the ribbons
and needles that protruded from his body, at least the ones that hadn't
made their ways under his skin into his flesh and bone. Emily hadn't seen

any of it? She hadn't known about any of it? But how?

Because Valéon still remembered all the nights that he sat at Emily's little two person table while they drank tea together in her kitchen, how she would speak to him, and her words would make the nightmare's hold on him lessen. It was a slow and gradual process, and sometimes a good deal of pain accompanied the healing process. It was the time Valéon had spent in Emily's company that freed him from the enchantment that bound him to the Ribbon Queen's nightmare will. It was Emily's presence that disintegrated the needles and ribbons one by one, and the way that she acknowledged him.

With this thought, Valéon admitted,

"I suppose Emily never saw my true condition.

She only saw how my condition should have been from the beginning."

"That's a good point," Ionthann said then.

"I wonder if that's related to your secret paper," Valéon wondered.

"What?" The captain of the guard asked.

"Maybe the key isn't looking at how things are now, but how they could be...how they should be," Valéon said.

"And maybe that Mirae Hope is connected to it."

But he stopped there, because they had made it back, and he hauled Ionthann up and through the invisible doorway back into the gardens. There were some snowbanks along the edges on the ground, presumably from the passing snow storm that had come and gone so quickly on the other side of the doorway. Valéon landed on solid, stable, unchanging ground and heaved a sigh of relief, along with Vandek and Iris, who had been waiting for Valéon and Ionthann to return.

"Did you enjoy your foray into the Changing Lands?"

Vandek asked in wry amusement.

"Glad you both came back so soon. Iris and I were afraid you'd be there for months."

Valéon shivered.
  "That short time was enough.
  How long were we gone for?"

"Not even a half an hour," Vandek said.

Valéon ruffled his wings
  and then murmured to Ionthann,
  "Let's not do that again."

"I wasn't planning on it," Ionthann said
  as he closed the invisible doorway
  and pulled out the little square mirror.
  "That's enough adventure and mystery for the day."
  To Iris, he gave a loving apology and kissed her cheek.

The royal gardener only shook her head and sighed.
  "So did we learn anything useful through that near disaster, gentlemen?
  Aside from always watch your step?"

Valéon and Ionthann started at being addressed as "gentlemen" yet again,
as if they could hear the secret seller through Iris.
  "Actually," Valéon started and glanced at Ionthann.
  The captain of the guard took the cue.
  "We met the merchant who gave me that crystal wolf all those years ago.
He gave us a lead but we don't know what it means."
  Ionthann pulled out the folded square of paper and passed it to Iris.
  "Does Mirae Hope mean anything to you?"

19

Nightmare Infestation

I n all his life, Darkon had never seen an entire country taken over by a nightmare.

A single individual, yes.

Even a palace or a fortress or a tower.

Those cases, the King of Kites had witnessed with his own eyes.

But to see the land of a whole nation

taken over by oily, sticky strands,

with some parts looking like

piles of chopped up carcasses

and detached body parts,

was something new.

Not to mention, the stench was terrible and made Darkon sick to his stomach.

He heard Falleyne whimper and knew that she could hear the twisted songs that emanated from the nightmare infestation. But she didn't say a word as she sat by Darkon on their fireproof kite.

Tal, on the other hand,

who flew beside them on a different kite,

shook his head and said,

"I haven't seen anything like this before.

And we thought the Ribbon Fortress was the worst. This is…"

the ink enchanter tried to find the words to describe this terrible scene.

"...A whole people taken captive by their own country."

Where were the people? Darkon couldn't see them. At least, not at first. But the deeper they moved into Kalos Fyrian, the more he began to see the citizens of the land of fire, desperately trying to extricate the nightmare strands from their homes, the trees, their land.

The first who took notice of Darkon, Falleyne, and Tal was a tall, middle-aged woman, who was clad in armor that was smeared from head to toe with the tar-like substance from the nightmare. She was calling out directives to the group of workers who toiled to deal with the mass of limbs and nightmare fangs, eyes, and voices.

"Chip away as much as you can,

then burn the rest," she called.

"Don't listen to the voices!

For Prince Blazewick,

we must continue."

Falleyne jumped onto her feet.

Darkon had to balance the kite at the sudden movement.

"Pardon me,

do you know Prince Blazewick?"

Falleyne called. "Is he well?"

The woman took one look at Falleyne, and must have recognized the royal regalia of the princess of Vinduren, because she bowed at once and said,

"Princess Featherfall!

How did you get past the firewall?

We haven't had any contact with anyone outside our borders for years."

"I called for reinforcements!" Falleyne motioned proudly to Darkon and Tal.

"I come with Darkon, the Kite King;

Tal, the master ink enchanter and former royal advisor of Inkaien;
and three fireproof kites! Do you welcome our aid?"

Darkon almost chuckled at that paltry number of "reinforcements," thinking that they should have come with an entire army of aid, instead of three
people and three kites. But when he saw the look of relief on the woman's
face, he thought again. Perhaps it was the fact that someone had come at
all that mattered most, not the actual number of people present.

"We welcome your aid, dear princess,"
the woman bowed once more.
To Darkon and Tal, she said,
"We greet you in the name of Eladan with greatest thanks.
Come this way. I'll take you to Prince Blazewick.
He'll be pleased to learn of your arrival."

Darkon offered their third fireproof kite and was glad to see that the
woman seemed to have full knowledge of how to mount the kite and sit
on it without instruction. She thanked Darkon for the kite and promptly
introduced herself as Bella, Chief Advisor and Refiner. From this brave
woman, they learned that there was an accident in the mines about ten
years ago.

At first, they thought they hit a major fire vein, to cause all the flame
to erupt from the ground. But later they discovered it was contaminated
with a nightmare. So the nightmare spread with the flames and grew to be
unmanageable. The nightmare made it so they couldn't refine the flames,
like they usually were able to. It just burned three times as hot and never
went out. Even water did nothing to quench the flames; the nightmare
prevented the flames from dying.

So that was what accounted for the firewall…Darkon mused to himself,
beginning to comprehend the mysterious occurrence
that no one outside understood. He ventured to ask,
"But your people are nightmare free?"
He had never heard of a nightmare taking over a country, but leaving its

228

people alone.

"We're all untouched by the nightmare," Bella nodded.
"Prince Blazewick included. Speaking of, there he is.
What is he doing outside of the capital again?"
The chief advisor raised her voice and bellowed,
"Elias! I thought we agreed you'd rest before coming out again!"

"I did rest," the prince replied as he turned and stood by a bonfire that burned three times his height. He tossed a gnarled piece of nightmare into the flame, and there was a burst of flame and screams from the nightmare voices. Prince Blazewick continued to pick up pieces of nightmare as it told him what a pathetic ruler he was and how his people hated his very being and how help would never come.

"I leave for five minutes, and you call that a rest?" Bella shook her head in disbelief.

Darkon wondered how the two could carry on such light-hearted exchanges in this situation.

The nightmare spat out such terrible lies
even in the face of actual help that had arrived.
The lips and mouths on nightmare strands
sneered that even if help came,
it would withdraw after seeing
how horrible the Blazewick Royal Family was.

Elias Blazewick, however, remained oblivious to the accusations and casually chucked his armful of twisted nightmare into the fire with aplomb. As he kept this up, he said,

"Look who's talking, my dearest workaholic advisor...you're worse than I am..."

He stopped as he registered the sight of the outsiders.

"Bella, did you manage to break out of the firewall?
We lost so many soldiers last time..."

"No," Bella answered with a gleeful smile.

"They broke through it to us.

All of those calls for aid weren't in vain.

Now, I leave our guests with you.

I'm going to see what I can do to take care of the nightmare in the metal district."

She bowed politely and took her leave.

"I knew I heard cries for help!" Falleyne couldn't contain herself anymore.

"I was right!

Elias, I didn't hear from you in so long, I was worried. How can I help?"

Elias laughed.

"You don't happen to know how to deal with a nightmare infestation of massive scale, do you, Falleyne? We've been at our wits end, trying to figure out what to do. But I have to ask, how did you get inside? And don't say you flew in on fireproof kites, because you would have been nothing but ashes by the time the kites came through."

"We did, but that was after Darkon got us in," Falleyne said.

"It was Tal's musical ink enchantment that helped," Darkon tried to give Tal credit. Tal shrugged and pointed at Darkon as if to say, "Stop being so modest; it was all you."

At being introduced to Darkon, Elias brightened considerably, which was saying something, because he already seemed to be quite chipper even while facing a long-term crisis.

"Ah! If it isn't the Kite King himself!" Elias bowed deeply and then piped up.

"I always wanted to meet you, and now look at how things turned out! I'm meeting my hero face to face. Granted, my kingdom is a complete mess, but I'm very glad to meet you, sir."

Darkon laughed. In a strange way, it was like seeing a younger version of himself. From a completely different country and with a very different sort of people – ones who were expressive and vocal and openly loving – but yet still so similar in cheer and optimism. Darkon found himself opening

up and admitting,
"My kingdom is a complete mess too.
I hope you could help me clean things up,
after we help you, of course."

"Seriously?" Elias asked in surprise.
"I mean, of course, it would be an honor, sir."

"Darkon is fine. Going by a first name basis makes things easier," Darkon said.
"We came through the Blade Pass after I drew this sword out of the mountainside."
He held out Valor.
"It...well...the sword
ate all the fire in the pass.
I'm not sure how that happened."

To say that Prince Blazewick was thunderstruck
would have been an understatement.
"How did you draw out the one sword
in the pass that can do that?" Elias wanted to know.

Darkon just looked at him
and was tempted to reply,
"By complete accident."
Instead, he said,
"I reached for the closest sword I could, and it came out.
Would you like it? I'm not a swordsman,
and I don't plan on becoming one any time soon."

"If you drew the blade, then it's yours," Elias said.
"In any case, I don't need a swordsman. I need someone who can help me regulate the fire levels and take care of this nightmare. The sword will

serve well for the fire. As for the nightmare, I don't know. It's been a beast, and it's only gotten worse."

"Have you tried liquid light?" Darkon suggested then.

"It's a good deterrent and eats away at nightmare. I learned that from Ionthann, the captain of the guard at Eld Mané. When he infiltrated the Ribbon Fortress, he used liquid light to keep the nightmare at bay for a time."

Elias shook his head.

"Our stocks of liquid light ran out years ago."

"We could go and bring you liquid light," Tal said then.

"If Darkon stays to help regulate some of the fire levels,

Falleyne and I could go to Eld Mané and bring back some liquid light."

Darkon listened as Falleyne asked why she needed to go with Tal, and Tal just said she was the one who had requested aid in the first place, so it would make sense if she could come and make a second request. Avorne would have no objections, especially since they succeeded in entering Kalos Fyrian and connecting with Prince Blazewick. In fact, the update might lift everyone's spirits and renew their efforts.

Seeing that Falleyne wanted to stay, Darkon nudged her on.

"I'll make sure the Blade Pass stays clear of fire. Bring back liquid light so we can take care of this. In the meantime, showcase those excellent diplomacy skills of yours."

He was relieved that Falleyne understood her importance and left willingly with Tal by kite.

Once the two were out of sight, Darkon turned to Elias.

"This is your kingdom, so I'll follow your direction.

Which places need the most fire regulation?

If you show me, I'll see what I can do with Valor."

He lifted his sword with a willing hand

and held out another to help Elias get up onto the kite

232

so they could scope out the land from above.

"You named it Valor?" Elias was pleased to learn that little fact as he showed Darkon the spots he planned to take care of first.

"Falleyne said the blade sang of a different sort of valor, to set things right. So I thought Valor would be a fitting name," Darkon explained as he directed the kite towards the first tower of flame that Elias wanted to take care of. From a distance, it looked like pillars of fire were holding up the cloudy sky.

"Falleyne can hear everything,"
   Elias said then,
   and Darkon didn't miss
   the tone of endearment
   in the prince's voice.

"Once everything settles down,
   I'll ask her if we can send
   a dual declaration of loyalty
   to Avorne Ehrthann in Eld Mané."

Darkon frowned in confusion. Why would the Prince of Kalos Fyrian and Princess of Vinduren have any need to declare loyalty to the King of Eld Mané? He received the explanation from Elias. It was the second peace treaty attempt.

As children, the two young rulers had made a pact with each other in the Inkstone Mountains on the border of their nations, ten years ago. They had vowed that for as long as they ruled, they would support the peace efforts with their all, their everything. Of course, then the firewall had erupted in Kalos Fyrian leaving Elias to fight the nightmare in his country alone, and Vinduren suffered upheaval in its royal house, resulting in Falleyne being secreted away to Eld Mané to be hidden until her throne could be restored.

Now that Falleyne and Elias had finally reunited, the two seemed even more eager to settle this matter and declare their united intention for all to see.

Elias told Darkon in no unclear terms it was widely considered that Darkon and Avorne represented the hope for the North and South. Somehow, in these twenty years, in the process of trying to right so many wrongs, the two kings had become a beacon for everyone else. It was much like how many regarded Valéon as the one who represented the peace effort, since he ended up being the keeper of the treaty draft and suffered from both the north and south influenced by nightmares.

It was uncomfortable, to say the least, to hear himself be referred to as a beacon of light and a leader of the peace efforts. Darkon had no objections to being support from beginning to end. He just didn't want to be crowned the paragon of leadership, especially when his kingdom was in shambles, and his kites nearly spent. Darkon wondered if this was a modicum of what Avorne felt when he urged his younger friend to pursue the second peace treaty. The pressure of such high expectation was heavy, and Darkon had no desire to take up the burden of this role.

"Elias," Darkon said, "Falleyne shares your high regard for the peace efforts. You both must have been infants when the first treaty attempt took place. How is it that you two are so set on supporting this cause?"

"Simple," Elias shrugged.

"We have a history we're proud of.

We want a future to be proud of too."

That single comment reminded Darkon why he had worked so hard to help the nations and their respective rulers for all these years – why he still worked hard to help them. And though the idea of being considered the hope of the North made him squirm, the King of Kites felt vindicated that even the upcoming generation believed that Avorne was the key to the peace efforts. As he sat beside a ruler of the next generation, Darkon considered all that he had learned.

Perhaps, Darkon thought, if he were willing to take up the title of Hope of the North, and do his best to be the beacon Elias believed him to be, he would not only take some of the pressure off of Avorne, but help this second peace treaty come to pass.

20

Extending the Invitation

Finding the ink portal on the parapet of the palace of Eld Mané was easier than Emily expected it to be.

Thanks to her scarf, which had designated itself to be her trusty guide and flown up ahead of her to lead the way, she found a way up one of the watchtowers built into the wall. From there, Emily climbed up the stone steps until she was up on top. The circle of ink that had been painted in brush strokes on one of the palace walls was impossible to miss.

It also made her curious. Emily studied the ink portal for more than a few minutes. Although she could see the kingdom of kites through it, she was completely mesmerized by the movement of the ink and all of its strokes and characters that wavered and shifted along the portal's border. It was like the ink was alive, and when Emily touched one character that looked like a hawk in flight, it circled the tip of her finger twice before settling back into place.

She would have stayed longer to look at all of the intricate designs, but at that, her scarf lightly tapped her shoulder, and then flew into the portal in a hurry. Right. Emily sighed. She'd come back and take a closer look later. She stepped through from the stone palace to grassy cliffs. On one side was the sea, on the other were the hills.

Kites fell from the sky,
fluttering down,

being blown about
by the strong winds.

Emily felt a jolt of dread hit her stomach.
   She didn't know why she thought of Scott just then,
   but the sight of so many kites failing around her
   made her think of his deteriorating health.

It was a morbid thought, and Emily shook her head.
   This was a kingdom that had a failing kite system.
   It was not a person who had a failing health system.
   The Kite Kingdom was not Scott.

Emily refused to draw unnecessary parallels to these two separate situations.
But she couldn't help but wonder.

Was the kingdom that Scott had lovingly created
   all those years ago to comfort his grieving wife
   falling apart because the creator was physically ill?

She didn't want to think about it.

So Emily pushed it out of her mind and focused on following her scarf,
which led her deeper and deeper into the kingdom. It led her on the edge
of the cliffs by the sea until she spotted a castle in the distance. But even
from where she was, she thought she could see a kite approaching. It didn't
fall from the sky like the others. It flew sure and steady, and upon it sat
someone Emily did not recognize.
   He recognized her, though,
   because he called,
   "Emily! You made it!
   Thanks for coming.
   Dad so wanted you to come,

even though he couldn't ask."

Somewhere in the back of her mind, Emily recalled the stories Scott had told her when she was a child. In the Kingdom of Kites, the King and Queen of Kites had three sons. The oldest was the noblest of the three, kind and skilled in the craft of kite making. The second was the bravest of the three, brash and loud but always willing to lend a helping hand. The third was shyest of the three, though intelligent and wise beyond his years.

Emily still remembered the names that Scott had given them: August, Griffin, and Den. When she was young, she had accepted that without thought; now that she was an adult,

Emily felt a pang recalling the names of the three sons

that Katarina had miscarried before giving birth to Ryan.

So she looked at the man who greeted her from that kite and remembered that the one who was older than her but closest to her in age was indeed the oldest.

So she asked somewhat cautiously,

"August? Is that you?"

"Who else could talk Dad into calling you when he's stressed out of his mind?" the oldest son of the Kite King laughed.

"Of course it's me. Come on. Mom's working with Queen Renadé to preserve the kites that have gone down until we know what to do with them. Grif and Den are there too. We told Queen Renadé that we were expecting you, so everyone's waiting."

Oh, that was right. Emily remembered why she had come in the first place. Avorne had mentioned that Renadé might help Emily with wisdom, whatever that might look like.

But as she was escorted to the castle, she enjoyed catching up with an old friend she hadn't met in years. She also delighted in the fact that she'd be able to tell Scott and Katarina how much their sons had grown in this kingdom designed to house the memory of the sons they never had.

She hadn't considered what the sons of the Kite King might be like after they became adults just like her. And it was a new thought that as first prince and eldest, August would one day be seriously considering taking the throne after his father.

"I prefer kite-crafting over governing people," August confessed.

"Honestly, Den would be a great fit
if he gets over his chronic shyness.
But he's intimidated that Dad can talk to anybody, anywhere.
No one expects him to be like Dad. Even Dad doesn't.
But that's Den for you;
he's set on being a royal kite archivist for life.
And Grif said himself that he'll give our citizens
high blood pressure if he takes the throne,
with his reckless disposition.
So that doesn't give me much of a choice,
but I'll do it since I'm the firstborn."

"Ah, the plight of the oldest child," Emily said with a wry smile.

She thought of how she had been saddled with raising her younger sisters, Crystal and Abby, after their parents began working overtime and were increasingly absent from home.

"Remember to enjoy yourself and take some time to do what you want to do, not just what you should do."

August nodded.

"I knew it was a good idea to call.
Glad the sash got to you so quickly."

Emily discovered with interest that her scarf from Katarina and Scott had served as a sash for August and his royal garb. It still led the way to the castle with great pride and made sure to move with graceful loops and twists, letting its golden tassels flutter in the air. It was as if it was celebrating a mission accomplished and wanted its fair share of recognition, which amused Emily to no end.

But eventually, the scarf wrapped itself back around her neck and settled down comfortably about her shoulders. Emily could almost sense its deep satisfaction and sleepy contentment in a job well done. She gave it a gentle pat to congratulate it, and then followed August into the castle.

The castle was different than what Emily had imagined as a little girl. It looked as if it had been made with stones carved out of the cliffs, and yet, it had many windows to let in the sunlight. There were banners and tapestries that told tales of kite-crafting, releasing, or taming. There were histories of the people of the kite and its kingdom woven in ornate detail, and culture preserved in the many intertwining threads.

But kites were also strewn all along the halls
    and in the various rooms, lifeless and still.

But in the face of all this gloom,
    Emily felt a strange feeling of anticipation light up in her chest.
    And she thought she could hear Scott's voice
    speaking softly in her ear:

Once upon a time, in the Kingdom of Kites,
    there was a loving King and Queen with three sons.
    They lived in a castle tall and bright,
    with kites to take them from place to place.

Emily spun around
    to see if Scott was
    somewhere close by.
    He wasn't.

"Something wrong?" August asked her.
    "Um, no." Emily said,
    thinking it must have just been
    her imagination. "Sorry."

But as she continued to walk down the halls with August,
    she could still hear Scott's storytelling:

One day, however,
  the kites in the kingdom began to fail, one by one.
  No one could go anywhere,
  because their kites would drop
  out of the sky,
  into the sea,
  onto the earth.

Not even the king or queen
  or their three sons
  knew what to do.

And so, they called for help
  from one they loved and trusted,
  though they had not seen her for years.

And because she was true to her word,
  the Ribbon Princess came to their aid.
  But she did not come bearing
  swords or spears or grand armies.

Instead, she came with
  a humble heart,
  a keen eye,
  and a sharp mind.

Because that is what all must have
  when they face a challenge.

Willingness to learn is the key to wisdom.

The storytelling stopped after that.
  Emily wasn't sure if it was because that was the end of the story, or if it

was because she was warmly greeted by the rest of the royal family.

Queen Katarina looked identical to Ryan's mother, from name and looks to personality and mannerisms. She hugged Emily the same way Katarina did back at the hospital.

Griffin looked like he belonged on a kite, wandering the lands in search for a wild kite to tame, nearly taking off Emily's arm as he shook her hand vigorously.

And Den wouldn't even look Emily in the eye, but managed to raise his hand in shy greeting and mumble,

"Hi there, Princess."

Oddly, Emily felt like she was meeting up with old friends though she had only just met them. The only one who was not part of Darkon's family was Queen Renadé, who was seated at one of the wide tables that had dozens of kites on it, with various ink enchantments spun around them for preservation. But once everyone else had greeted Emily, Queen Renadé stood up and said,

"Welcome back."

Emily recalled the one time she had met Renadé, which had been near the end of her first adventure into this vast world. Renadé had come to thank her for helping to keep her husband, Avorne, safe. That had been the extent of their interaction, so Emily wasn't sure how to go about addressing this queen who spoke the least out of everyone present and had ink designs rippling all along the left side of her body.

So Emily decided to keep things as simple as possible. She said,

"I'm on the path to leadership and have traveled in the directions of strength and honor. Wisdom and kindness are next. Avorne sent me this way saying you could help me with wisdom."

She was surprised at herself for not offering help regarding the kite situation, but something in her wouldn't let her go that way. Perhaps it was because deep inside, Emily understood that what had gotten her to exhaustion and apathy was offering so much help without replenishing her reserves.

Renadé seemed to pick up on Emily's unspoken plight.

"Did he now?"

The queen of Eld Mané remained unruffled.

"Of course he would."

But instead of offering advice, Renadé offered Emily a seat as she worked to patch up a kite with ink characters that rose off of her skin and into the air. Emily watched as Renadé would lay out the characters of ink suspended before her and study them with a frown before changing the configuration. With a sweeping of her forefinger, she would take one stroke out of one character and add it to another. Sometimes she would take one line and bend it into a circle, twisting the ends together with a deft movement of her fingers.

Emily waited for the moment of grand insight, when she would be endowed with some profound epiphany that would solve all her problems instantly. None came. The transfer of wisdom came not through advice or suggestions, but through silence and then a single question:

"From where you currently stand,

what is something you can do

that only you can do

to help the vision come to pass?"

After waiting so long for a response and receiving this unexpected question, Emily found herself sitting in thought just to give an adequate reply. It made her do the work of considering all her challenges and her one desire that trumped them all. She thought of what she most wanted to do at the moment, which was help Avorne and the others to realize the second peace treaty.

After struggling in the silence,

Emily found her solution.

"I can extend the invitation."

It was then that Emily told Renadé about the nature of the conversation she had shared with Avorne earlier. It wasn't a long telling. Emily expected that she was relaying information that Renadé already knew, since it made sense that the King and Queen of Eld Mané would communicate regularly. Emily just mentioned that Avorne had a vision for the second peace treaty that was in the Inkstone Mountains behind the palace that she couldn't see yet.

"I still want to be a part of this," she told Renadé.

"If I write the invitations, would you back me up as Queen of Eld Mané? It would mean more with your endorsement."

Emily had expected some sort of verbal acknowledgement; she didn't expect to end up working with a willing ink enchantress who was an expert at design. It turned out that Emily hadn't been the only one who wished to help Avorne reach this vision that only he could see. Emily was pleasantly surprised with the stocks of paper and boxes of ribbons that were provided by the royal kite family to aid Emily and Renadé in their massive project.

Renadé designed individual ink enchantments along each card, while Katarina and her sons got busy tying the ribbons – blue and gold – to the completed invitations. Emily would have spent days handwriting each invitation had it not been for Renadé's simple – or so the Queen claimed – ink enchantment that replicated Emily's handwriting and laid it upon each card. It saved Emily hours of work and cramped fingers.

The final result on the cardstock read like so:

I, Emily, Ribbon Princess and Legend of Silkairen
as new keeper of the first peace treaty draft,
on behalf of Avorne Ehrthann, King of Eld Mané,
do ask for your heart, mind, will and strength
to do all in your power to support
the long-awaited fulfillment of the second peace treaty.
I uphold the heart of the King in this matter.

Do you?

If so, please sign your name on the back of both attached cards.
Keep one for yourself and let the other make its way to our leader.

On the reverse side, the card read:

I uphold the heart of the King in this matter.

Underneath that was a line on which one could sign one's name. Perhaps the part that awed Emily the most came when she signed both copies of the first set of invitations. She kept the one with the blue ribbon for herself, and so the card with the gold ribbon took flight from the work table, and made its way out of the castle into the kingdom of kites and journeyed towards the King of Eld Mané.

The same happened when Renadé, Katarina, August, Griffin, and Den signed their copies as well. Everyone kept a card with the ribbon color of their choice, and the one that they did not keep also took flight to find the King they were meant to encourage. As for the rest of the cards, each blue and gold ribbon paired up with each other and began the long sojourn to all the surrounding countries.

"How many do you think we need to make?" Emily asked, never quite having undertaken an endeavor of this scale before.

"How much paper and ribbons do we have?" Renadé asked with a gleam in her eye that said she was more than willing to keep going and test her limits.

"I've got plenty of ink."

Shaking her head, Emily realized that she had discovered wisdom with the help of this highly capable Queen of Eld Mané, who willingly lent her gifts and skills to an upcoming leader still finding her way. It made Emily confess,

"If I ever hold a high and honored position like yours, I hope I'll do the same for those who are beginning on their journey to be a leader."

Renadé smiled.

"To remember where we have come from is wisdom.

But the aid we extend to others

that was first extended to us is kindness.

You'll find that the last direction will come easiest to you.

It is the hardest for most others, but for you,
I doubt it will be an issue."

Emily paused to absorb that and consider the weight of the words offered to her. Kindness was the last direction of the four to the path of leadership. So with strength, honor, and wisdom, she had helped different allies along the way.

She wondered with whom
   she would travel
   the direction of kindness,
   and who it would benefit along the way.

21

Collecting Courage

I t began with a single card
that flew into the King's Heart,
dangling from a golden ribbon
that carted its delivery
with faithful determination.

It fluttered about around Mirae, distracting her from designing the hall of healing, which Halas had requested after mentioning there needed to be a place where people could go to recover from any unseen or unspoken wounds.

It flitted briefly by Halas, who caught the card in his hand to study it. When he read it, Halas nudged Avorne in the shoulder to get his attention and handed it to him.

At first, Avorne thought Mirae had come up with some small flourish for the King's Heart on a whim. When he saw the contents, he thought otherwise. The edges of the cream cardstock were decorated with an exquisite calligraphy design. He could recognize Renadé's ink enchantments and personalized inklines anywhere. It bordered the front and back of the card. But more than that, were the words that were written in the center of the card:

I, Emily, Ribbon Princess and Legend of Silkairen
as new keeper of the first peace treaty draft,
on behalf of Avorne Ehrthann, King of Eld Mané,
do ask for your heart, mind, will and strength
to do all in your power to support
the long-awaited fulfillment of the second peace treaty.

I uphold the heart of the King in this matter.

Do you?

If so, please sign your name on the back of both cards.
Keep one for yourself and let the other make its way to our leader.

The words made Avorne's breath catch in his throat.
He turned over the card slowly and read Emily's commitment:

I uphold the heart of the King in this matter.

-Emily
Ribbon Princess
of Silkairen

Then a little stream of five cards on blue or gold ribbons followed. Avorne swallowed as he read each of the commitments and signatures:

Renadé, Queen of Eld Mané;

Katarina, Queen of Kites;

August, First Prince of the Kite Kingdom;

Griffin, Second Prince of the Kite Kingdom

(best kite tamer in all the land);

Den, Third Prince
   and aspiring archivist of the Kite Kingdom.

Those names by themselves did wonders to boost Avorne's morale. But it didn't end there.

A card fluttered in some minutes later, this time carrying in the commitment of Sylasienne, Ribbon Queen of Silkairen and a note saying how pleased she was that the best and latest ribbons she had designed were being utilized to further the peace efforts.

Another came from Raiidran, Ink Prince of Inkaien,
   which also had
   (*Ryan*) scrawled underneath it in parenthesis
   and the note,
   "Best of luck, Avorne.
   My one request is that you host this in a place
   worthy of the peace treaty."

Shortly after, one came from Crystal, Sky Maiden with a penciled comment of
   "Aw, I wish I could be there!
   But I'll wait until Em comes home
   to tell me all about it.
   You can do it!"

Another card came signed, Cassan/Vince with the comment,
   "Good luck, man. Or should I say, Majesty?
   Did I mention that this peace treaty is a big deal?
   Big as in epic proportions?
   No pressure or anything.

I expect nothing but the finest, my friend."

But the card that moved Avorne most was handed to him by Mirae, who was completely distracted by this point at the flood of cards that swarmed around them in a flutter of gold and blue ribbons.

This one was simply signed "Scott,"
  and on the bottom was written,
  "On behalf of Darkon, King of Kites,
  I would like to offer our complete support to this cause.
  He has never doubted your heart or abilities; neither have I.
  Eagerly waiting to see your next move."

Avorne remembered that Emily had mentioned that Scott, Darkon's counterpart in Emily's domain, was ill, so he wondered how this card had reached him and come back. But then again, Crystal, Ryan, and Vincent were also in that domain, and they had responded immediately. Perhaps there was a connection somewhere that Avorne wasn't aware of.

In any case, he was brought back to the present by a nudge in the ribs from Mirae.

"A King is nothing without his people, huh?" Mirae grinned.
  "I bet all the rulers out there are totally jealous of you."

"What do you mean?" Avorne asked.

"You pretty much just stole the hearts of their people.
  If you want proof, just look around you."

She looked into the air that fluttered with clouds of cards and ribbons. Then she eagerly snatched one out of the air.

"Oh, a blank one! I'm signing it."

After she did, she handed one to Avorne.

"There. Though, I'm disappointed I wasn't the first.

Who started this anyway?"

Avorne cleared his throat and looked at the card that fluttered gently by his shoulder and did not mingle with the flock of cards that swirled around them.

It was the first one that had come – Emily's card.

He understood that Emily had made it to Renadé in her search for wisdom. He saw the front, and then the back, both with Emily's name and open declaration of dedication.

"Emily did," he admitted.

Then he noticed the tiny postscript

that Emily had crammed at the bottom of her card:

Here's to your heart of gold, Avorne!
And to your vision, which I fully expect to see once I'm back!
Save me a seat at the peace treaty. I'll be there.

Avorne thought about that wish he had made on the dandelion at the beginning of all of this, when he had desperately wanted someone who could help him. Little by little, one by one, the people who shared his heart and vision for the second peace treaty were coming together and helping him in whatever ways they could.

True, no one but Mirae and Halas could see the inner workings of the King's Heart, but there were plenty who were close and on their way.

"Emily?" Mirae was saying to Halas.

"Do you know her? She's a leader, isn't she?

Look at the way she wrote this...

it's like she's a complete natural."

251

Halas chuckled.

"I know of her; I haven't met her – yet.

I have a feeling she'll be here soon enough.

You'd be pleased to know that she created

a smaller version of the King's Heart

for her younger sister, Crystal, once."

"For real?" Mirae looked impressed.

"What materials did she use?"

Halas laughed and tapped his chest.

"It was her heart. If you ask her when she comes,

I guarantee you she'll have no idea that she did,

just like Avorne didn't know he created the first King's Heart

all those years ago when he fought our first nightmare."

"But if she hasn't seen the King's Heart," Mirae said,

"and she doesn't know that she created one,

then how could she know to say 'uphold the heart of the King?'"

"She has our vision," Avorne said at last.

Something about hearing Halas mention the parallel between him and Emily reminded him of something she had said to him the last time they worked together to defeat the nightmare that took over the Ink Prince.

Emily had claimed that their hearts matched.

He had always considered that comment to be metaphorical, not literal. He hadn't thought their hearts matched, as in they both had created a time and space for the King's Heart to appear for their loved ones.

But now, he considered the result of their first collaboration, which had been a dome of sunlit, watery stained glass that had surrounded them. It had, in a way, resembled the King's Heart that Mirae was currently designing, in color scheme, intent, and atmosphere.

That memory made Avorne want to redouble his efforts, especially when

252

he thought about the yearning that had come over Emily as she listened to his vision the last time they had met. He knew that yearning in her had birthed these invitations and declarations of loyalty and support.

"Emily's a leader with a matching heart," Avorne said.

"Well, if she shares our vision and our heart, then we better not let her down," Mirae said as she rolled up her sleeves.

"With all of these responses coming in,

there's going to be a high expectation.

I don't want to disappoint,

so we've got our work cut out for us."

Avorne nodded in agreement, and said nothing as Mirae went back to bringing a long hallway filled with rooms on each side into existence. Mirae asked Halas to check them out to see if it was similar to what he had envisioned.

Halas went with the blithe comment that knowing Mirae, everything would be pretty much perfect,

just like the kitchens,

the dining hall,

the spare bedrooms,

ballroom,

and various lounges

she brought into being earlier.

He diagnosed her as a helpless overachiever, and the young architect just snorted and said to quit with the flattery and go check anyway. Avorne was grateful that Halas and Mirae had built up such a good rapport with each other. It comforted him to see the playful banter, and it also gave him some room to think on his own, without needing to engage in conversation.

Ironically, Mirae picked up on Avorne's quietness

and engaged him first, asking,

"Are you okay?"

Avorne nodded.

"I was thinking.

253

Is there a way we could modify the door to the King's Heart?
I know it was perfect for me,
but it could trip up everyone else trying to come in.
Could you make it so it's a tailored door
for each person who wants to enter?"

A thoughtful look came upon the architect's face, and she said,
"That's a good point.
We should make it as easy as possible.
Especially if the first thing they see
is the door instead of the whole place.
I can change that right now."

Mirae walked from the reception hall towards the front doors.
"Um, Avorne?" She called then.

"What?"
Avorne asked.
"Is it too hard?"

"No," Mirae said.
"I already changed the entryway configuration.
That's not the problem. Are you ready to have guests?
Because there's someone out here waiting to get in."

"Who?"
Avorne jumped up.
"What do they look like?"

"Eh," Mirae started.
"Dark skin, dark hair,
and wearing a standard issue Silkairen uniform?
The insignia on it is the same as the one on your tunic, though.

Looks like one of your higher ranking soldiers?"

"That would be Ionthann," Avorne said, pleasantly surprised.
     "He's the captain of the guard. How did he come here?"

"Well, you can ask him yourself, because the door's opening from the other
side. He'll be in any minute."
     And then, Ionthann must have entered, because Mirae said,
     "Hello, sir! If you want to see Avorne, he's just in this way."
     "And you are...?" Ionthann was saying.

"Mirae," the architect said
     as she led the captain of the guard inside.
     "I built this place."

"Wait, Mirae?"
     Ionthann had now made it to
     where Avorne was sitting
     and shot him a perplexed look.
     He asked Avorne,
     "She's with you?"

Wondering how they were going to
     explain everything to Ionthann, Avorne nodded.

But instead of demanding an explanation
     from the King directly, Ionthann asked Mirae,
     "You're not Mirae Hope, by any chance, are you?"
     "How did you know?" Mirae asked.
     Ionthann held up a small square of paper that had "Mirae Hope" written
on it.
     "I was told that everything I needed was contained in this."

But Mirae wanted answers of her own.
  "Where did you get that?
  How did you get in?
  Can you see the King's Heart from outside?"

"Whoa, slow down," Ionthann held up his hands.
  "The aura around this place is curious;
  I didn't notice until today.
  I got this," he gave the paper to Mirae,
  "from a secret seller in the Changing Lands.
  He gave me this when I was a boy,"
  he took out a crystal wolf from his pocket and frowned.
  "Somehow it was the key to letting me inside,
  which makes no sense to me."

Avorne made a note that Ionthann's crystal wolf was very similar to the crystal whale shark that Mirae had given to him. And then he wondered if they were made of the same material, and if that wolf had been shaped in the same way and from the same sort of material as the whale shark and even the King's Heart. But he thought it interesting that Mirae cared more for the paper Ionthann had brought with him instead.

"This is a secret of mine," Mirae whispered.
  "How did you get it?"

Then she got a hold of herself and asked,
  "Do you have some time?
  Because I'm sure you have questions too,
  and this is going to take a while to explain."

"Yes, I –" Ionthann began to say, but stopped mid sentence, because Halas had just come back to join them.

Ionthann pointed to Halas and said,
   "Halas, if that's really you
   and I'm not seeing things,
   then you better have
   a good explanation for being here.
   What is going on?"

"Yeah, that's..." Mirae sighed and looked to Avorne and Halas.
   "Want to help me explain?
   It'll help us figure out what to say
   to every other person
   that comes in from now on."

Avorne took one look at Ionthann, Halas, and Mirae,
   and took in a deep breath. "Sure.
   Halas, why don't you do the honors?"

"Slacker," Halas rolled his eyes.

"Hey, you're the dead one here," Avorne pointed out.
   "Also, you're the one who gets the King's Heart best."

To Ionthann, he said,
   "I'll just preface everything by saying
   this is my vision for the second peace treaty
   that's being brought to life by Mirae.
   She's an architect from the Invisible Lands
   who's been designing this place for years.
   Turns out her heart for her leaders
   matched up with my vision for the peace efforts.
   And with that, Halas, it's all you."

Halas just sighed and said.

"This is the King's Heart.
It's a time and space for all of us to get our bearings
before we go back to our current situation.
Usually it's a temporary state between dreams and reality,
but with Mirae's gifts and abilities,
it's become a tangible reality
that responds to the desires of her leaders.
It also allows me to be present with you in this space."

Avorne watched as some sort of understanding registered in Ionthann's
eyes.

"I think I know why I'm here," Ionthann said.
  "Once, years ago, in a dream,
  I vowed to defend the King's Heart.
  I suppose I'm here to fulfill that vow."

Hearing that admission
  from his captain of the guard
  gave Avorne hope.

He was on the right track.
  They were all on the right track.

Sure, the explanations would take some time to sort out.
  Everyone seemed to have more and more questions they wanted to ask
each other. But things were actually moving into place. When he heard
Ionthann ask if they knew of any way he could fulfill his vow to defend the
King's Heart, Avorne happened to see a blank set of invitations being toted
around by a pair of gold and blue ribbons in the air.
  Avorne reached out to grab both cards and held them out to Ionthann.

"You could begin with this.

It's just a starting point,
but it's something."

He didn't know why it made him so happy to see the captain of the guard read those invitations and sign his name on both commitment cards. Ionthann pocketed one and handed the other to Avorne. The King of Eld Mané tried to articulate what he felt in words.

"Is it strange if I feel like I'm collecting courage?"
He asked the others.

Ionthann shook his head.
"Not at all. The aura around every response is the same.
Each one is emanating that quality.
You are literally collecting courage."

"Hold onto that," Halas suggested
as he signed a set of his own and followed suit.

"You'll need it," Mirae added.

Avorne couldn't have agreed more.

22

Flight into the King's Heart

Valéon got increasingly restless as he waited for Ionthann to return to the gardens. The captain of the guard had said he'd only be a few minutes when he left with the small square of paper that had "Mirae Hope" written on it.

It had been a few hours.

Iris didn't seem concerned and said that Ionthann might have run into Avorne in the mountains and that could account for the delay in his return. But Valéon wasn't just thinking about Ionthann. He was also thinking about Emily, who had gone to stretch her legs and never came back. He had picked up her deck of blue and gold cards which she had left here, for safekeeping. Valéon knew that she treasured them from the time she had passed them to him across from the table at breakfast. He would hate to have her lose something so meaningful.

So, because he was so accustomed to taking care of minute logistics like this while serving the Pondragai Household, Valéon took it upon himself to keep track of the small things that others seemed to forget. It was something that Vandek made note of as they sat there waiting, mentioning that Valéon really should consider taking up an occupation that let him use the full capacity of his skillsets. Which included flying from place to place, Iris chipped in.

When he admitted that it was hard to see future possibilities, Iris told him they'd come soon enough and that he just had to look for them. Vandek added that sometimes those opportunities came to you. The royal advisor pointed towards the south entryway of the royal gardens and said,

"We have guests on the way.
　　They're in a hurry."

Iris placed her hands upon the trunk of a tree,
　　closed her eyes, and confirmed Vandek's perception.

"It's one of our kites.
　　Tal Roethal is on it,
　　as is...oh, that's curious."

Iris looked to Vandek and said,
　　"Have you been in contact with Falleyne lately?"

Valéon watched
　　as an expression of surprise
　　and fondness came over Vandek's face.

"No," the royal advisor said.
　　"I haven't. Not since, well...
　　it's been quite some time."

"I suppose Falleyne is one of the many secrets
　　that Vandek kept hidden with his influence,
　　and she is one of his most treasured
　　victories and success stories," Iris said.

That got Valéon's attention.
　　"How so?"

That was when Valéon learned of what Vandek had done
    to hide the princess of Vinduren in Eld Mané for a time.
    It had taken place nearly ten years ago,
    when Valéon had still been held captive
    in the Ribbon Fortress.

And because of Vandek's enormous influence,
    none had noticed the youngest of Vinduren's royal family
    being secreted away during its upheaval or
    being restored to her throne when stability returned.

"How come we didn't know this?" Valéon asked.

"No one was supposed to," Vandek shrugged.

"Her safety depended upon no one knowing her status or whereabouts. Even now, the only one who knows of the extent of the measures for protection that were taken are Falleyne's advisor, the princess herself, and me."

But by then, the story was cut short by the arrival of Tal and Falleyne. They were in a hurry and asked for Avorne and Renade. Valéon said they were both out. Was the matter urgent? Yes, they told him, very much so. At this, Valéon motioned to Vandek and asked if the royal advisor could help them instead. Falleyne immediately brightened at the sight of Vandek.

"Hello, Vandek! I mean, greetings in the name of Eladan," she made a hurried bow and series of hand gestures.

"May He grant you the breakthrough always desired but never gained."

"Likewise, may He return such favor upon you, Princess," Vandek said with a bow of his head and mirrored hand gestures.

"What is it that you need?"

"I found a way into Kalos Fyrian with Tal and Darkon after Avorne sent them my way. But there's a nightmare outbreak that's taken over their fire veins, which accounts for the firewall at the borders. Darkon is helping Elias with the fire calibration, but they asked us to bring back liquid light. Could we borrow whatever liquid light you can spare?" Falleyne asked.

"I'll repay you for whatever we use."

Iris offered, "You could ask Theia down in the healing wards. I'm sure she'd offer to give you however much liquid light you need."

At the mention of Theia and liquid light, Valéon felt like Falleyne was a younger version of Theia.

Theia was the light representative who had come to the first peace treaty attempt with her counterpart, Crescens Umbra, the shadow representative. Now they both oversaw the healing wards in the palace of Eld Mané. It must have been in the fierce dedication and love in the way Falleyne spoke.

But he came back to the moment
when Vandek asked how much
the nightmare had taken over.
Had it taken over
the capital city
or the ruler?
Or both?

"The whole country," Falleyne said
with a slight tremor in her voice.
"But the people are nightmare-free.
And so is Elias, thank goodness.
It's only the land and fire veins.
Darkon thought that liquid light could do it,
but is there any place that has that much liquid light available?"

"You don't need much," Vandek said slowly.
"Just enough.
Pour it in the right place,
and it should spread throughout the fire veins
and cure the land of the nightmare."

"Want to come back with me?" Falleyne asked suddenly.
Valéon noticed how uncomfortable the royal advisor became from that

sudden request.

And though he didn't have the affinity of perception, Valéon knew that Vandek still struggled with guilt over what he had done under the influence of the nightmare all those years ago.

So Valéon said,
"You should go, Vandek.
Ask Theia too. She won't say 'no.'
Plus, she could take care of
any remaining nightmare areas
with her affinity for light."

It amazed him how well his suggestion was taken, how quickly Tal ushered Vandek and Falleyne out of the gardens and towards the healing wards with a silently mouthed "thank you."
Valéon was left alone in the gardens with Iris,
who studied him with a pleased expression.

When he asked what it was,
the royal gardener replied,
"You still have a voice of power,
and it affects all those who listen to it.
Have you considered what you will do,
now that the peace treaty draft
has safely been transferred to Emily?"

Valéon shook his head.
It was part of why he felt out of place,
even as people rushed from one place to another
trying to help out with the peace efforts.

Where was his place?
What was his role?

Valéon didn't know.

He knew he had a part to play in all of this,
   understood that his voice was
   an important element
   in the future second peace treaty.

But as far as
   where to go
   and what to do,
   he was at a loss.

But Valéon recalled the description that Crystal had written of him to give to Emily. He'd been deemed a messenger, and so that was what he would seek to do.

   He asked,
   "You don't have any messages
   you'd like me to deliver, do you, Iris?"

"Actually," Iris smiled, "I've been collecting these."

   The royal gardener pulled out a small bundle of cards that were tied together in a supple chain of gold and blue ribbons.

   "What's this?" Valéon asked as he received the bundle with care.

   And when he recognized the cards he exclaimed,

   "I saw one of these while I was putting the last set of books back on the shelves in the library on the third floor. It kept following me while I worked through the stacks, but I ignored it. *What* are they exactly?"

   "Emily's contribution to the peace efforts," Iris surmised.

   "I'd offer you a pair, but it looks like the one that found you in the library is still following you," She pointed behind him.

   Valéon turned his head and was promptly bumped in the forehead by a pair of two cards held together by blue and gold ribbons.

   Emily sent them? Well, she was the Ribbon Princess, he told himself as

265

he took hold of this very silent but persistent disturbance. When Valéon read the cards,

his annoyance gave way

to a swell of pride.

His friend was growing in leaps and bounds, and it gave him joy that she was finding her stride and style of leadership.

He signed his own set and asked Iris,

"Would you like me to deliver these signed replies to our beloved King?"

Iris laughed.

"Avorne will cry if you use his title.

But yes, please do.

I need to keep up the surveillance in the palace,

since Avorne, Renadé, and Vandek are out.

But I will attend the second peace treaty.

Send Avorne my regards."

"I will," Valéon answered.

He took flight, traveling up towards the glass domed ceiling and exiting through one of its doors. It was as if he became a homing beacon the minute he exited the palace. Valéon wasn't sure where they came from or how they knew he was on the way to make a delivery to Avorne, but the invitations came fluttering to him on gold and blue ribbons from everywhere. Valéon laughed at the absurdity of it all and remembered the time he had first helped Emily arrive on the shores of Silkairen. There, they had been swarmed by countless scarves and ribbons.

This time, there was no Emily,

and Valéon was the one who was greeted

by eager invitations with every

"I uphold the King in this matter"

signed with a name and title.

He was pleased to be joined by one that was signed

"Raehn, Singer of Eles Teare, Cantabelle."

Another fluttered close by with
   "Haliien, Owner of the Hourglass, Honoraire."

There were signatures of rulers and citizens
   of southern and northern countries.

And they all hovered around Valéon in the air,
   under the clear sky, waiting for his command.

Valéon held back a chuckle and called out,
   "If you're for the King and his heart, follow me.
   I'll show you the way."

He began to make his way into the mountains, flying over the ink signs that had been frozen in all sorts of shapes and contortions from the last rainfall. He looked for any sign of Avorne or Ionthann or even Emily down in the mountains, but didn't see anyone, which was odd. Where was everyone? He flew in wide circles from above, trying to see if there was something that he had missed.

Then he saw it. He almost flew right into it. A door. A double door, in fact, made of swirling wind and cloud. To anyone not from the Realm of the Sky, it would have just looked like a wispy patch of windswept cloud. But Valéon was a native of the Sky, with an eye trained to see any architecture of his homeland. That looked exactly like the doors of the Pondragai Estate. But the estate of his beloved Lord and Lady had been dismantled and dispersed in cloud and wind and rain. Valéon had scoured the Realm of the Sky for any remnant of his former Lord Leutheros and Lady Laehna and come up with nothing. The doors before him, however, were identical to that of the nonexistent Pondragai Estate.

Valéon closed his eyes,

swallowed,

and opened his eyes once more.

The doors were still before him.

The signed invitations hovered about him, but now they crowded close

around Valéon and collectively nudged him forward, as if to encourage
him to enter.

"If I go in,"
   he asked the invitations
   that seemed determined
   not to go ahead of him,
   "will you follow?"

The nudge became a rather forceful push.

Valéon got the point.
   He reached out,
   placed the palms of his hands on the doors,
   and pushed with all his might.
   Valéon entered the building that had the doors of the Pondragai Estate,
but housed something quite different on the inside. It was an enormous
hall filled with rooms with open doors filled with people walking in and
out, visiting with each other and speaking in hushed but excited tones.

For a moment, Valéon thought he was seeing things.
   All the people before him were supposed to be dead.
   They were the people who had been present
   at the first peace treaty attempt
   and had gotten killed by the ink explosion
   that had taken place in the treaty chamber.

Valéon hadn't seen them in years,
   but he could recall their faces,
   the countries they had represented,
   the stances they had held
   in the discussion for peace
   that had devolved into

heated debate and
bitter arguments.

. He thought he could recognize
the late King of Eld Mané, Avorne and Halas's father,
who was relaying some important message
to his oldest three sons, who had also been killed
that fateful day from the ink.
The resemblance he shared with Avorne was uncanny.

One of the former princes of Eld Mané, it looked like he could have been
the oldest, noticed Valéon first and strode over with a wide smile and open
arms.
"You made it!" He called back to the late King of Eld Mané,
"Father, Valéon's here. Our messenger arrived!"
"Excellent!" the late King said as he came to greet Valéon.
When Valéon began to bow, King Ehrthann stopped him and bowed
instead.
"I cannot tell you how grateful we are to you for keeping our legacy alive
through all the years of trial and suffering. Where's Annette? She'll be most
pleased to see you. She's the one who insisted that we can't go down to join
everyone until we saw you first. She only let Halas go, because she said
he'd help Avorne to prepare his heart."

King Ehrthann glanced behind him and then said,
"There she is! Oh, fancy that –
she's with Lord Leuthe and Lady Laehna.
She must have wanted them to meet you first thing as well.

Annette,"
he called to the late queen of Eld Mané.
"Valéon has finally come."

When Valéon stood before Queen Annette,
    and his Lord and Lady, he murmured,
    "Either I'm dead or I'm dreaming.
    How is this possible?
    What's happening?"

Queen Annette laughed a small laugh,
    "You are alive and not dreaming."

Lord Leuthe took Valéon by the shoulders warmly,
    "Welcome to the King's Heart, Valéon.
    It's certainly been a while, hasn't it?"

Valéon nodded and looked his former master in the eye. "
    It has, Lord Leuthe.
    But I read and remembered
    the peace treaty draft,
    and I haven't forgotten."
He didn't know why he felt so comforted by the cordial clap on his shoulder and wondered at how strange it was to feel as if Lord Leuthe considered him as an equal here.

Lady Laehna clasped Valéon's hand next and explained,
    "We're getting ready for the second peace treaty.
    Those of us from the other side of life are waiting here,
    because the preparations aren't complete yet,
    but the second peace treaty will happen soon.
    But seeing as you're still alive,
    and that you would boost the morale
    of Avorne and his team downstairs,
    would you mind delivering
    our replies to these lovely invitations?"

She motioned to all the people
who held similar signed cards in their hands.

Valéon held out his hand to receive the written replies.
"When everything is done,"
he dared to express his wavering hope.
"Would you two have a moment to spare?"

"I can spare many moments,"
Lord Leuthe reassured him.
"Long ones, too, at that."

Lady Laehna added,
"We'll have plenty of time.
But don't keep the others waiting!
We heard Avorne say himself
that he can't have the second peace treaty without you.
Go on." And she ushered him down the hall.

Valéon wondered as he accepted the signed invitations from his former Lord and Lady along with the late King and Queen of Eld Mané and their first three sons. He walked down the hallway, which gleamed like stained glass bathed in sunlight, and he collected the remaining invitations from all of the representatives who had either perished in the first treaty attempt or lost their lives in one way or another after.

The invitations that had followed Valéon in and still fluttered around him in a buzz of anticipation apparently grew impatient and hurried him through the hall and to the staircase at the end of it. But the cards hoisted him up into the air to get him a head start and prompted him to fly down directly, bypassing the spiral staircase to reach the ground floor.

By the time Valéon landed, the air around him was thick with invitations. The cards and ribbons nudged him forward to Avorne, Halas, Ionthann, and a young woman that Valéon didn't recognize. She shared the same silvery-white hair as him and her eyes were a lavender-blue. Valéon thought she could have been of the Sky nobility.

But Ionthann said,
  "Valéon, meet Mirae Hope.
  She's an exceptionally talented
  architect from the Invisible Lands.
  As you can see, her work
  and capabilities speak for themselves."

The two mystery words clicked in Valéon's mind.
  "So Mirae Hope is a 'who,'" Valéon smiled.
  "Nice to meet you. We went through a bit of a harrowing situation to get that piece of paper with your name on it. The secret seller did say that everything we needed was contained in there, and I'm beginning to understand what he meant."

Then, seeing Halas for the first time in years,
  Valéon heard his voice waver.

"It's nice to see you, Halas.
  You look good."

"For a dead man," Halas laughed.
  "I feel good. I think it's because I stopped worrying.
  Avorne always did say to quit worrying."

"Yeah, I did. But did you listen?"
  Avorne rolled his eyes. "No."

Halas gave Avorne a playful shove.
  "I got over the chronic worrying.
  Give me some credit here."

Valéon laughed, but he was interrupted by a hesitant tap on his shoulder. It was Mirae. She grew shy as she asked,

"As living legacy of our peace treaty,
would you mind giving me some input
on the treaty chamber? I'm having trouble
with the design for the speaking area."

"The speaking area?" Valéon asked.

Mirae nodded.
"No ink. That's the rule.
So if there's no ink,
it'll have to be words only.
Well, I thought that since you're a speaker,
we'd have a speaking room. What do you think?"

His thoughts overwhelmed him so much he was at a loss for words. Thankfully, Mirae seemed to understand and suggested,

"If we flew to the top of the King's Heart,
then you could point out where
you'd like to have the speaking area.
Would you mind?"

Mind?
No, Valéon didn't mind.
Not one bit.
He was much obliged.

In fact, it gave him a way to show her his appreciation without saying another word. The words "thank you" seemed so very inadequate when he had just been given an opportunity to meet his beloved Lord and Lady along with all those who had given their lives for the first peace treaty attempt.

In this case, action seemed to trump words. Valéon swept the young architect up as he took flight with her in his arms. He heard her gasp in surprise and then let out a soft "wow," as she held onto him as they ascended up the King's Heart and its dazzling stained glass structure.

"It's so beautiful from up here,"
    she murmured.
    "I never thought I'd see it like this."

"It's beautiful from anywhere," Valéon said.
    "Especially if you fly into it the way I did."

When Mirae asked him where he'd like the speaking area to be, Valéon just pointed to the ground floor where Avorne and the others still stood.

He saw the golden crown design
    in the center of the floor with its bold
    "A KING IS NOTHING WITHOUT HIS PEOPLE."

Seeing that view from such a high place in mid-flight,
    Valéon thought it was perfect and said so.

When he saw the tears well up in her eyes, Valéon said,

"You're doing a good job.
    We'll help you with the rest.
    We're almost there."

23

Recalibration

As King of Kites,
Darkon never once imagined
that he would help quell
an entire nightmare outbreak in a country not his own,
wielding a weapon he never would have selected for himself,
with a southerner who once tried to incite war
between the north and south by claiming northern treachery.

It was a bizarre day, no matter how Darkon looked at it.

But he hovered above the heart of the fire veins in Bright Haven with
Elias on his kite, joined by Tal and Falleyne, and two others. One was
Vandek, royal advisor of the palace of Eld Mané, and the other was Theia,
former light representative and overseer of the healing wards.

Darkon bowed his head to the two newcomers in silent acknowledgement
as he tried to concentrate on the last tower of flames that remained in Kalos
Fyrian. He was sweating profusely from all of the close work he had been
doing to take care of the fire calibration, and though no one looking at him
would have guessed, he was actually quite tired and shaky.

Elias had mentioned off-handedly as they were coming here, that anyone
who used a sword the caliber of Valor had to be in excellent shape, because
its ability to absorb flames reflected its wielder's strength and vitality.

"Not bad for an old man,"
    Elias said as he clapped Darkon on the shoulder with a grin.

But he steadied Darkon's hand,
    as Valor nearly slipped
    out of Darkon's grip.
    "You all right?"

Darkon just shot him an amused look.
    "For an old man.
    Is this the last fire to take care of
    before we address the nightmare?"

"Yes," Elias answered.
    "Though, I'm not sure how
    we're going to do that
    with such a small amount of liquid light."

He eyed the vial of liquid light
    that Theia and Vandek had brought.
    "Are you sure that's all we need?"

Vandek nodded.
    "I checked with our light expert,
    and she said it's plenty."

Theia confirmed.
    "It's more than enough to take care of the job."

Elias shrugged his consent.

To Darkon, he said,
    "Take all the fire you want.

We've got a surplus to last us for years.
You taking this much off of our hands would be a favor."

How anyone could have a surplus of fire was beyond Darkon.

But he had gotten the hang of reaching out with Valor and touching the blade to the flames. It didn't have to be a wide swing or thrust, as he learned from Elias. All the blade needed to do was touch some part of the flame, and it would begin to absorb the fire. The deeper the blade was bathed in flames, the quicker the fire would be absorbed, and in greater volumes.

With this last tower of fire, Darkon let the blade go into the fire halfway. He wanted to be able to sufficiently handle the physical strain of holding Valor steady while it took in all of the flames, but he also was tired and wanted to get the job done as quickly as possible. Even as Valor touched the tower of flame, the intensity of heat around Darkon flared up. The jewel upon Valor's pommel gleamed brighter and brighter as more and more fire was absorbed into the sword. And after what seemed like hours, but most likely was a few minutes, the job was done.

Darkon saw the amount of flames dwindle down. Now that the veins no longer were inflamed, they could address the nightmare contamination that pulsed within them. Darkon felt his legs grow shaky and so he sat down and set Valor beside him on the kite. He heard the musical ink enchantment from Tal sing a little louder, and wondered at the way strength seemed to be slowly restored to his limbs as he rested.

They flew down to the ground now,
and Elias pointed to the core of the fire veins.

"That's the center of the veins."
He didn't hide his puzzlement from Vandek and Theia.

"When we poured in buckets of liquid light,
  it only ate away at parts of the nightmare.
  How is that single vial going to take care of
  the nightmare in the whole country?"

Theia explained that the effects of liquid light were amplified through the flames in the fire veins and that it would serve as a boost to both light and fire, letting both disintegrate the nightmare immediately. She also pointed out that if you poured the light into the heart of the veins, then it would pump the light into the rest of the land, which would save them the hard work of pouring lots of liquid light on every nightmare area simultaneously. But she said it would make more sense if they saw it instead of just listening to her talk.

The light representative turned to Vandek and asked,
   "Would you like to do the honors?"

Vandek took the vial of liquid light and nodded.
   For a minute, he almost seemed overcome by emotion,
   but eventually he composed himself enough
   to look Elias in the eye and say,

"Once, I threw an entire peace effort into chaos
   with an inkwell of northern ink
   by pouring it into the water system in Eld Mané's palace.
   Many have told me that I've done
   more than enough to atone for what I did,"
   and here, he looked at Falleyne,
   who only gave him a painful smile.

"But I always felt like something was missing
   to set things right by my own personal standards.
   I think this may be it."

Vandek asked Elias,
   "With your consent,
   Prince Blazewick,
   I would like the opportunity

to right one wrong from long ago."

Darkon watched as a soft understanding seemed to come across Elias's demeanor.

The Prince of Kalos Fyrian said gently,
  "If it will help you be at peace,
  by all means, go ahead."

Vandek took in a deep breath,
  and addressing the nightmare
  that simmered below
  in the veins of fire
  in a mess of
  scoffs and mocking,
  sneers and derision,
  he said,

"Release this land and its people.
  They are not yours to take."

As he spoke,
  he poured the liquid light
  into the nightmare-infested flames.

The reaction was immediate.
  Liquid light met fire
  and blazed
  into a dome
  of flowing flames
  and searing light.

Darkon shielded his eyes

with his arm
from the blinding light.

The first pulse came and went
from the core of Bright Haven,
all the way through the remaining fire veins
that traveled through Kalos Fyrian.

It ate away at the nightmare strands
like acid corroding metal.
The screams and cries that came
from the disappearing nightmare were terrible.

Darkon could see Falleyne curled up next to Tal
holding her ears with her hands.
He was glad to see Tal hold her steady in a tight embrace.

The second pulse came and went
from the core of Bright Haven,
and this time,
all the horrible lies and taunts
dissipated.

The nightmare's
multitude of voices
burned away into ash.

Darkon saw tears
streaming down the cheeks
of Theia and Vandek
as they forced themselves
to watch every bit of this moment.

The third pulse came and went
  from the core of Bright Haven,
  and this time,
  all of the detached body parts
  and unnatural limbs,
  eyes and tongues,
  fangs and claws
  dripping in the black
  tar-like substance
  were
  lit upon,
  broken,
  seared away.

Beside him, Darkon beheld Elias
  jump to his feet,
  raise his fist in victory
  and shout with the joy
  of one who
  had gained
  freedom
  at
  last.

Prince Blazewick wasn't the only one who shouted. From every part of Kalos Fyrian shouts could be heard, the voices of young and old, a people who had collectively sought to support the peace efforts for years and had been unable to until now.

Seated on the kite, Darkon was moved beyond words or expression. He heard the call and response between Elias Blazewick and his people, the echoes that rang through Kalos Fyrian:

What shall we do with victory?

Pursue peace.

What shall we do with freedom?
  Take up our joy.

The call and response became a mantra:

Victory gained.
  Now for peace.

Freedom claimed.
  Now for joy.

And that mantra became a four word cheer:
  Victory. Peace. Freedom. Joy.

Darkon looked down at Valor and realized that the characters he had seen engraved all along its blade lit up at that rally cry.
  It held the same four words:
  victory, peace, freedom, joy.
  His most prominent thought was that he had to bring those four things back to Avorne to encourage his friend in his pursuit for what seemed impossible.

Sometime after the restoration of Kalos Fyrian,
  after Tal, Falleyne, Theia, and Vandek
  were on their way to their respective homes,
  Darkon was left alone with Elias,
  checking the remaining fire veins
  to make sure everything was clear
  and in good working order.

The two rulers said nothing as they worked side by side.

What more was there left to say?
Darkon was content working in silence.
He still savored the victory over this nightmare,
especially the part Vandek had played in it.

In a grand reversal, the man who had thrown
    the first peace treaty attempt into chaos,
    was now responsible for ushering in
    the second peace treaty attempt.

Apparently, Elias was overwhelmed by many thoughts as well, because he
didn't say anything until they finished checking all the fire veins. Then he
asked what reward he could offer Darkon for helping his country to be
whole again. Darkon laughed at that.
    Fireproof paper?
    That's all he had ever wanted.
    No jewels or riches or extravagant wares.
    Just paper that could be used to craft
    good quality, robust, and trusty kites.
    But Elias Blazewick was not satisfied with the idea of sending off Darkon
with nothing but a stack of fireproof paper. Especially when he learned
that Darkon's kite system was failing.
    Did Darkon plan to replace all the kites?
    Darkon thought it was obvious. What else could he do?

"But what about all the kites you have right now?
    The ones that failed?" Elias asked.
    "They're a vital part of your infrastructure."

"It's a huge loss," Darkon sighed.
    "But we can start over again."

"I'll give you something better," Elias offered.

"I'll teach you how to fireproof your kites."

The Prince of Kalos Fyrian was eager to start building up a good reputation for his country. It was good for public relations to have Kalos Fyrian bring the "fire cure" to the Kingdom of Kites and help it to get back on its feet, Elias pointed out.

Plus, having a chance to work with a longtime role model wasn't an opportunity that came around every day. Darkon unsuccessfully tried to hide his smile and gave way to the prince's enthusiasm. He agreed to stay long enough to learn how to fireproof paper from Elias.

It turned out that Elias was big on trading principles and processes. It was how his country refined its fire not to burn, being able to take out the burning element if desired. It was also how they became experts at their craft, which included pottery, metallurgy, and glass working. Even during the nightmare outbreak, interesting discoveries had been made. For instance, a special blend of glass allowed one to see things that were invisible.

Darkon perked up at that.

"How do you reckon it works?" He asked.

Elias shrugged.

"We can see the barrier by the Invisible Lands and the cities behind it. Honestly, it was shock to see their architecture. I understand why none of them want to leave. If you come out of there at the cutting edge of everything and then are forced to make do with what we have here, it would feel like a step backwards. Can you imagine the demand on their resources?

The crystals that they use are from the crystal archipelago beyond the Changing Lands. It's a challenge just to collect the raw material; it takes a fortune to cut and refine it. So the fact that they possess a method to build their cities with that crystal material is a huge trade secret. It made me wonder if a representative from the Invisible Lands was at the treaty attempt."

Darkon thought about this.
  "We did. I helped dress and deliver
  the body of their representative.
  His entire uniform was of lighter colors,
  white and pastels. There was a unique design to it,
  which delineated a sort of ranking system,
  but I couldn't tell you what it meant.
  He was a high official, though.
  He never spoke once in the entire debate
  about the wording of the peace treaty.
  The expression he wore was of someone there
  because they had to be. Unimpressed, bored,
  and wanting to be somewhere else attending to
  something more important."

Elias choked back a laugh of disbelief.
  "What's more important than the peace efforts?
  I hope this time around their representative
  will be one who actually cares."

Darkon silently agreed.
  He did not share with Elias how difficult it had been to see to the dead bodies of the representatives when he had witnessed the attitudes of his fellow northerners at the meeting. Darkon remembered the feeling of being acutely embarrassed on behalf of his neighboring countries after seeing the way they acted towards those of the south.
  Granted, those of the south like Ionthann might have felt the same about their fellow southerners, like Vandek, who was a very different man twenty years ago. But he didn't want to set off an already indignant young ruler with such musings, so Darkon kept that remembrance to himself.
  Instead, he let Elias run him through the basics of fireproofing paper,

which consisted of three steps.

The first step was one he had already done, which was to absorb flames from the fire veins into Valor.

The second step required releasing controlled amount of the flames from the blade into the paper. That took some work, as Darkon realized that releasing the fire in smaller amounts was actually more difficult than absorbing vast amounts of fire through Valor.

The third step required letting all the flames be absorbed into the paper. If they were taken out before the flame was fully absorbed into the paper, one could unwittingly set something on fire.

Darkon learned quickly, maybe too quickly.

Elias was disappointed that Darkon would be leaving so soon. Darkon reminded him that there was plenty of time to share in the future, and that Elias was free to come and visit any time, now that the firewall was down. Elias reluctantly agreed, and gave Darkon enough fireproof paper to last him an entire year.

To top it all off, he gave Darkon a glass lens.

As a thank you, the prince said.

Something that could give him a different perspective

to see what no one else could see.

That made Darkon think of how discouraged Avorne had been when he said he could see a vision that no one else could.

Darkon received that lens with anticipation and spent most of the flight back to Eld Mané looking through it. He was tempted to go towards the Invisible Lands, because as Elias had said, the architecture of its cities beyond its gleaming barrier was exquisite. But he needed to drop the fire proof paper shipment back at home for Katarina and the boys. And then Darkon needed to see how Avorne was doing. If there was one thing this unexpected foray had taught him, it was that there were many who looked up to his example, and he didn't want to let them down.

It was the crystallized structure in the Inkstone Mountains surrounded by a firewall that made Darkon come to a halt. He lowered the lens and saw nothing but the mountains behind the palace of Eld Mané.

When he brought the lens back to his eyes, he could see this mysterious structure that towered up above even the palace, encircled by flames.

It was like a portion of the Invisible Lands had been plopped down in the mountains and then wrapped in a fire vein from Kalos Fyrian for good measure.

Why was it invisible though?

Darkon thought this very strange.

And then he wondered if this was

what Avorne had been referencing

before they had parted.

Well, there was only one way to find out. Darkon flew the kite down towards the ground, dismounted, and then sent the kite off to the ink portal so it could get to the Kite Kingdom safely. He directed it to make haste, and the kite obeyed. As for Darkon, he took a good long look at this giant crystal structure encased in a tower of flame. He still could only see it through the lens. So with one hand holding the lens to his eye, and the other hand holding Valor, he set the edge of his sword to the tongues of flame.

At the meeting of blade and flame, Darkon felt the familiar drain of energy, the physical strain that came as he held the sword which absorbed fire. But soon, the fire had gone into Valor, and Darkon stood before the crystal structure by itself.

That was when he noticed the kites

strewn all around on the ground.

Behind the wall of fire,

were mounds of lifeless kites.

Again, they were only visible through the lens.

Darkon found himself exercising his one-handed solution again, still holding the lens to his eye to see where all the kites were, and lightly touching Valor to the paper to fireproof them the way Elias had taught him.

At first the flames that came out of Valor engulfed the kites completely.

Darkon was afraid that he had released too much fire, and that it would consume the kite's paper and wooden frame. But they absorbed the fire, and then, they came to life.

The kite gleamed like an ember in the fire, and giving a great shudder, it trembled and then rose into the air, circling around Darkon and then hovering in the air. It brought him joy to see these kites come back to life, each and every one of them. Darkon took away the glass lens and found he couldn't see any of them.

How bizarre. He put the lens back to his eye, and saw that the kites were arranging themselves into a winding pathway, a staircase of kites that wavered and rose into the air to what looked like a door. Clearly he was meant to walk up the steps of kites. Darkon found each one hold steady as he put his entire weight on every kite. He ascended up the staircase until at the top, he found himself in front of a door.

It was a double glass door that slid open
as soon as he stood in front of it.
Darkon had never seen a pair of doors like this one.

The smell that met him was one
that made him wrinkle his nose in distaste.

But on the inside, he saw a room, white and sterile,
with what looked like a stretcher made into a bed.

On the bed was a man who looked identical to him
in features and age and mannerism.
He was hooked up to a mechanism
that Darkon couldn't recognize.

"Scott?"
Darkon whispered.
He had met his counterpart many times in the past, even before the first peace treaty attempt. He received no response from the man, who was

either asleep or unconscious. Darkon lowered the lens from his eyes and found that he could see even without its aid. He put the lens in his pocket. Darkon approached Scott, reached out to touch the other's forehead.

What was wrong? The machine beside him only beeped and showed him images and pulsing lines that meant nothing to him. Darkon received no reply or explanation, heard nothing but his own heightened heartbeat and breathing.

Somehow, he knew.

It was the same as the kites that suffered in his kingdom.

Darkon took up Valor and wondered if it could do to a Legend what it could do to kites and paper. He decided not to dwell on any doubts or fears, and with a resolve that lit up bright within him, the King of Kites took Valor and laid it upon Scott's chest. With one hand on the hilt to steady the blade and another hand on Scott's shoulder, Darkon let the flames emerge from Valor and engulf Scott. The fire set upon the man's body and limbs, seeped through skin into flesh and bone.

"Come on, Scott," Darkon whispered.
    "We've got work to do. Are you with me?"

"I'm with you," a faint reply came,
    and Scott opened his eyes
    and grasped Darkon by the hand.
    "Thank you. Whatever you did worked.
    The doctors couldn't find what was wrong."

Darkon smiled as he withdrew Valor and helped Scott to sit up.

"Don't ask me to explain it;
    I couldn't tell you.
    Let's just be thankful you're back.
    Speaking of, where are we?"

"That I can answer,"
  Scott stood on his feet with care.

As soon as his feet reached the floor,
  the hospital room faded away
  and made room for
  a beautiful space
  made of stained glass.

"Welcome to the King's Heart, Darkon.
  Why don't we go to find the others?
  They're waiting."

24

Kindness

Once again, Emily stood in the Inkstone Mountains behind the palace of Eld Mané. She stood where she had first met Avorne and stared at the space where he had said the second peace treaty would be.

She couldn't see it.

She knew it was there,

because all of the signed invitations

would reach a certain point and then disappear.

It was the same with people who went in, like Vandek.

A couple went,

who took the time to say "hi" to Emily before going in,

calling themselves Theia and Crescens.

They were the ones who were in charge

of the healing wards in the palace.

Tal and Raehn came with their two children.

Renadé came with

Katarina, August, Griffin, and Den.

Then came Haliien and Cassan from the Hourglass.

Iris greeted her before entering as well.

Others came, many people that
    Emily didn't recognize or know,
    like a Falleyne Featherfall and Elias Blazewick.

If anyone came asking for the King's Heart,
    Emily just directed them to the path
    where she knew Avorne's vision was.

Emily was glad to be able to assist others to joining the second peace treaty attempt. But she also really wanted to see the King's Heart, and she very much wished to go in.
    But how could you go in to a place you couldn't see?
    She tried walking slowly in its direction, expecting that she'd at least run into a wall or a door or something to let her feel her way in. But she just kept walking through the mountains alone.
    She resorted to waiting there in the mountains for others who sought the King's Heart.
    Well, she'd at least make sure that others could make it in.
    Sometimes, people would have trouble seeing it.
    "I can't see it," they'd say,
and Emily would patiently wait
before suggesting,
"Try looking again.
Can you see a part of it?
A window maybe?
Or a banner?
Or a door?"

That prompt would be enough for the person to say,

"I got it! I can make it on my own now.

Thank you!" And they'd leave too.

It wasn't like she didn't try taking her own advice.

Emily looked and looked hard.

She would try to search out some small piece

of this vision that Avorne had.

She saw no window,

no door,

not even a corner of a building.

She tried to imagine a beautiful castle cathedral that practically touched the sky made entirely of crystal glass, because that was what Avorne had said the King's Heart looked like.

But nothing came into view,

and Emily knew she couldn't fool herself

into believing something that wasn't there.

What could she do

when everyone else

around her could enter,

but she couldn't?

What had she missed?

Emily went over the directions she had previously taken, from strength to honor to wisdom to…kindness. Emily realized that she still needed to take the direction of kindness on the path to leadership. Was this kindness? Leading people to a place she couldn't get into herself? Or was kindness the patience to listen to the fears and doubts of those who couldn't see the King's Heart? The encouragement to prompt them to try one more time and not give up?

Emily got tired of pacing, so she sat down on the ground to think. She opened *Gold: Leadership at Heart* and reread the note from Scott and Katarina that said,

To our Ribbon Princess,
who was born to be a leader of the highest caliber:
Today, we celebrate your heart of gold.

Proud to be yours,
The King and Queen of Kites

As she sat there, running her fingers over those words, Emily wondered. Did being a leader mean that you led people forward even if you couldn't reach the vision yourself? She wasn't sure what she thought about that, but she didn't have much time to dwell on it, because she was interrupted by Valéon, who had flown down and swept in from above out of nowhere.

"Forget something?" He hovered in the air before her, holding out her deck of cards.

"Hey, Valéon." Emily was happy to see him.
She took back her cards and said, "Thanks."

"So are you planning on sitting here forever?"
Valéon asked, crossing his arms and looking amused.
"Everyone's waiting.
Especially after they got that showy set of invites you designed."

"Yeah, about that..." Emily said.
She looked at Valéon and wondered
how in the world she could explain to her friend
that she couldn't see the King's Heart.
Valéon seemed to pick up on her hesitation and landed on the ground. He sat down next to her and let his wings settle across his back.
"You don't want to come?" He asked.
"Of course I want to come," Emily said. She picked out the original invitation she had received from Crystal, Ryan, and Vincent that invited her to the second peace treaty from the book she carried.

She showed it to Valéon.

"I said 'no' to a whole bunch of people to come here.

And I've loved every minute of it.

Meeting Ionthann, Iris, and Vandek was really nice.

And designing those invitations with Renadé

and the rest of Darkon's family was great."

"Then what's the problem?" Valéon said.

Emily closed her eyes, took in a deep breath, and said it.

"I can't see the King's Heart."

"But you have the same heart

and vision as we do," Valéon insisted.

Emily nodded.

"But you can't see it?"

Valéon asked.

"Yet," Emily said, wanting to make sure

that Valéon knew that she hadn't given up on getting in.

"I can't see it yet. But I will. I know I will."

Valéon put a hand on her knee and said,

"I'll get Avorne. Wait here."

"Why bother Avorne when he's trying to get everything ready?" Emily protested.

But Valéon had already taken off and flown up into the air, flying higher and higher until he disappeared from sight, presumably into the King's Heart, which Emily still couldn't see. She couldn't help but feel embarrassed when shortly after, she was approached not just by Valéon and Avorne, but Darkon and Ionthann as well.

"Oh, great," Emily muttered under her breath. The last thing she wanted was a pep talk to just pull herself together and try harder. She *had* pulled herself together and tried harder. It hadn't worked. She just needed time to figure something else out.

When she looked down at the four men who stood before her,
Emily raised a hand in awkward greeting and said,
"Hey, guys."

To Emily's great relief, they didn't give her anything resembling a pep talk. They also didn't tell her to pull herself together and try harder. Instead, they all turned to Ionthann and waited for the captain of the guard as he studied Emily with a keen eye. Emily fought the urge to look away, but she forced herself to lock gazes with Ionthann. She was caught off guard by the question he asked after a minute of silence.
"What's holding you back?"

Emily blinked.
"What do you mean?"

"Something's holding you back
from seeing the King's Heart,"
Ionthann pointed out.
"There's reservation
surrounding you like a thick cloud.
There's a good chance that
it's preventing you
from seeing the King's Heart."

At the mention of reservation, Emily frowned and thought hard. Did she have any reservations about going into the King's Heart? She didn't think she had a reservation regarding that. She had always desired to be a witness at the second peace treaty, to see Avorne, Valéon, and Darkon and their allies fulfill their long-sought dreams. She had always wanted to spend time with them, work side by side with them, support them with everything she had. Granted, she had barely been able to see any of them this time around, and it was all she could do seeing Darkon to refrain from hugging him and asking if he felt all right.

Because she was reminded of Scott and his mysterious decline in health, and that brought back the issues that she was helping so many of her friends work through and deal with.

Everything Emily had done so well to ignore until now came
flooding back
to the forefront
of her mind.

Emily looked at the deck of cards she held and nearly dropped them when she saw that they had turned from their blue-gold design to
black tattered ones
with blood-red lettering.

She turned the cards over and read the issues that she had been listening to, counseling and advising people out of: anxiety attacks, eating disorders, depression, suicide, estranged family members, dysfunctional relationships, lawsuits, financial trouble, death in the family or loss of a loved one, gossip, bullying, car accidents, drug addiction, alcoholism, marital issues, struggling children, myriads of health problems, passive aggressive friends, bad parenting, escapism, workplace challenges, home challenges, social challenges, and more.

Emily knew exactly what was holding her back. She looked at Ionthann, held up her deck of black cards, which she knew Ionthann would recognize and understand.

"This is holding me back," she admitted.

"I'm stuck. If I see the King's Heart, then I'll be able to go in.

If I enter the King's Heart, then we'll fulfill the second peace treaty. If we fulfill the second peace treaty, I'll have to go home back to everyone else's problems and pain. This is the first time I feel like I've lived life for myself.

I don't want this to end.

I don't want to go back."

No one said a word then. Ionthann was the only one who could look Emily straight in the eye. Avorne, Valéon, and Darkon looked away.

"I'm not saying I want to stay here forever,"
Emily tried to qualify.
"I'm just afraid that
I won't be able to come back to visit again.
That somehow you won't want my company
after we accomplish this."

"Emily," the King of Eld Mané
gave a command for the first time. "Stand up."

Emily didn't waste any time following his directive.
She stood up in front of Avorne.
Avorne crossed his arms across his chest, bowed his head, cleared his throat, and then sighed a deep sigh. The King pulled something out of his pocket and handed it to Emily.

"Tell me," he said.
"Who came up with this invitation?"

Emily let out a small laugh.
Were they really having this talk?
But she said, "I did."

"What did you declare twice?
Once on each side of the card?" He asked.

Emily stood straighter as she answered,
"I uphold the heart of the King in this matter."

"So long as you do," Avorne said,

"you can always come back."

For a moment,
   the black cards
   in Emily's hands
   flickered
   blue-
   gold.

Darkon stepped in this time
   and lightly rested the pommel of his sword
   on the top of her deck,

"We always welcome your company."
   He smiled the way Scott did,
   and it brought a fiery warmth back into Emily's heart.

This time,
   the black cards turned blue
   and remained that way.

Valéon nudged her in the side with his elbow.
   "Avorne and Darkon say all that,
   but neither of them can bring themselves to admit
   that we saved a seat for you…and a podium."

"Wait, what?"
   Emily started.
   "A podium?"

"We're the four who will be
   presenting the second peace treaty
   at the King's Heart," Valéon grinned.

"Seeing as we all hate public speaking, we decided that we could suffer through it together if you gave the opening remarks and possibly the closing remarks on top of that."

"That…" Emily began, not quite sure how to object.
  "I did not sign up for that…"
Ionthann sheepishly admitted, "It would have been me, but seeing as you're the keeper of the peace treaty draft now, it's all you."
  The captain of the guard didn't hide his obvious relief.
  "Thanks for sparing me. I owe you one."

Emily laughed. She couldn't help herself.
  "Fine then. I'll do the opening and closing remarks."
  In her hand,
  designs of gold
  emerged upon
  the blue cards
  and stayed.

"Now would you look at that?"
  Ionthann said as he gently tapped her cards with a finger.
  "You chose the path of leadership, just like in your dream."

"You got your heart of gold back,"
  Darkon said as he clapped her on the shoulder.
  "Scott will be pleased to know."

"You talked with Scott?" Emily asked in surprise.
  "When? Where? Is he all right?"

Darkon smiled.
  "I did. He showed me into the King's Heart after I healed him.
  But he went back home after, because he didn't want to worry Katarina or

Ryan. He also said something about expecting a good story for Christmas?"

Darkon looked bemused.

"He said it began with the
Kite Kingdom and the Ribbon Princess,
but wanted to hear the end from you."

"I almost forgot about that," Emily felt relief course through her and breathed easier. Then looking at her four friends, Emily said,

"Thanks, everyone. Kindness was the last direction I needed on my path to leadership. I'm glad I got to learn it from all of you."

That was when Ionthann got a knowing look on his face and asked Emily to review the path of leadership and its directions. Out loud? Now? Emily wasn't sure where this was going. She shrugged when the captain of the guard confirmed: Out loud. Now. So Emily hoisted the deck of cards in her hands and shuffled them with movements that came naturally to her.

"The path of leadership
has four directions,
and they are…"

Emily held the deck out to the King of Eld Mané first.

Avorne drew the first card,
held it up, and said, "Strength."

She held the deck out to Valéon,
who drew the second card and read, "Honor."

She held the deck out to Darkon,
who drew the third card and said, "Wisdom."

She held the deck out to Ionthann,
who drew the fourth card and read, "Kindness."

Then, Ionthann said something that Emily remembered well. It was what he had said when he was about to give her the first peace treaty draft.

The captain of the guard asked,
    "Will you revive the King's Heart?"

Emily replied without hesitation,
    "I will revive the King's Heart
    by traveling the path of leadership,
    the directions of which are
    strength, honor, wisdom, and kindness."

Avorne asked,
    "What will you do with the strength you gain?"

Emily replied,
    "Strengthen the hands of all who rebuild."

Valéon asked,
    "What of the honor you will receive?"

Emily answered,
    "Honor the memory of those who first came."

Darkon asked,
    "What of the wisdom you will find?"

Emily said,
    "Wisdom will speak to those who would hear."

Ionthann asked,
    "What of the kindness you will claim?"

"Kindness will bind what is broken and mend every hurt."

Emily spoke loud and clear.

"Then by choice and right, the King's Heart is yours.
   May the breath you breathe bring new life,
   and may the words you speak bring hope and healing,"
Ionthann concluded.

He gently closed her eyes with one hand and said,
   "May the King's Heart no longer be a dream,
   but become reality."

"Just so," Emily replied
   as she put her hand over Ionthann's,
   her eyes still closed. "Just so."

She felt Ionthann withdraw his hand.
   When she heard Avorne cough and clear his throat, she asked,
   "Is that my cue to open my eyes, Majesty?"

Avorne choked.
   "Don't you start with the titles like everyone else!
   And yes, that would be your cue to open your eyes."
   Emily laughed, opened her eyes, and then promptly gasped. Surrounded by Avorne, Darkon, Valéon, and Ionthann, she stood in the middle of an enormous sunlit, stained-glass structure. It was the beautiful castle cathedral that practically touched the sky made entirely of crystal glass that Avorne had described.

Only now, she could see it with her own eyes. There was a golden crown embedded in the design on the floor with the letters "A KING IS NOTHING WITHOUT HIS PEOPLE" written around it. There were so many upper floors and halls and doorways, and people that were coming in and out of various places. There was even a library that had "Welcome to the Library" written above it.

"But how...?" Emily could barely begin to find the words to form her questions. It was beautiful here. Much more beautiful than the words Avorne had used to try to describe it.

Valéon was the one who decided to break the news to her first.

"We didn't know how to tell you," he said.

"You've been standing in the center
of the King's Heart all this time.
You just couldn't see it."

"Until now," Emily murmured in amazement.

"Until now," Valéon agreed.

"We figured that Ionthann could find out what was keeping you from seeing the King's Heart, since you clearly came in without a problem on your own."

Darkon was the one who informed Emily of the details.

"You actually came in first, before the others. We thought it was strange that you looked around and then walked out. We figured that you wanted to make sure everyone else could find their way, especially when you kept showing others the entrance. It wasn't until you came back and sat down that we realized something was wrong and you couldn't see it."

Ionthann just shook his head.

"You nearly had me worried, with that reservation aura around you the whole time. Iris said it would dissipate eventually, and she was right. We just didn't realize all the things that were holding you back."

Emily felt a well of gratitude rise from within her as she looked at her friends.

"Thank you for not giving up on me. I'm glad I made it."

"So are we." Avorne smiled the brightest smile.

"Welcome to the King's Heart, Emily. It's about time."

25

Fulfillment

Somewhere in the middle of seeing to arrangements, exchanging greetings and pleasantries, and requesting assistance as needed, Avorne realized that he couldn't find Mirae anywhere in the King's Heart. He had finally met up with Renadé, who had returned from her extended stay at the Kite Kingdom. His wife had taken it upon herself to explore all the various halls and rooms designed by Mirae and returned to him quite impressed.

"You've been busy, I see,"
  Renadé said as she came up to lightly kiss him on the cheek.
  "And without a single drop of ink on top of that. I'm impressed."

"I didn't come up with the design,"
  Avorne reminded her.
  "That was all Mirae."

"But you had the heart and the vision," Renadé said.
  "This couldn't have come into being without you.
  It was a good collaboration by the looks of it."

"It was," Avorne agreed.

"Where is Mirae? I can't find her anywhere."

"Have you tried the library?"
Halas practically appeared out of nowhere
as he posed the question and
followed it up with a suggestion.
"Try the architecture section."

Avorne nearly jumped. He sighed,
"Halas, we've got to work on this."
It had been so long since he'd been with Halas, he had forgotten how well his brother could use his influence to come and go unnoticed. But then he registered what Halas had said.
"What's Mirae doing hiding out in the library? She never had trouble talking with you or me, or even Ionthann or Valéon."
"She got overwhelmed after seeing everyone's reactions when they came in," Halas explained.
"Every person who enters the King's Heart has said something along the lines of, 'How does this place know what I've wanted my whole life? I never told anyone...' and then half of them break down into tears because they're so moved."
"Looks like her heart
for her leaders reached theirs,"
Avorne said. "It certainly did mine."

"And mine," Halas agreed.
"Mirae probably never expected to reach
so many people to this degree and on this level."

"She's in the architecture section?" Avorne asked.
"Is she planning on coming out any time soon?
I'd hate for her to miss the second peace treaty."

"I doubt she'd miss the event, seeing as that's why you're both working together," Halas smiled.

"But you may want to coax her out, maybe by offering to introduce her to Emily. From what I gathered with my perception, she's wanted to approach Emily for some time now. But with you, Valéon, Darkon, and Ionthann all focusing on Emily, Mirae got intimidated. I think she gets shy around groups of people, even though she shines with one-on-one interactions."

"Why would she get intimidated by us as a group? She's so friendly with us. She bonded with Valéon the minute he flew in, and she's gotten along fine with Ionthann and Darkon. I don't see why she'd be any different with Emily in the mix." Avorne frowned.

Renadé pointed out,

"It's not every day you can meet a leader of your caliber. Also, Emily is a peer. You said yourself that Mirae admired the invitations that Emily designed. She might worry about what Emily might think of her. Maybe I can help with introductions."

It was at times like this that Avorne was glad his queen was as perceptive and considerate as she was.

"To the architecture section it is, then,"
he agreed. "Shall we?"

Halas looked content with this arrangement and offered to go find Emily, who herself seemed to have pulled off a disappearing act of her own, claiming she wanted to arrange her thoughts for opening remarks. So Avorne entered the library with Renadé, and there, in the architecture section, they found Mirae huddled up against a shelf with a set of small crystal tiles stacked beside her. The young architect had a deep sea green tile that she'd flip between her fingers. In a nervous twirl or twist, she'd shape the crystal material into one form and then another. One moment, she turned it into a fish, the next a lizard, and then a sea turtle.

"I thought you of all people would want to meet the leaders who came here," Avorne said as he knelt beside her.

"I do," Mirae confessed.

"It's just there's so many here
and all at once. How do I start?"

"You start with one," Avorne said with amusement.

"You say 'hello' and introduce yourself.
If you want someone to practice with,
I brought Renadé, my one and only queen."

Mirae's eyes grew wide as she looked up, but Renadé smiled and settled down on the ground across form the young architect.

"What Avorne means is that if you want so much to speak to those you look up to, you shouldn't hide yourself from them. It's probably overwhelming to have so many see you and your work outside of the Invisible Lands, but it will do your heart good to spend time with the people you labored to reach for so many years."

That seemed to sink in, and then Mirae voiced her concern.

"I don't have to speak in front of everyone at the peace treaty, though, right?"

"No," Renadé said.

"All that will be done by Avorne, Darkon, Valéon, and Emily. Speaking of which, Emily wanted to have something to help keep track of her notes. She's trying to pull her speech together. Would you mind helping out?" Renadé asked.

"After doing something of this magnitude, that detail should come easy to you."

Mirae perked up at that.

"I can do that." She picked up her crystal tiles eagerly, and her enthusiasm overcame her timidity.

"Thank you, Queen Renadé."

"Renadé is just fine. Now get going. Wouldn't want to make her wait."

Once Mirae was gone, Avorne said,

"Ren, have I ever told you you're a genius?"

He was pleased to see her stifle a laugh.

"Thanks for talking with Mirae. There were times when I thought she deserved to work with women leaders she could look up to, but Iris was covering surveillance at the palace, and you were in the Kite Kingdom with Katarina, and Raehn was busy overseeing Eles Teare. And Emily was apparently all over the place. Somehow the first positive leader interactions Mirae got were with me, Darkon, Valéon, and Ionthann."

"Don't feel too bad," Renadé laughed.

"You were the one who saw this first. Anyone can see that you have a special place in her heart just because of that. And if she decides to stick around a little longer, then she may have time to work with all of us women leaders too."

Avorne had to agree with that. Ironically, after getting Mirae to leave the library, Avorne spent most of his remaining time there in the architecture section, trying to organize his thoughts for his speaking part in the second peace treaty.

Avorne hated speeches. At least Valéon had a voice of power, which seemed like the perfect affinity for public speaking. And Darkon could speak with ease to anyone, just by virtue of his personality and charisma. And Emily? Well, she had a voice of power too, though she tended to bury it and deny that she had the gift of speaking.

But even as King of Eld Mané, Avorne dreaded the idea of standing up in front of so many people and addressing the peace efforts. He wanted to do well for the sake of those who had lost their lives to try to make the first peace treaty a reality. Renadé's advice was simple and straightforward:

Just be yourself.

Don't spout nonsense.

Acknowledge who came before us,

what it took to get here,

and what you hope for our future.

Avorne sighed. She made it sound so neat and clean cut.

Did she want to speak for him?

No, had been the amused reply.

But she expressed her faith in his ability to succeed by laying an ink character upon the back of his right hand that read, STRENGTH.

Whether it was his wife's faith in him or the ink charm she laid upon his hand, Avorne did find the strength and clarity of mind to pull his thoughts and words together. By the time he emerged from the library, he had a good idea of what he wanted to share with everyone who had come to the King's Heart. He also found that Mirae had made some last minute modifications. There in the reception hall area, a speaker's platform had been raised. It almost looked like the giant golden crown design on the floor had been elevated up to become a stage. And upon it was not only a podium, but four seats, three of which were already filled. Darkon, Valéon, and Emily already sat there waiting.

And from one end of the room to the other, were seats that had been completely filled by those who had entered the King's Heart. He saw rulers and citizens from so many countries, both north and south. He thought he was seeing things when he glimpsed people who had already passed away, like certain representatives from the first peace treaty attempt. But he saw them, and he thought perhaps it was the King's Heart that allowed them to be together in this time and space. Avorne even saw his family – his father and mother, Diurne, Gavin and Okten.

How everyone from this side of life and the other had known to come here and at this time was a mystery to Avorne. He knew it wasn't everyone, because that wasn't feasible. But there were enough people from every country, ruler and citizen alike that gave Avorne the reassurance that this was only the beginning, not the end. He wasn't expected to bring about a time of ultimate peace and prosperity for all the years to come. He was only expected to begin the change that would naturally follow if people's hearts changed.

With that comforting thought, he stepped up onto the speaker's platform and looked at Darkon, Valéon, and Emily.

"When are we starting?"

They all replied,

"Now."

Avorne coughed, and then made his way to his seat, very glad he was not in charge of opening remarks. As soon as he sat down, Emily got up and made her way towards the podium. Whether it was a mechanism built into the King's Heart, or people were unusually attentive to what was going on at the speaker's platform, the buzz of murmuring and chatter died down to a respectful silence.

Emily reached the podium, held up her hand in greeting, and began with a cheerful,

"Hello, everyone!"

Avorne had to chuckle at that. Leave it to Emily to set the mood in a way that fit her. He saw her take out her invitation from her pocket and hold it up for everyone to see.

"For those of you who don't know me, which is probably most of you, I'm Emily. If you received a set of invitations tied with blue and gold ribbon, that was me." Emily continued.

"On behalf of Avorne Ehrthann, King of Eld Mané, I'd like to thank everyone for coming. Whether you were a part of the peace efforts from the very beginning, or you joined later in this long endeavor, your presence is very much appreciated. We're all coming from different places and experiences; all of us have had our own challenges, myself included. But the most important thing is that we uphold the King's heart in this matter. Am I right?"

Avorne could see the heads nodding in agreement, hear the murmur that rippled through the audience. He felt a swell of pride to hear Emily speak this way. He also thought that she should have more than just the opening and closing remarks. He listened to Emily again.

"Today, while they are not the only valuable voices to this peace effort, you will hear from those who have been seeking to bring about this second peace treaty from the beginning. Your speakers will be: Avorne Ehrthann, King of Eld Mané, speaking on behalf of the South; Darkon, King of Kites, speaking on behalf of the North; and Valéon, our first keeper of the peace treaty, speaking on behalf of the peace effort itself."

311

Avorne wished that Emily could have a say in this. She had been the one who had come in hopes of witnessing the peace treaty, had specifically expressed her interest in it and invested a good portion of her time and energy into helping out as best as she could. Avorne shared a silent glance with both Darkon and Valéon and knew that they shared the same thought as him. They thought that Emily should speak as well.

Up front by the podium, Emily looked down at her crystal tile and coughed. She tugged at one end of her blue-gold scarf and absentmindedly played with the tassels before clearing her throat and adding,

"I'm sorry, let me correct myself. Valéon will speak on behalf of the past peace treaty attempt, and I will speak on behalf of the future of the peace efforts before sharing the closing remarks."

Avorne's breath caught in his throat. Whatever crystal tile Mirae had given to Emily must have picked up on the shared sentiment of the other speakers and given her an immediate update. Avorne had no idea how Mirae had managed that, but he forced himself to focus, because that was when Emily said,

"And so, without further ado, I present to you our first speaker, Avorne."

As she passed by him,
Emily shot him an unimpressed look
and whispered, "Seriously?"

Avorne suppressed a chuckle and said,
"You'll do great. We're all in this together."

By the time he got to the podium, Avorne felt decidedly prepared. He was certain that Mirae was helping him out with the atmosphere of the King's Heart, because he found that for the first time in his life, he wasn't afraid of speaking in front of this enormous crowd of people. He didn't get nervous, didn't break out into a cold sweat, or struggle with a dry mouth. In fact, he felt like he was talking to people he had known his entire life – genuine friends and family.

So he spoke his mind and heart.

"As you know, this has been a labor of love, brought about by much sacrifice, pain, tears, and hard work. If I were to tell you every single person and every single effort that went on to make this second peace treaty possible from the past twenty years, we may be here another twenty years just from that list alone. I will say instead, what I learned as both King and citizen, a southerner and – for a short time – a northerner in disguise."

Avorne tried to search the crowd to find Renadé and Haliien. They were both sitting in the front row.

"As a southern king, I learned that I had citizens who supported me with more love and loyalty than I knew what to do with. I found allies in those of the north, both rulers and common folk alike. And in a six-week period, when I was a northerner in disguise – specifically a refugee from the Invisible Lands," Avorne smiled as he caught Mirae's proud look.

"I learned that there were southerners who took me in and gave me safe haven, a means to support myself, and friendship. I believe the keys to reconciliation are at the core of those experiences."

Raising his hand, Avorne listed his three points on his fingers.

"The first key is support through love and loyalty.

The second key is willingness to partner with allies.

The third key is establishment of protection and stability.

What does this look like?

Well, it will be different for every person and situation.

But I give you the secrets that took me twenty years to discover."

Avorne looked at this sea of people in silence for just a moment before saying,

"I would not be standing here if it were not for all of you. I thank you for all you have done, all you are doing, and all you will do in days to come. With that, I will let you listen to Valéon, our voice for the peace treaty and all those who worked to defend it in the past."

It was the most natural thing for Avorne to turn to Valéon and motion

313

for his friend to come up. Of course, then Valéon made a quick motion pointing to Darkon, and Avorne realized that it was supposed to be Darkon next.

"Oh. I've been informed
   that it should be Darkon who's next,"
   Avorne laughed. "Darkon?"

26

Valor of a Different Sort

Valéon felt his heart skip a beat when Avorne turned to call his name and motioned for him to come up to the podium.

What was Avorne doing, making his speech so short?

Valéon had expected Avorne to go on for another half an hour with details and examples and whatnot.

Apparently the King of Eld Mané had forgotten
    to mention some of the important details,
    like the nightmare outbreaks and what to do about them.
    Also, it was supposed to be Darkon who was next, not him.

Oh well. Valéon couldn't blame Avorne's lapse in memory. This was a huge crowd of people, and it was pretty nerve racking to speak in front of them all.

Thankfully, Darkon was a master of improvisation and walked up to the podium without even getting ruffled. Valéon wondered how the King of Kites could maintain such a composed and cheerful demeanor. He also wondered what Darkon was doing with that sword, which seemed to be out of place in the Kite King's hand. He watched bemused as Darkon hoisted the sword up onto the podium, frowned and drummed his fingers upon the blade in thought.

In the front row of the audience, Mirae was clearly aware that a different set up was needed for the speaker's platform, so she held up her forefinger to let Darkon know she understood his need and to wait one minute. The podium changed itself into a stand for the sword, complete with a deep scarlet and gold cloth draped beneath it.

Valéon heard the collective "wow" travel through the King's Heart in hushed tones. Like everyone else, Valéon wondered what Darkon would say and what this sword was meant to signify.

Of course, Darkon lightened the moment
by looking at Mirae and saying,
"Can I walk the stage?
I do better when I'm moving around."

Mirae looked at him with a raised eyebrow as if to reply,
"What are you asking me permission for?
It's your speech."

Darkon gave her a friendly salute
and then turned to give a grand bow to everyone present.
"I have had the joy and honor of working with many northerners and southerners over the years, mostly providing alternative modes of transportation. I'm sure you all are familiar with my kingdom's specialty," Darkon smiled and made a sweeping gesture with his arms.

As if on cue, kites floated down from above, circling above the audience, and the speaker's platform. The kites gleamed as if they were embers in a fire, and Valéon recognized them as the fireproof ones.

"Just recently," Darkon continued,
"my kingdom suffered a kite infrastructure failure, leaving my country and myself in a difficult situation that I'd wish upon no one. But in the process of giving help and receiving it, I learned something valuable. Being humble enough to ask for help and accepting it with a grateful heart is a great gift, not only to myself, but to those who offer aid."

Darkon strode from one side of the platform to the other.

"Not that we look to hold up a scoring board stacking up our debts to each other – that's not the point. Rather, this is the true nature of being a good neighbor and a good friend. And while I have seen many such examples in my lifetime, I'd like to acknowledge two individuals who exemplify this perfectly."

Valéon looked over to Avorne at this, and Avorne just gave him a shrug in response. Obviously, none of them had communicated with each other before what they would be saying, so this was completely new, even to the King of Eld Mané. Avorne nodded his head towards Darkon to say they'd find out soon enough.

Then Darkon said the two names,
"Falleyne Featherfall, Princess of Vinduren,
and Elias Blazewick, Prince of Kalos Fyrian."

Ah. Valéon had a feeling he knew exactly where this was going. It was certainly different from Avorne's short and concise speech that had three main thoughts and corresponding takeaway points. Darkon's style was more free-flowing and revolved around storytelling. He continued to listen to Darkon.

"Neither of these two young rulers know it, but they opened my eyes to see what true friendship between the south and north could look like. Just by being themselves, they helped bring about the healing of not only my kingdom and kites, but also my heart."

Darkon walked back to the center of the platform and picked up the sword from its stand.

"This sword is from the Blade Pass between Vinduren and Kalos Fyrian. I drew it rather by accident when we searched for a way to reach Elias and his people. It has the ability to absorb flames and was what allowed us to enter Kalos Fyrian after consuming the fire in the Blade Pass."

Darkon placed the sword back on the stand with care and admitted,
"As most of you know, I am for peace.

You can imagine my discomfort
toting around a weapon that is meant for war.
But I was told that this blade sings
of valor of a different sort,
the valor to set things right.
That is what I'd like you to take home with you,
this idea of valor. To pursue the peace we all desire
requires just that. It is easy to fight a battle or a war,
isn't it? It is hard to stand for peace. Because what
renown or high honor is bestowed upon those who
rebuild a broken place or restore a broken people?"

Darkon turned to Emily at this and said,

"It often is overlooked and underappreciated. Hard work, long nights, lots of patience and even more listening. It's usually a thankless job. Not much glory to be found in that, am I right?"

Seated right beside Emily, Valéon could see his friend give a painful smile and small nod in response.

Now the Kite King turned back to the audience and looked straight at Mirae.

"One could liken it to doing work that is invisible. Much like the King's Heart. Raise of hands – how many of you had trouble seeing the King's Heart in the beginning?" Darkon said then, raising his own hand.

"I can see that just about everyone's hand is raised. Except Mirae, well, yes, you are the one exception, dear. And Avorne – the other exception."

Darkon chuckled when he looked back to see Avorne decidedly not raise his hand.

"Well, it is no mystery that pursuing peace requires labor that often goes unnoticed. But once we catch sight of the vision, much like how we caught sight of the King's Heart, we will find that rebuilding is actually the most beautiful, exquisite, and advanced undertaking. So with that, I say, let us take for ourselves and for our people, valor of a different sort."

Darkon picked up his sword once more
  and held it aloft with a noble air and said,
  "The valor to set things right."

As Darkon turned and began to approach his seat between Avorne and Valéon, the entire place erupted into a huge applause. Valéon felt a tap on his shoulder and found Emily leaning over to say,

"I swear Darkon and Scott have the same storytelling style. I totally can't speak like that. Is your speech going to be like Darkon's?"

Valéon laughed.

"No. I can't speak like that either. I'd like to think I'm somewhere between Avorne and Darkon style-wise."

And he thought that was an accurate statement. Because Avorne was short, to the point, and linear, while Darkon was a sprawling storyteller who moved seamlessly from personal thoughts to public acknowledgements to visual examples.

When Emily asked him if he thought one style was better than the other, Valéon thought about it briefly. When he did answer, Valéon said,

"It's not about preference or style.

It's about your heart
and if it matches the King's Heart.
As long as you share the heart and vision,
the expression and style are secondary."

A thoughtful look came upon Emily's face.

"I suppose you're right about that. Avorne and Darkon complement each other really well." Then she grinned.

"That means we should try to complement each other's styles too. What's your style? I'll try to do the exact opposite."

Valéon laughed.

"Just be yourself. I'll be me. That's it. Besides, I don't think Avorne and Darkon were trying to get that result on purpose. It just happened."

"Fair enough," Emily shrugged.

"Oh hey, it looks like Mirae wants to ask you something before you start."
She pointed towards Mirae, who was waving her hand trying to get Valéon's
attention.

"My turn already," Valéon swallowed
    and tried to calm his heart,
    which began to race.

"Yep, and before you know it,
    you'll be done,
    and it'll be me
    getting all flustered."

"You've got a voice of power,"
    Valéon grinned.
    "You've got no excuse."

"Look who's talking,"
    Emily gave him a light-hearted shove.
    "I expect nothing but the best,
    especially with that voice of yours.
    Anyway, you better get going
    before Mirae says something."

Valéon took that advice, getting up from his seat, and walking to the edge
of the platform.

He bent down on one knee
    as Mirae stood up on her tiptoes to ask him,
    "Would you like the podium back?
    To hold your notes?"

Valéon looked at the stand that Darkon had used to display the sword, which still had the scarlet and gold cloth draped over it.

"I don't have any notes. Would it be possible to not have anything in the front? I can just stand and speak."

Mirae's eyes grew wide.

"You're going to say everything by memory?"

Valéon tapped his forehead with his finger.

"That's the plan."

"How do you do that?" Mirae asked in awe.

"Easy," Valéon answered.

"Practice. Not that exciting and pretty repetitive. But it works. Is it too complicated to clear the front of the platform?"

Mirae shook her head,

"Nope."

She pointed to where the stand used to be,

and Valéon saw it melt into the floor of the platform.

This time it was Valéon's turn to ask,

"How do you do that?"

Mirae smiled.

"Same as you.

Practice."

Valéon was impressed.

"When this is all over,

I'd like to see a practical demonstration."

Mirae looked pleased and rubbed her nose absentmindedly.

"Okay, when this is all over."

Then, she stood on her toes,

    kissed him lightly on the cheek,

    and said, "You can do it!"

Perhaps it was the expectation and full confidence that Mirae had, but that brief interaction was enough to set Valéon at ease. His heart rate returned to normal, and he went to the center of the stage. By the time he turned around to face the audience, he had received a thumbs up from Emily, a salute from Darkon, and a nod of encouragement from Avorne. Valéon was ready. He took in a deep breath and brought to mind the first sentence of his memorized speech. Valéon did decide to add one impromptu transition and began with,

"Thank you, Darkon. I have a hard act to follow. I hope I will not disappoint."

Then, Valéon began the memorized portion of his speech. "I would like to share with you that which I committed to memory twenty years ago. They are the words that have survived from the first peace treaty attempt, and I believe it is vital to remember the legacy of all those who sought to bring about the peace efforts. Would you like to hear them?"

27

Legacy of Words

When he sat down in his seat after finishing his speech, Darkon was promptly prodded by Avorne, who congratulated him on a job well done.

Darkon was more concerned
   that he had gone on too long
   and might have lost the audience,
   but Avorne said it was perfect.

He also said that he knew who to call
   if he ever needed an inspirational speech
   complete with theatrical flair
   and sincere teaching moments.

Darkon felt heat rise into his cheeks at that compliment.

"You're a complete natural," Avorne was saying.
   "How do you not freeze up in front of all those people?"

Darkon shrugged. He could see Valéon heading to the front of the platform and bend down on one knee to talk with Mirae. Then he looked to the

people who sat waiting and could hear the casual buzz of conversation fill
the air around them.

"They energize me.
I speak better the more there are.
But when I first became king,
I was so nervous about speaking in front of anyone,
that Katarina set me up
in the middle of the kite archives
so I could practice.
Every night, I'd speak to hundreds of thousands of kites, and soon, I
gained my confidence and my theatrical flair, as you put it. I performed for
those kites, who really were my first and best audience, and that ultimately
helped me to become comfortable in my own skin."

"Teach me sometime," Avorne said.
"I could use that inspirational bit to raise people's morale.
I can never escape my linear outlines and points of presentation."

"There's nothing wrong
with being linear or concise," Darkon pointed out.
"You'll never lose your listener that way.
A lot of people used to say
they'd get lost listening to my messages
because they didn't know what the main point was."

"Hm," Avorne said thoughtfully.
"Never thought of that before.
Oh, looks like Valéon's done ironing out logistics with Mirae.
Is he going to speak without notes?" Avorne asked.

Darkon saw the stand that had kept Valor on display melt into the platform
and disappear.

"Apparently. No notes or props..."
　　Darkon shook his head and let out a low whistle.
　　"That's something."

"I would feel very exposed
　　without a podium," Avorne admitted.

"I would feel very exposed
　　without a prop," Darkon agreed.

But they both fell silent with the rest of the people in the King's Heart,
because Valéon began with a brief thank you to Darkon, which Darkon
replied to with a salute.

It was when Darkon realized that Valéon
　　was going to recite the actual words
　　from the first peace treaty draft
　　that he felt something in his gut wrench.

He looked to Avorne,
　　and saw the King of Eld Mané
　　grip the arms of his chair so tight
　　his knuckles went white.

"He's really going to do this, isn't he?"
　　Avorne whispered.

"Yes," Darkon replied
　　and prayed that Valéon would make it through
　　without any adverse effects or anxiety attacks.

He watched and waited for Valéon to go on.

"We are weary.
　　After forgetting our purpose
　　and creating a history of injustice,
　　we are ready to search for peace.
　　No more shall we rise up
　　against each other,
　　as north and south.

Though we know the challenges before us,
　　we vow to do whatever necessary
　　to see this dream become reality.

In place of a jealous rivalry,
　　our nations shall assist any in need.
　　We shall take up respect,
　　consideration, and honor
　　as our joy and responsibility.

While acknowledging the strengths
　　of others and ourselves
　　we recognize that all possess
　　shortcomings.

Alone, we cannot stand strong,
　　yet together an alliance will be formed.

This is what we vow,
　　and this is what we strive to attain:

Peace. Redemption. Harmony. Hope.
　　Life with the King of Light.
　　Leyana arothan, Eladan."

Darkon realized he had held his breath while Valéon was speaking. He let out a sigh and could hear Avorne exhale slowly beside him as well. Valéon had recited the words of the peace treaty draft without a mistake or mishap, not fumbling even a single word. And it occurred to the King of Kites that what enabled Valéon to speak like this was a combination of discipline and sheer will power.

There was a painful moment of silence.

It wasn't the words themselves that had such an effect, but the knowledge of what the speaker of the words had suffered for nearly eighteen years while keeping those words alive and safe. Though he couldn't see where Vandek or Sylasienne sat in the audience, Darkon wondered if they were the ones who felt the worst, as they were the two who had done the worst to Valéon while under the influence of their respective nightmares.

But Valéon spared everyone from agonizing even more by continuing.

"Those are the words roughly penned during our first peace treaty. As most of you know, I have become a symbol of our peace treaty, the living legacy of the first attempt and its unfinished words."

He ruffled his wings
    as if to shake out a bad memory,
    and then said,

"When the ink explosion
    took place twenty years ago,
    my former master, Lord Leutheros,
    gave me the draft of the peace treaty
    for safekeeping with the direction
    to read and not to forget.
    At the time, I merely was obeying an order.
    I never would have imagined that a seemingly
    insignificant transfer would become the cornerstone
    upon which so many would base their hope."

327

Darkon wondered how Valéon could speak so honestly yet with such gentleness. It was in the way Valéon stood, the tone that he used, and perhaps the voice of power with which he spoke. Darkon marveled at how peaceful Valéon appeared, even as he continued.

"It is common knowledge that I have suffered in the hands of both the north and south with their subsequent nightmare outbreaks. Neither will deny it, and I can assure you that neither side is proud of that fact. However, I am not here to remind us of our past failures and shortcomings. Instead, I would like to take this time to remember and acknowledge everyone who came to the peace treaty attempt and the vision they sought to reach."

For a moment, Valéon turned to face Avorne, Darkon, and Emily.

"Twenty years,
  and we
  haven't
  reached
  the
  vision
  yet.
But we're closer."

Valéon turned back around and motioned at the King's Heart.

"As living legacy of the first peace treaty attempt, I urge every one of you to let go of the past with its pain and failure and twisted nightmares. Instead, recall the good that was ever-present, even in our darkest times. Because there has been much good in our past, in the people that we met, the friends we gained, and the courage we found along the way."

Here, Valéon held up his hand.

"If you wish to attain true peace,
  the key to that future is forgiveness.
I give you that key, but it's up to you to open the door."

There was no thunderous applause

following Valéon's conclusion,
only silent weeping.

Darkon found himself in tears
and was relieved to see Avorne
was in more or less
the same state as he was in.
Perhaps the words held more weight and meant more because it came
from Valéon, who really had suffered the most out of anybody there. And
perhaps, Darkon thought, the words were the most encouraging, because
the unspoken but shared sentiment was that if Valéon could do it, then so
could they.

When Valéon took a seat once more,
Darkon reached out
to take a hold of his friend's shoulder
and murmured,
"Well said, Valéon. Well said."

Valéon let out a shaky breath and nodded.
"I didn't think I'd be able to say all of that
without breaking down somewhere in the middle."

"Well you did make it," Darkon said.
"And you made all of us break down instead."

"You know who helped me hold through?"
Valéon said after a moment of silence.

"Who?" Darkon asked, genuinely curious.

"Vandek," Valéon replied.
"His influence held me steady when I wavered.

And when I forgot my lines
because of all of the memories,
I saw the prompt for my next sentence
hovering up above in the very back in ribbons.
That was Sylasienne.
She must have gotten a hold of the paper
I wrote my speech on and directed her ribbons
to help me find my place again."

Darkon frowned. He couldn't remember seeing anything. But then again, he had been so focused on Valéon, everything else had faded from view. It did him good to see Valéon so comforted. Darkon didn't know what to say, but to his relief, he found he didn't need to say anything.

Valéon kept speaking.

"After those nightmares used the two of them the way they did, Vandek and Sylasienne wanted to make sure that nothing would stop me from speaking on behalf of the peace efforts. I don't know how I'll thank them."

"You already did," Darkon said.

"And I think they're the ones who felt that way towards you, which is why they did what they did."

Valéon nodded.

"I'm glad I'm done.
Now it's just Emily,
and then we can breathe."

Darkon laughed.

"Have you seen her face?
She's never going to forgive us
for making her do the last speech.
I don't know how she's going to wrap this all up."

Valéon laughed. But he smiled fondly after that and said,

"She'll be able to tie it all up.
It's Emily. Besides, this is for her
as much as it's for us. We wouldn't have
come this far without her. She really is our future."

But their conversation was interrupted by Emily, who had stood up at last, composed herself, and wiped her tear-streaked cheeks with the back of her hand.

"We are going to have a long chat after this is all through, gentlemen," she gave a withering look to Avorne, Darkon, and Valéon.

Then it melted into a helpless smile
as she held out her hands and said,
"Wish me luck."

"I have no dandelions on me," Avorne said.

"You're a Legend," Valéon pointed out.

Darkon just laughed and said,
"You don't need luck.
You're a leader of the highest caliber
with a heart of gold. Go lead."

Seeing Emily tear up at that and smile the biggest smile was more than enough reward for Darkon. He saw Emily make a quick motion to Mirae to request the podium again, and lo and behold, the podium rose up in its rightful place. Emily placed her crystal tile on it, checked her notes, and then drummed her fingers on the podium.

"Did she write something while we were all speaking?" Avorne asked from bedside him.

"I wouldn't be surprised if she did," Darkon leaned back in his chair and got comfortable.

"This is going to be good, isn't it?" Valéon asked.

"Oh, it won't just be good," Darkon said.
"It'll be fantastic. Just watch."

28

Final Remarks

Emily was not thrilled to be following up after Avorne, Darkon, and Valéon, who were all excellent speakers in their own right and perfectly capable of wrapping up this second peace treaty by themselves. She was still confused as to why they had all insisted that she do the last speech, which Mirae's mysterious crystal tile had informed her, like an email notification without the electronics or the internet.

Emily held back a sigh.

Well, it wasn't like she could back out now.

Besides, if she could address a whole slew of scarves and ribbons the last time she came, then she could address a whole bunch of people she didn't know this time.

With that, Emily plunged into the closing speech.

"And that leaves me with the task of opening the door to our future. No pressure, right?"

She was comforted by the trickle of laughter that traveled through the King's Heart.

"So we're left with the question, 'now what?'"

Emily glanced at the crystal tile and was glad to see her mental notes that she had haphazardly pulled together during the transitions between her friends' speeches had been adequate enough to give her the semblance of a conclusion.

"I can't tell you the solution to all of your challenges," Emily said.

"We all know that once we step out of the King's Heart, we'll be going home to our current problems. I for one, have thirty nightmare situations to address after this, so I can totally understand anyone who wishes they could hide out here in the King's Heart until things magically get better."

Emily raised her hand in admission and said,

"I've been there."

She paused and took a deep breath.

"But as you and I know, that's not how leadership works."

Where was Ionthann? Emily searched the sea of faces and found Ionthann sitting in the front row, several seats over from where Mirae was sitting. Iris was beside him, and Emily decided she'd focus on those two first.

"We have been placed in the crossroads of our lives with all of its hardship not so we can give up and be broken, but because we are called to overcome and be a beacon of light to those around us."

Emily remembered to look at the rest of the people before her and said,

"I can almost hear some of you asking, 'how can I be a beacon of light when I can't even see where I'm at or where I'm going?' Well, let this be your vision until you do see. Things will become clear as you progress. On your path to leadership, there are four directions: strength, honor, wisdom, and kindness. They will serve as your compass as you find your way. You will find allies in every situation as I did, and you will become the leader you are meant to be along the journey. And as I was reassured by a good friend," Emily turned towards Avorne and saw him give a broad smile. She turned back to the people who listened attentively.

"So long as you uphold the King's Heart in this matter, you can always come back. So let's all go and do our part, and let's all meet again one day, here, in the King's Heart. Thank you."

And then, just like that, it was over.

Emily couldn't remember if there was an applause at the end, because she was more or less buried in a group hug right after finishing. After that, Emily was overwhelmed by congratulations, thank you's, and many introductions to so many people she couldn't keep track of their names.

There were more requests for advice than Emily knew what to do with, especially on matters she didn't feel qualified to answer, so she tried to redirect them as best as she could to Avorne, Darkon, and Valéon.

Eventually, Emily managed to leave Avorne, Darkon, and Valéon on the speaker's platform and run into Mirae.

"You don't know of a quiet place I could hide out in for a while, do you? Until most of the people are gone?"

Mirae steered her through
the many people that surrounded them.
"This way."

Whether by chance, irony, or just good fortune, Emily ended up in the back corner of the library, which was blissfully quiet and empty.

"The architecture section is the best," Mirae said.

"Though, I'm a bit biased. I'll give you a heads up when it gets quieter out there. Great job, by the way. You sounded like you practiced your speech for hours, even though you wrote it while you were on stage."

"Well, you did help me out a lot," Emily gave back Mirae the crystal tile that had kept track of her notes.

"This was really helpful. Thanks."

"No problem," Mirae took the crystal tile and then handed Emily her book, which she had been holding onto like a manager's assistant.

"Here's your book back, safe and sound."

Emily had never been so thankful to have someone like Mirae guard her time and need for space. She made a mental note to find a friend like Mirae back at home who could do the equivalent there. Left alone in the back of the library, Emily settled down on the floor, opened up *Gold: Leadership at Heart* and became completely absorbed in her reading. Sometime later, when she had gotten about halfway through the book, Emily heard a quiet cough and then the question,

"Do you mind if I join you?"

Emily looked up and saw a vaguely familiar person standing before her.

He was Avorne's younger brother, Halas, who she had briefly met before when he was connecting her with Mirae before the second peace treaty. She had wanted to speak with him, but there had been no time. How convenient that he'd come by now.

"I don't mind. It's Halas, right?" She asked.

"That's right," Halas sat down on the floor and leaned against the shelf, placing himself not directly across from her, but more to the side to allow for enough leg room.

"Thought I'd take the chance to talk with the one person I know so much about but never actually met before."

Emily tilted her head in curiosity.

"How's that?"

Halas answered,
"Crystal used to talk about you all the time.
Every time I came to visit,
it was Emily this, Emily that.
She always talked about
the good things you'd do for others.
Crystal missed you a lot that year
she was in eighth grade
and going into high school."

"Yeah, it was her worst year," Emily recalled then.

"Crystal lost her friends after getting accepted into the high school for the arts. She had a rough time getting to her next set of friends. But she had you in between, so thanks for being there. I think you gave her a reason to wake up in the morning and go to school even when it was torture. You saved her life more than once," Emily smiled.

"Thanks for helping her to make it through, even though you gave up so much."

"It wasn't much of a sacrifice for me,"

Halas answered. "I loved her."

Emily nodded.

"I know. She loved you too. Still does.

I think secretly, she hopes to meet you again,

even if she isn't writing. Would you mind seeing her if I sent her this way? She deserves some good quality time with you."

"I would love to see her again,"

Halas said fondly.

"But Emily, I wanted to thank you."

Emily half-laughed.

"Whatever for?"

"For two things," Halas said.

"First, for taking care of Crystal the way you did.

For being her lifeline when she needed you the most.

She said I was just like you once,

and it came at a time when I felt

I was completely alone.

Knowing that there was someone like me

out there somewhere gave me hope."

"Oh," Emily didn't quite know how to reply to that unexpected compliment.

"You're welcome, I guess. And the second thing?"

Halas smiled.

"For supporting Avorne and helping him to reach the fulfillment of this second peace treaty. It isn't final by any means, but it was a solid start, a good beginning. And it was something that he lost so much sleep over; it was wonderful to see him achieve what so many of us fought to reach for twenty years."

"Oh, that…" Emily still found it hard to find an adequate reply.

"Honestly, I can't even tell you why I care so much for a peace treaty that's in a world completely separate from mine."

"It's a reflection on who you are," Halas offered an understanding smile.

"I suppose so," Emily agreed.

"I hope it's a good one."

Halas chuckled.

"It's a beautiful one.

You should try to see that beauty back at home."

Emily shook her head.

"I still want to stay a little longer.

Until I get my reserves back."

Halas shrugged.

"No one's stopping you.

Did you find anything to take back with you?"

"You mean like a takeaway?" Emily thought about that.

"The strength, honor, wisdom, kindness thing, for sure. I'll remember what energized me after I burned out and find ways to set my boundaries and say 'no' when I need to. Now I know my limits."

"I would add one thing," Halas said.

"When you've done all you can do, listened and helped as much as you can, then let go. You can't live their lives for them. At some point, they need to stand on their own. Worrying won't help anyone. Plus, you have your life to live too."

"I keep telling myself that," Emily said, knowing she had been working on that for years.

Halas grinned.

"Take it from an expert. Avorne always did say I was a chronic worrier. He was right. I'd like to help others to not be that."

Emily nodded. Then she had a new thought.

"I'd like to come up with a King's Heart equivalent back at home. It's done me so much good, I'd like to do that for others."

Halas hesitated at that.

"You already have."

This was news to Emily.

"I did? When?"

"The last time you came," Halas explained.

"You made a smaller version of the King's Heart for me and Crystal. It wasn't big at all; it was actually modeled after Crystal's room, only with the typical stained glass patterns you find here. It's how Crystal and I met after I died, and it did a good deal to heal Crystal's heart."

She hadn't expected to find that out.

"So I'm capable of doing that already?"

Halas nodded.

"It's probably why you were able to come into the King's Heart Mirae designed, even if you couldn't see it, because you created a smaller form of it before."

Emily felt more confident about the idea of bringing the King's Heart with her.

"Thanks, Halas. I'm glad I got to talk with you finally."

Halas shrugged.

"Anytime.
Darkon and Valéon both said
that you had meant to ask
about what to do with your double affinity
some time ago. I forgot about that until now."

That was right. Emily had forgotten about it too. She had mainly wondered if Halas had ever wanted to bury his double giftedness and live a normal life. But sitting by him now and speaking with him, she realized that Halas had embraced his double affinity of perception and influence and no longer struggled with being different.

Halas picked up on her realization and confirmed it by saying,
"It's not so bad, having a double affinity.
Some days it feels like a double burden,
but if you push through that,
you'll come into your own well enough."

A thought rose to Emily's mind, about when she went back home, if any of this would amount to anything in the face of the challenges that she was helping people work through.

Halas gave her a knowing look and said,
"Don't go there."

Emily sighed.
"It's a shame that
strength, honor,
wisdom, and kindness
are invisible."

"There's no shame in traveling a different path," Halas said.
"If you live long enough, you'll find that those are the things that matter in the end, like the King's Heart. You're lucky enough to have seen it when you're young. Don't lose sight of it while you live your life."
It was a good reminder and an encouraging one at that. But Emily and Halas were interrupted by Mirae, who let them know that the King's Heart was all clear, save for their friends and family. So Emily ventured out of the library and back into the main section of the King's Heart.

Of course, when she arrived, she was subjected to a good deal of teasing from Avorne, Darkon, and Valéon about pulling yet another disappearing act. Was she learning from Halas? Was he teaching her the secrets of becoming invisible? Or was it Mirae instead? Emily was pleased to see Halas and Mirae counter with their own claims about how Emily was just more like the two of them, and more naturally aligned to the gifts of invisibility than the rest of them.

Emily stayed out of the bantering for the most part, though she was quite amused at the silliness that was beginning to exude out of everyone present. She was given the small square mirror by Ionthann, who had held onto it for her. He was accompanied by Iris, who said,

"It wouldn't do to come all this way to forget your way home."

Renadé stood to the side, content to listen to everyone else socialize.

No one wanted to leave, and no one wanted to be the first to bring it up. Other topics of conversation were brought up and bandied about as the afternoon turned into evening, and the good cheer and laughter continued on for quite some time. Mirae changed the reception area to a cozy gathering place, complete with couches, chairs, tables filled with food and drink, and bright fireplaces that provided plenty of warmth and light. Emily ate more than she probably should have, and knew she wasn't the only one.

But perhaps because she was the one who came from outside, Emily was aware of the time. She had to go. Emily could feel her reserves, once completely empty, now filled to the brim. The exhaustion she originally had felt coming in was replaced by a vigor and readiness to face the challenges that waited for her at home. But she could see in the way that Avorne lovingly sat on the couch next to Renadé while chatting with Darkon and Katarina, that no one wanted to say goodbye. Valéon was talking with Tal and Raehn and playing with their kids, and Ionthann and Iris were talking with Vandek and Sylasienne.

It was Halas,

who must have sensed her feelings

amid the festivities.

"Are you leaving?"

Mirae, who had spent the entire time close to Emily
    but too shy to say anything, asked, "So soon?"

"I have to," Emily said.
    But she considered what additional kindness
    she could give her friends, both old and new.

She placed a hand on Mirae's shoulder and whispered,
    "Can I borrow you for a second?"

Mirae couldn't contain her curiosity. "What for?"

Emily smiled.
    "You'll see. It'll be a team effort. Do you have any spare materials that
you used to build this place?"

Mirae laughed.
    "Oh, I have spare materials all right. What do you want?"
    And she raised her right hand in a grand sweeping motion.
    Mirae's warehouse of materials rose up in the middle of the room,
complete with a standing work station. Not surprisingly, it got everyone
else's attention and all conversations came to an abrupt end. Emily just
shook her head, thinking that for someone from the Invisible Lands, Mirae
sure had a flashy flair to her style.
    "You really are a workaholic *and* an overachiever," Halas teased Mirae.

"Hey," Mirae was indignant.
    "This isn't work. It's a gift."
    She looked to Emily
    with expectation,
    "Isn't it?"

342

Emily said,

"It was supposed to be a secret.

But yes. It's my gift to you all before I go."

She had been hoping to do all of this in relative secrecy, but now that everyone was aware of her about to leave, they had come to crowd around the work table that she and Mirae stood at. So Emily decided to turn it into a more interactive farewell gift. She had Mirae gather up a bunch of tiles that she was fine parting with in an empty crate. Then she had Mirae bring it around to each person present and have them choose one that they liked. After that, she had them all place them on the work table on top of one of Mirae's empty blueprints.

Emily paused.

"I've been told that I made my own King's Heart before, only I wasn't aware of it. I'd like to make one for you with Mirae's help. Mirae, could you give me a hand?"

She saw the happy look that wouldn't leave Mirae's face, and wondered at how easy it could be to bring joy to another person, especially if their desire was to work side by side with someone they looked up to. Emily put her hand on the tiles, and Mirae put her hand on top of Emily's. The multi-colored tiles melted into the paper and became a blueprint of Emily's apartment, which was much smaller than the King's Heart that Mirae had designed, but still kept all of the stained glass patterns and designs.

It was amazing that everyone found a place to stand inside of it. Some were in the kitchen, others were in the hall or in the tiny living room area, or in Emily's bedroom. But Emily stood in the kitchen with Mirae, Halas, Avorne, Darkon, and Valéon. And she finally found the right words to say.

"I hate to be the first to go, but I wanted to extend an invitation to all of you. I'm planning a small get-together on Christmas, here at my place. Just me, Crystal, Ryan, Vincent, Scott and Katarina. They're expecting me to tell about my visit with all of you. In story form. It won't be in writing, but if any of you would like to join me in my storytelling, and chime in with your own, you're free to come. I'm also not sure how I'll fit everyone, but maybe Mirae can help us with the sizing of the place, since I plan on starting them at the King's Heart."

Emily wasn't sure why everyone looked so shy and pleased all at once. It was like Mirae's bashfulness around Emily had spread to the whole group, kings and all. Then she said,

"No pressure, though. It's just that I'd love to see you all again sooner rather than later. And why not have an excuse to come meet again in the King's Heart?"

Mirae saved Emily by saying,

"I'll come. I've never been to someone else's rendition of the King's Heart, so I want to see how you build it. Plus, your style is unique. I like it."

"Scott will be there, right?" Darkon said.

"I wouldn't miss seeing him for the world."

"Count me in," Valéon said.

"I can help you serve tea, if you'd like."

Halas paused.

"I'd like to come to see Crystal and Ryan,
but how will we find our way?"

"Leave it to me," Mirae beamed.

"I'll modify the King's Heart to connect with Emily's."

"Then it's settled," Avorne smiled.

"We'll come by your place on Christmas."

Emily said,
"All right.
Christmas,
my place.
Take care and I love you all.
See you soon."

The others voiced their agreement and raised their hands in farewell. As they did, they faded from view, and Emily stood once more in the kitchen of her apartment, no longer made of stained glass, but back to its ordinary state. She found it was easier to say goodbye when she knew she'd be seeing her friends again very soon in the future. Out of curiosity, because she held her deck of cards, Emily flipped over the top card.

In beautiful golden letters was the word GLADNESS.

How fitting that this particular blue-gold card mirrored what she felt at that moment.

Emily got started right away. She had a lot to do if she wanted to be ready for Christmas.

29

Meaning in the Mundane

Avorne spent most of the time after the second peace treaty in a daze. He couldn't keep track of how many friends and family members, new and old, came up to him to congratulate him on this auspicious moment, and how thankful they were for him to step up to spearhead the second peace treaty on his own. Of course, he had to keep telling everyone that he hadn't done this on his own, and that they had all helped him along the way, but for some reason, no one paid any attention to his efforts to share the credit.

Avorne shook his head, convinced that this was all wrong, but he was tired of arguing with pretty much every person who came up to greet him. Truth be told, the enormity of what had been accomplished didn't start sinking in until after Emily had left for her domain. Avorne had said his goodbyes to Valéon and Darkon and wandered off on his own to a quieter corner of the King's Heart to give himself time to consider all that had happened.

He thought he would have felt more of the excitement that had emanated from those who had congratulated him. It was a huge accomplishment, setting up the second peace treaty in such a different but beautiful way. But while Avorne felt a huge relief that this had gone as well as it did, he felt as if he were being confronted by a looming unknown. Now what? Avorne wandered into one of the spare rooms down a hallway and was shocked to find his three older brothers at a long wooden table just about to play some extensive strategy game. It was just like the dreams he had dreamed, only this time, Diurne, Gavin, and Okten were actually present in the King's Heart.

And like in his dreams, they were kind and warm, not at all the terrible brothers Avorne had known as a child. It was surreal.

"Thought you could use a grand distraction,"

Diurne said after calling Avorne over.

"You're thinking too much, which is never a good thing."

Avorne looked at Diurne.

"Who's the one who always said I couldn't think for myself even if my life depended on it?"

Diurne coughed, somewhat embarrassed.

"I was just jealous that Ionthann always chose to show you the heavens on those late night excursions. Astronomy was my best class, and even though I aced every exam and paper, you still got Ionthann's attention every time, complete with one-on-one tutorials."

Avorne blinked, not expecting this confession at all.

"Ionthann did that mainly to keep me from sulking, which I was prone to do – a lot. You three didn't help at all."

Gavin cleared his throat.

"Not only that, but you got Iris as your tutor. She was the mysterious northerner who graced our palace out of nowhere, and you landed her as your personal teacher from the start. We all were hoping to get her."

Avorne laughed.

"Seriously? You do know that Halas had her longest right?"

The others nodded and agreed unanimously.

"Halas was her favorite."

They heard Halas's voice float in from the hall.

"I heard that.

And Iris will deny it."

"She'll deny it," Okten said,

"But we all know it's true.

Halas, why don't you come to join us?

Avorne will get cold feet otherwise and leave.

But if you stay, he will too."

Halas poked his head into the room and chuckled.

"Isn't this a bit late in coming?" He walked over to them, pulled over a chair and tapped the empty board on the table with his fingers.

"We should have done this when we were boys."

He asked for the pieces then, and was handed a cloth bag that held pieces that clinked together inside.

When Halas took a handful of the pieces out, he paused before studying one and handing it to Avorne.

"Am I seeing things, or does that look like me?"

Avorne took it and looked at the crystallized figure.

"No doubt about it. Look, your name is on the base, along with your double affinity."

Halas shook his head and continued to pass more figures to Avorne.

"There's Iris, Valéon, Ionthann, Uncle Vandek...oh wow, even Theia and Crescens. Raiidran. Tal and Raehn...hey, look, here's you."

Avorne stifled a laugh as he studied the various crystal figures of his friends, family, and himself that were all quite detailed and accurate.

"What are all of these doing here? What kind of game could we play that has all of us in it?"

Gavin took the figures and began setting them up along the board, which had gained an appearance like a world map that zoomed in on Eld Mané.

"We all agreed that after accomplishing a feat so great as the second peace treaty, you might like to look back at how it all began and what it took to get there."

Diurne helped with the set up and added,

"We decided to split it into four rounds. That way, you can review the major events and give credit to where credit is due. You were the one so set on trying to give credit, you couldn't even accept your own."

"Was that somehow wrong?" Avorne asked.

"No," Okten replied.

"It was just like you to want to share it all with others, even when you really did deserve most of it."

Avorne would have argued against that, but he was stopped by Halas, who suggested,

"Why not listen to what they have to say? They do have a point."

The whole thing was bizarre.

Avorne thought so and said so.

But he humored his brothers by "playing" the rounds of this strategic game, which was really a recreation of the major turning points of his life. There were four rounds, and each round emphasized some decision Avorne made that distinctly changed the course of events.

In the first round, it was his determination not to kill Uncle Vandek, even though the nightmare was intent on killing Avorne by taking his crown. It was Avorne's declaration that "A King is nothing without his people" that ultimately defined his way of living. Without Vandek, they would have lost a very powerful and valuable ally in rounds two, three, and four – his brothers pointed out. Not only that, but it was Avorne's sacrifice of heartbeats that created the first space that Halas and Iris had deemed the King's Heart all those years ago.

In the second round, a few new players were added. Their beloved captain of the guard, Ionthann came to the forefront in an effort to rescue Valéon with Iris. Avorne's piece got moved south of the palace to Honoraire after his crown went missing. Avorne's piece remained in one place while Halas's was in motion constantly. What was the decision that was so important in this round? Avorne questioned his brothers and was surprised by the answer he received: it was the decision to defend the thief who stole his crown. If Avorne had taken care of Cassan through the usual means of punishment, then the next round would have been quite different.

The scenes upon the board changed, as did the players and pieces. The presence of Legends came to the forefront, as did new pieces for Crystal and Ryan, the Sky Maiden and Ink Prince respectively, and for Vincent – who was really Cassan suffering a bout of amnesia – and Emily, the Ribbon Princess. Avorne thought he had his brothers at last. This round was all focused on the Legends and their feats; he was just on the fringe really.

Diurne, Gavin, and Okten – even Halas – disagreed with him.

"Why are you disagreeing with me
    when you died in this round?"
Avorne asked Halas.

Halas shrugged.

"Crystal told me how you talked with her at a time when she didn't want to be there and she didn't want to talk to anyone, but you kept trying. It was your idea to ask her for help in rescuing Ryan when the Ink Prince was lost to the nightmare. You worked side by side with Cassan when he had gambled so many of his memories away that he kept saying his name was Vincent. And you created that makeshift King's Heart-like dome with Emily while you fought the nightmare. Not to mention, you were the one who invited Emily to come back for the second peace treaty attempt. If you hadn't invited her, Emily never would have come."

Avorne could see where this was going. He knew they were saying the fourth round wouldn't have happened without his actions over the previous years. The fourth round was the most familiar one. The main pieces were those of Avorne, Darkon, Valéon, and Emily, but there were some new ones, for people like Mirae, Falleyne, and Elias. There was even one for the secret seller, which Avorne knew nothing about. But that was with Ionthann and Valéon anyway, so Avorne decided to ask them about that little detail later.

He didn't need anyone's help to know what his defining decision had been in this round. Avorne already knew. It was seeing the King's Heart when he thought it was an ink sign, and it was entering in and meeting Mirae and letting her stay and work on the King's Heart instead of making her go elsewhere. Nothing else would have progressed without that. Avorne got the picture. He knew this was his brothers' way of telling him that he himself played a bigger role than he took credit for.

Avorne relented at last. When he confessed that he felt overwhelmed at the prospects of what to do now that the second peace treaty had happened, he received a surprising encouragement. His brothers took each figure that represented an individual in the sprawling timeline of twenty years and lined them all up on the table before him. There were dozens upon dozens of people there. If it took this many people to work towards achieving what had happened earlier that day, then it would most likely take as much time and people to progress from this point. It was a burden meant to be shared by everyone, not just shouldered by Avorne.

During all of this, Avorne grew quiet and introspective. It was so unlike him that Halas put an arm around his shoulders and asked,

"Where are you, Avorne?

If you think any more deeply,

we'll lose you to the mysterious deep."

Avorne shrugged.

"If we were to record all of this for history, we would include every nightmare outbreak and how each one was defeated. We'd mark down the first peace treaty attempt, the captivity and rescue of Valéon, and the second peace treaty attempt as well. But for me, the things that stuck are much more mundane. Is that strange?"

"Finding meaning in the mundane?" Okten asked.

"No. Most can't see it, but that doesn't make it strange. Why? What sorts of things were you thinking of?"

"How hard Uncle Vandek worked to make up for his actions in the first peace treaty attempt," Avorne began.

"That six week time frame when I got to live like a northern refugee and met Renadé and fell in love with her."

He smiled at Halas.

351

"All those times you came to check in on me while I was sick at the Hourglass, and when I tried to get you to say what was on your mind while you were worrying."

Avorne stifled a laugh as he added,

"Winning the pot of our collective betting for calling the place where Ionthann and Iris would get engaged. I'm so glad I guessed the Sunshade House."

Avorne went on,

"Meeting Mirae and finding out the extent of what she could do, which was mind boggling. Being able to work with her and in the process meeting everyone I thought I'd have to wait to see after I died myself. Watching all of those invitation responses flying in on their own and finding out that the one who started them was Emily. Seeing her expression when Valéon said we saved a seat and a podium for her. And when she found out she'd be speaking with the rest of us."

He could have kept on going, but he didn't. Avorne realized that it was the little things along the way that had given him meaning, contentment, and purpose. The big things were important too, of course, but they weren't the only events of significance in Avorne's view.

"Do you think it's too un-kingly?"

He asked then.

"To find meaning in the mundane?"

"No," had been the reply of Diurne, Gavin, and Okten.

"It suits you completely."

Avorne couldn't figure out if that was a compliment or not.

Halas picked up on it and confirmed,

"That would be a compliment."

It was this entire shared interaction with all of his brothers in the King's Heart that comforted Avorne that night, after the second peace treaty had been completed. It was the fact that he regained time lost with his family and was able to enjoy the relationships with his brothers that he had never been able to have while they were still alive. While it would most likely be relegated to the most mundane of activities and conversations, to Avorne, it was still meaningful and very much needed.

The aching emptiness that had loomed with the dark unknown of the future had been filled with contentment and camaraderie that Avorne never would have thought possible. Perhaps, he thought as he fell asleep on one of the spare beds in Diurne's room, it was just another gift of the King's Heart, which Mirae had designed so lovingly for her leaders. It was entirely possible that the young architect from the Invisible Lands understood that what brought healing to one's heart often came through the mundane filled with meaning.

30

The Perfect Honor

Valéon hadn't expected to return to the Sky Maiden's domain for quite some time. But here he was, carrying a message that Emily had left with him in the King's Heart before she had gone home. Emily hadn't given him any explicit directions on what to do with it, but Valéon knew the expectation was self-explanatory. The folded piece of paper had the name "Crystal" written on it. Valéon decided to make the delivery since he could and thought it fitting.

Flying high above the ground among the occasional cloud, Valéon savored the feeling of the winter air, enjoying the cold, the rush of wind around him, and the sun that shone bright that morning. His wings skimming along the edges of the realm of the Sky, he did something he hadn't done for years. He began a playful test of his limits, seeing how well he could weave in and out of cloud formations, how many twists and turns he could take while rising up in the air or diving down.

If there had been one thing that had awakened in his accidental visit to the Changing Lands with Ionthann, it was his curiosity about his limits. Valéon thought about what it would take to be a messenger, and had concluded that if he wanted to take that part of his new responsibilities seriously, he would need to build up his stamina and make sure he was fit for the role. What had brought about this thought? An offer from Mirae, who had pulled him aside into the library on his way out of the King's Heart.

Valéon hadn't expected her to make him the offer, and hadn't known how to respond. The young architect had only rubbed her nose absentmindedly as she did when she was feeling shy and didn't know how else to proceed. She had asked him to think about it, and that he could let her know when he came back. Valéon had been glad for the chance to do so. It was also why he took his time before entering the Sky Maiden's domain. He wanted plenty of time to mull things over.

But the doorway to the Sky Maiden's domain had appeared sooner than Valéon had expected, that golden archway of mysterious characters that outlined the entrance to the world of Legends. When he first entered in, no one was there. Valéon could smell something delicious wafting in from the hallway. Leaning out of Crystal's doorway, he checked out the hallway and found it empty as well.

"Hello?" He called down the flight of stairs.

"Anybody home?"

He could hear music and sounds coming from below, so Valéon made his way downstairs, following the scent of baked goods and the strains of music that grew louder and louder. He made his way to the kitchen, where he found Crystal hard at work, moving freshly baked cookies onto the counter, sampling her work, humming along with the music, and reviewing what looked like a lengthy manuscript.

Crystal looked up and said,

"Hello, Valéon! I thought it might be you." She pointed to her papers and said,

"I've gotten my writing back, full swing! I tried to think of something to give to Emily all weekend, and I've finally got something."

When Valéon curiously tried to read what Crystal had written, she covered up her work and said,

"Don't read it yet; I haven't finished."

Valéon fought back a smile. For some reason, she reminded him a bit of Mirae. Of course, Mirae was still older, maybe closer to Emily in age than Crystal, but that passionate response was the same.

"If it's about me, then I expect to be the first to read it," he grinned.

Crystal sighed.

"You're worse than Halas. Next you'll be telling me to make sure I have you do something more than standing around and talking..."

Valéon was amused to no end with this lament, but he leaned over to pick up a cookie and sample one himself. As he enjoyed the warm sweetness and melted chocolate, Valéon asked,

"Are you going to Emily's for Christmas? Because she invited a bunch of us to come too. Avorne, Darkon..." He was about to mention Halas, but he was interrupted by Crystal.

"Oh, that's right," she said.
"Em was going to visit you all.
Did she? How did that go?"

It occurred to him that Crystal might only be vaguely aware of the second peace treaty. He answered,

"It went well – really well.
But I'll let Emily tell you the details herself."

"Did she have a good time?" Crystal asked.
"Did she stop worrying and enjoy herself?"

"Yes," Valéon smiled.
"Emily had a very good time.
She didn't want to leave."

"Oh, good!" Crystal was pleased.
"She needs to do something for herself every once in a while. I might send you to her now and then as an excuse to take a break."
Then she added,
"You wouldn't mind, would you? She actually talks with you about what's bothering her. Don't tell her I said so, but I'm pretty sure she thinks of you the same way I think of Halas."

Well, that was quite the compliment. Unexpected too.

Valéon felt a mixture of embarrassment and pride at that comment. He managed to murmur,

"I wouldn't mind."

Not knowing how else to respond to that, Valéon held out the message Emily had wanted him to deliver.

"This is for you, by the way."

Crystal took the note and opened it with interest. She didn't read the note out loud, but Valéon could see the note in Emily's neat hand. It read:

Hey Crys –

I've been to the King's Heart. Want to visit?
  I met a special someone there; I'll let you guess who.
  He'd love to see you again – told me himself.
  Oh, and no writing necessary. Just bring yourself.

Love,
  -Em

Crystal must have read it a second time just to make sure she got it right, because it took her a minute before she looked up at Valéon and asked,

"It's Halas, isn't it?

Em got to meet Halas, didn't she?"

Valéon took another cookie.

"Em met lots of new people this time around. But she did seem to bond particularly well with Halas." He loved seeing her delight at finding that out.

And so it was the most natural thing for him to offer,

"Want me to take you to the King's Heart?

I'll be sure to get you there and back in no time."

"For real?" Crystal asked, so very pleased with the prospects of seeing her closest friend again.

"Yes! Do I need anything?"

"You read the message,"
Valéon said.
"Just yourself."

He did make sure that the oven was turned off and not in the middle of baking another batch of cookies. He also took it upon himself to say that Halas might like one of the chocolate chip cookies or the sugar-cinnamon ones, which both came from Emily's specialty collection of recipes. Crystal swept a few into a napkin and wrapped them up with care. She asked if they were going to fly there.

Of course the answer was yes. The entrance into the Sky Maiden's domain was still the exit into his world. Valéon took great joy in being able to sweep Crystal up in his arms and show her the beauty of their sky and earth even in the winter season. He treasured her laughter as they flew to the King's Heart and was pleased that she had no trouble spotting it at all in the Inkstone Mountains. He considered how happy Mirae would be to learn about this development.

Interestingly, the entrance of the King's Heart looked like it was hanging from the sky like a banner. Valéon wondered if this was something that was tailored for Crystal specifically. That was curious, seeing the stained glass design unfurl and then ripple in the wind.

"Valéon?" He heard Crystal say quietly then.

"Hm?" He replied, his wingbeats steady. They were almost to the King's Heart.

"What do you think about the idea of being a librarian?" She asked.

Had he not disciplined himself to fly steady no matter the circumstances, Valéon would have missed a wingbeat. He said nothing for a minute before replying,

"What makes you ask?"

Crystal shrugged.

"A long time ago, I thought you were one. I tried to write you as a librarian. I never wrote that part, because I was so upset with what happened to Halas and I was scared about coming back. But related to that, Ryan suggested me to write a place that was bigger on the inside than it looked on the outside and hung from the sky like a banner. I definitely didn't write this place here, but it's the description Ryan suggested I try. It was supposed to be your place," Crystal confessed.

"Is…is there a library in the King's Heart?"

Valéon felt his heart beat faster
at this new insight and inquiry.
"There is."

"It's yours," Crystal said then, absolutely convinced.

"I know it's for you. It's the library I never was able to write along with the occupation meant for you. I'm so sorry it's taken me so long to ask you directly, but would you like to be the librarian of the library in the King's Heart? Because that would do my heart good," Crystal gripped him a bit tighter as she said.

"I didn't know what happened with your wings or that you were in captivity. And I'm sorry I never tried to write you out of that terrible situation. But if you'll forgive me, I'd like to give you what I never was able to all those years ago. What do you say?"

For the longest time, he couldn't find the words to speak. Valéon just flew the both of them to the entrance of the King's Heart. When he had let Crystal down on the front step, which floated in midair, he took in a deep breath. He didn't know how to tell Crystal that this was exactly the same offer that Mirae had presented to him before he had gone off to deliver Emily's message. Somewhere in the back of his mind, Valéon suspected this was just one of the many heart desires that the King's Heart not only picked up on, but addressed in its loving, specific, and tailored way.

The first set of words came naturally.

"There's nothing to forgive. It was for the best."

The second set of words took some time to say.

"I would love to be a librarian."

The third set of words was nothing short of a miracle.

"Serving in the library of the King's Heart is the perfect honor. How can I ever thank you?"

Crystal hugged him so tightly then, Valéon realized that the young woman had needed this conversation just as much as he had.

She murmured into his chest,

"You just did."

The banner opened up in unraveling threads, as if it were a tapestry with a secret entrance hidden within its weaving.

"Shall we?" He said as he motioned for her to go first.

It was with great joy that Valéon showed Crystal inside, taking her to the magnificent library as its official librarian. Ever after, he treasured the surprise, delight, and pride in the expressions of both Mirae and Halas as they received him and Crystal into the King's Heart.

31

Coming Home

I t was the best feeling, coming back home to the Kingdom of Kites knowing he had a solution for the kite crisis.

Darkon returned with a sense of immense satisfaction, even though he knew that the process to get his kite infrastructure up and running at full capacity would take a good amount of time. Still, bringing Valor back made the King of Kites feel like he was bringing back a real treasure, something that he planned on passing down to his sons when the time came for them to take up the responsibilities of ruling the kingdom.

He already knew that Griffin would want to "try it out" first, given his second son was the most prone to fall in love with anything new and exciting without fail. Den would want to document everything about the sword itself, not just how Darkon had pulled it out of the Blade Pass and how it could absorb and release flames, but also how old it was and its prior history, perhaps even to try to learn of its maker from many years ago. But for now, Darkon thought he would share the actual process of fireproofing their kites to August, since the eldest happened to be the best at craftsmanship and kite making to begin with. In that sense August was similar to Elias, holding an appreciation for processes and techniques, efficiency and good quality.

Lucky for him, it was August who greeted him when Darkon came back through Renade's ink portal, which the Queen of Eld Mané graciously offered to maintain until things had returned to normal in the Kite Kingdom.

"Let's get to work!" August had said upon Darkon's arrival.

"We've all been waiting to see how you revived that first batch of kites with that sword."

Darkon took the time to thoroughly enjoy working side by side with his son as they began with the kites that were strewn along the grassy hills and cliffs by the sea. As Darkon demonstrated the workings and mechanics behind the fireproofing process, he listened to August's update about the well-being of the citizens and the overwhelming reaction they shared in regards to the second peace treaty. Though no one came to express their congratulations to the King of Kites for his prominent role in speaking on behalf of the north, they were so proud their king was there to represent their people, especially as one of the four speakers.

The people of the Kite Kingdom had received the invitations that were designed by Emily, August pointed out. However, as most of the kites were unable to carry them to the peace treaty, and only a few closest to the ink portal could use it to get to Eld Mané on foot to enter the King's Heart, the majority of citizens had remained at home. But each had written their response to the invitations they received and sent the reply on its way. Still, to show their solidarity and support, each family had tied their invitation to their personal kites as a quiet but open declaration. For those whose kites had not been in working order, they displayed their invitations on their front doors or in their windows. This action in itself told volumes.

Also, according to August, it seemed that they all suffered the same case of chronic shyness that plagued Den. August said that Den was actually the most excited to enter the King's Heart of everyone in their family, and he had looked quite longingly into the library that you could see to the left side upon entering the grand reception hall. Darkon's youngest had actually snuck inside while everyone was getting ready, and been thrilled to find books on the Kite Kingdom that he had never read once in his life.

They told of tales and histories that were not contained in their own enormous royal kite archive, and Den had barely been able to tear himself away from the rare tomes. It was only when he saw Avorne coming out after preparing his speech that Den reluctantly put the books back on the shelf and found where Katarina and his brothers were seated.

August laughed as he retold the mysterious double-shyness that had overcome his younger brother, who never looked anyone in the eye the entire time they were there and never whispered a "hello" to anyone. He did manage a wave to Emily at the end, and blushed when she nodded at him in acknowledgement.

"Who knew that the rest of our citizens would be like Den on such an important occasion?" August laughed.

"I was shocked. Especially when Grif had the time of his life getting to meet new people. He found people he'd run across on his kite taming expeditions and he reconnected with old friends, and he made a bunch more. Meanwhile, Den and our people who did attend didn't say a word. They were so proud of you, though, Dad. I seriously thought they'd burst from all of that pride."

Darkon sighed.

What a shy people they were,
  his people of the kite.

So hard working and loyal
  and proud to lend a helping hand,
  but so very soft spoken and reserved
  when it came to meeting other people.

They would have to work on this,
  Darkon concluded.

He didn't expect them to become as outgoing or friendly as himself, for Darkon didn't even expect such a thing from his own children. But he thought, as he had thought many a time, that his people deserved praise

363

and credit and recognition for what they had done and still did without complaint.

August pointed out that the citizens leaned more towards what all the boys in the family fondly referred to as "Mom's life philosophy." This amused Darkon, because up until now, he hadn't heard any such thing from his wife.

"And what is that?" Darkon asked, fully intending on checking with Katarina later.

"Oh, it's something she said once to us, when we were mad that you weren't getting credit from the North or South for all that you were doing to help the peace efforts," August began to explain.

"You were traveling with Emily to address the nightmare in the Ribbon Fortress and the Ink Prince's Tower. We were upset that no one recognized your hard work."

Darkon found himself comforted by this admission.

"What did Mom say?"

August laughed,

"You know Mom. She said that she used to be like that, wanting everyone to get the credit for what they did, because it only seemed fair."

He had shared so much of his life with Katarina, Darkon couldn't recall if years ago, Katarina had expressed such a sentiment. But he let August continue.

"I'll never forget,"

August murmured.

"Mom said,

'You know, all those thank you's?

They come back to you.'"

Darkon felt a swell of pride hearing that. His Katarina really was the best, and though she did most of her work behind the scenes and was content to do so, the Queen of Kites had wisdom beyond measure.

"So were you satisfied with that very rare piece of wisdom?" Darkon asked.

"Not at all," August said.

"We thought it was just Mom being modest and humble, like she always is. Griffin accused her of giving up on fighting for what we deserved. Den went into a mild state of depression and didn't come out of the Kite Archives for weeks. As for me, I holed myself up in the highest tower of the palace to make and release my kites to work through my frustration."

Darkon shook his head.
"Poor Katarina.
All her precious gems of wisdom
wasted on our glory-seeking sons."

August shot him an indignant look of protest, which made Darkon grin.
But Darkon asked,
"So was Mom's life philosophy
completely rejected by you three?"

"No," August admitted.
"It sank in. I sort of accepted it a few nights later, when Mom came to make kites with me. We had just finished a batch – the first set of fireproof kites, actually. We went up onto the palace rooftop to release them into the night sky. Mom took one of those gleaming kites in her hand and sent it off while saying,

'Be brave and strong.
Even if you may be
the only one left standing.'"

August paused.
"She turned to me and said that in the same way we release kites so they can return to us later, it was the same with our actions. She pointed out that it's easy to think our kindness to others is in vain when we don't receive an acknowledgement right away – or ever. But in the end, the thank you's that we deserve do come back to us, sometimes much later, and sometimes

through people and circumstances we never would have expected."

August pointed to the sword in Darkon's hand and said,

"I'm pretty sure that's proof that the way you and Mom live your life is right."

"I have half a mind to tell her what I just heard," Darkon mused.

"Just so I can watch her say, 'I told you so.'"

"She already did when we were at the King's Heart," August said.

"She was so proud that you were the speaker for the North. She even cried when she was greeted by Prince Blazewick and Princess Featherfall. They spoke so highly of you and thanked her for all the support she's given you all these years. I think they were the ones who voiced the thank you's Mom deserved but never got. I'm glad you got to meet them and work with them."

"Hmm," Darkon nodded in agreement. That brought to mind a thought that he wanted to make sure that Katarina would feel fully appreciated and loved all the time, and not just on special occasions.

But he was pleased to learn that those in the Kite Kingdom were comforted with the fact that in their time of crisis, something noble and good was birthed in the whole process. There was word that once things settled down, those who wished to visit the King's Heart would be able to do so on their own time and of their own volition. Darkon was glad that Mirae had let him know that she had no plans on taking down the King's Heart any time soon, and wouldn't mind staying for an indefinite amount of time in the future.

The only regret that Darkon had left was that he barely got to work with Emily while she was here. When he mentioned this, he was curious at the thoughtful silence that filled the air. Darkon waited patiently, focusing on fireproofing kite after kite in the process, knowing that August would voice his opinion soon enough. He made a mental note that the work might go faster if they collected big mounds of kites and fireproofed them altogether.

Then he brought his attention back to August, who said,

"Don't feel too bad about that."

366

Darkon gave a knowing look to his son.

"You're only saying that because
you got to work with Emily instead, aren't you?"

A smug look came upon August's face, as he admitted,
"I don't deny it."

But then he got serious.

"Emily had a great time with Queen Renadé. Mom loved being able to host it at home, bringing out the best of her papers and ribbons. Den loved organizing everything, and Grif loved the challenge of keeping up with the sheer volume of invitations. And while we worked to help other people, the solution to our problem was sent back to us on a fireproof kite. From you."

Hearing that did good to Darkon's heart.

"Plus," August said,

"You got to work with Emily for the most important thing, which was speaking in the King's Heart."

"That's true," Darkon had to agree.

He did have a mind, however, to spend a little more time with Emily when visiting her at her place. He wanted to check up on Scott, yes, and he wanted to see how Katarina and Ryan were doing as well. But most of all, he wanted to thank Emily for spending time with his family in his absence.

It was the best gift she could have given him, and she didn't even know it.

32

Christmas in the King's Heart

mily had figured that someone would come by early as she was getting ready for her very last minute and informal Christmas get-together plans. She just never thought it would be Darkon knocking at her apartment door first. But it was the King of Kites who knocked quite politely on her door, and Emily opened it to find a very pleased-looking Darkon standing before her, holding his kite behind his back.

"Darkon," Emily said

as she motioned for him to come in.

"You're an hour early."

"I know," he beamed.

"I wanted to come before everyone else. Mirae is trying her best to keep everyone else from barging in from her side of the King's Heart. She insisted that everyone wait, but she let me come through on the condition that I help you with whatever last minute things you need."

"Oh," Emily felt better hearing that.

"Well, I could use some help moving this pile of gifts on the kitchen counter to my bedroom. I asked Crystal to do the baking this year, so she'll be coming in with all sorts of desserts and snacks."

Darkon stepped inside and looked around Emily's apartment.

"Do you not decorate for the holidays?" He asked.

"If I were to judge your level of festivities from decorations alone, I'd give you a zero," the Kite King mused.

"I used to," Emily said, as she closed the door behind him.

"But this year had more people problems than usual, and while I was taking care of them and working, there was no time for that sort of thing."

"Hence, Crystal baking for you?" Darkon asked as he swept up an armful of gifts and began to head towards Emily's room with some direction from Emily.

"Pretty much," Emily followed with the rest of the gifts.

"But it's the first time I set aside everything else to do what I wanted to do, so I'm content."

She didn't explain what she had been struggling with, but Darkon found it perched on her dresser drawer anyway on his way out of her bedroom. She watched as he stopped short, went back, and peered at a paper that listed names and issues and potential solutions. She wasn't surprised at the look of shock that came over his face.

"Is this what you're dealing with here in your domain?"

"Other people are dealing with them," Emily pointed out.

"I'm just the designated listener. I don't ask people much beyond 'how are you?' but I somehow end up with a lot of their life stories or woes. Not like they come all the time – only when they're in trouble. But it happened to be that it was all concentrated in one big wave this time around."

"No wonder you were exhausted coming to us,"
    Darkon whistled softly.
    "Valéon told us how worried he was for you,
    even after you left. Can you handle all of this?"

"No," Emily said honestly, relieved to admit the truth.

"I'm not qualified to deal with most of those issues, since I don't have the professional training. I'm like the stepping stone between people and the help they need to find.

I'm not the final stop,
and I can't take care of everyone,
but I can be the bridge to the help they'll receive.
I used to feel guilty saying 'no' to a whole bunch of people.
But I can't do this forever,
and I don't want to, either.

So I made a list. There are things I'm letting go of completely, others that I'm passing on to more capable hands, and a few I'm holding on to that I can take care of without burning myself out."

Darkon nodded thoughtfully.
"I see you only listed a few names under that column:
Crystal and Abby,
Henry, Luke and Lavender,
Ryan and Vincent,
Scott and Katarina."

Emily nodded.
Her immediate family and close friends.

Everyone else she had decided to let go of in one way or another. If there was one thing that she had learned during her last visit, it was that she was finite and human. And pursuing her calling would require her to shift her priorities and way of living, though it would cause a bit of discomfort in the beginning.

She felt validated when Darkon said,
"Good thinking. Wise choice."

But they didn't dwell on that topic much longer. Darkon asked what she needed and proceeded to assist her in getting it all done. Emily had to admit, it was nice to get last minute help from Darkon. He did a decent job sprucing up the apartment and making sure it was clean enough for guests. Darkon even took it upon himself to add a few well-placed decorations, which included a white and gold kite flourished with wintry cheer and red and green ribbons for the apartment's door.

About fifteen minutes before eleven, Crystal came, her arms loaded with a huge paper bag filled with baked goods.

"Hello, Darkon!" She said, pleased to see the Kite King.

"Merry Christmas! Did you come to see how Ryan's Dad is doing?"

"Merry Christmas!" Darkon said in reply.

"And yes, I did want to make sure Scott was all right after…"

"After that mysterious recovery, right?" Crystal said as she began to unpack the cookies, brownies, cupcakes, and pies one after another.

Then to Emily, she said,

"Don't you think this is way too much for desserts? And we've got dinner with Mom and Dad later tonight back at home. Abby is so excited, she's practicing up a storm on her cello. Says she wants to give us all a private concert in the living room tonight."

"We can send everyone home with something. I'm sure Vince wouldn't mind lightening the surplus of sweets, since he's not seeing his folks this Christmas." Emily said.

She noticed the look of relief that passed Darkon's face and realized that he was glad he didn't have to explain that he was the cause for Scott's "mysterious recovery." She patted her friend on the shoulder and said,

"Darkon, could you help me move these two chairs into the living room area? Where my couch is with its bookshelves – and the TV."

Darkon was more than happy to oblige. A moment later, he came back saying,

"You call that a living room? It's more like the size of a very large closet. How are you going to find room to fit everyone?" He didn't hide his amusement.

"Hey, I make do with what I've got," Emily said.

"I've made it so far. Plus, once we open up the King's Heart, it will feel huge."

"We're going there?" Crystal asked, delighted

"More like it's coming here," Emily said.

"Mirae said she'd open the door on her side once she got the signal."
"Who's giving the signal?"
Darkon asked
at the same time Crystal said,
"What signal?"

There was a knock on the door. Emily went to open it and was met by
Vincent, Avorne, and Renadé.

"Emily!" Vince greeted her
    as he shoved Avorne' shoulder.
    "Look who I brought!"

Avorne looked bemused and said,
    "We brought ourselves.
    Seems like Cassan is suffering
    a mild case of amnesia…again.
    I take it you'll insist
    on being called
    'Vince' like last time?"

"Got that right," Vince said.
    "Oh, by the way, Ryan said he's coming with his parents. He said Scott
would be here, so that's cool." Vince snagged Avorne's crown off the King's
head with ease – too much ease, in Emily's opinion.
    She and Avorne both gave him a look, and Vince coughed, spinning the
crown between his hands with a bit of guilty pleasure.

"Sorry, my bad.
    Couldn't help myself,
    you know."

Renadé cleared her throat.

"Would you like to
keep your fingers
for the holiday season?"

Vince swallowed.
   "Why yes. Yes, I would."

He was quick to place the crown back on Avorne's head and patted it
nervously. He then handed the drinks he had brought with him to Emily
as a peace offering, which Emily accepted before ushering everyone inside.

   Ryan did come with Scott and Katarina soon after, bringing sandwiches,
and Emily was hard pressed to find enough room for six real people and an
additional three – albeit fictional – others. She sent everyone to the living
room area and organized the food and drinks as best as she could on the
counter.

   "So let's take a vote," Emily called from her kitchen.

   "Food first or story first?"

   She was somewhat surprised when the response came as a unanimous
decision: story first. Well then. Emily decided that she could use a
brownie before launching herself into the telling of a not-quite epic, but
still intriguing tale. She popped one into her mouth and chewed hurriedly,
washing everything down with her tea from earlier that morning that had
gone cold as she cleaned the house.

   When she was ready, Emily came to the living room area and found Scott,
Katarina, Crystal and Ryan all snugly seated on the couch, and Vincent on
one of the chairs. He patted it and said,

   "We saved you the seat of honor. The beloved storyteller's seat."

   Emily rolled her eyes and tried not to laugh. She noticed that Avorne,
Renadé, and Darkon stood more in the hallway than in the living room
space. They'd take care of the space issue soon enough.

   "Right," she said as she plopped herself down in the seat.

   "So, my disclaimer is..."

"Don't say you're not a storyteller,"
   Vince stopped her before she could get there.
   "Especially when you just offered to tell one."

Emily shook her head.
   "Fine then."
   She took a breath.
   "It started with a place."

Ryan perked up at that.
   "What sort of place?"

"One that no one else could see," Emily began.
   "An invisible place, in fact."
At those words, Emily's apartment began to become translucent. Crystal gasped and grabbed Ryan's hand. Ryan blushed and ducked his head. Katarina and Scott waited with eager anticipation.

Vince quipped,
   "Okay, you've got the setting,
   but what was the conflict?"

"The conflict," Emily said.
   "Was that there were only two people
   who could see this invisible place.
   One was on the inside;
   she was the architect of the place.
   And one..."
   she looked at Avorne with a smile.
   "One was on the outside,
   and he could see this place,
   but no one else around him could.
   This story is how he helped everyone on the outside

see the vision he saw from the beginning."

"This is related to those invitations we got that you wrote, isn't it?" Ryan asked then. Crystal still hadn't let go of his hand, and he looked like he had no objections about it either.

"It is," Emily held up her forefinger,
  "But I haven't gotten there yet."

"Tell them what it's called!"
  Crystal leaned forward then.
  "Tell them its name."

"Its name,"
  Emily said then,
  "is the King's Heart."
At that admission, Emily's translucent living room and apartment began to gain patches of color, like a quilted masterpiece of stained glass windows. And where Avorne, Renadé, and Darkon stood, there wasn't just Emily's hall. It gave way and opened up into the enormous King's Heart that Mirae had designed her entire life. It wasn't just the King's Heart that Crystal, Ryan, Vincent, Scott and Katarina saw, either. Emily knew that they could see the people who waved their greeting and called out an enthusiastic,
  "Surprise!" and "Merry Christmas!" simultaneously.
They saw Valéon in flight, who circled high above the crowd. Darkon jumped upon one of his fireproof kites and proceeded to bow deeply. Avorne just smiled and shared a happy look with Renadé. Emily was pleased to see so many she had seen at the second peace treaty, like Iris and Ionthann, Falleyne and Elias, and of course the rest of Darkon's family as well.
  But it was Mirae who stepped forward shyly, and said once the initial cheering had died down,
  "Welcome to the King's Heart, Everyone. We've been dying to meet you ever since Emily asked us to come. You will stay to listen to her story,

right?"

It was the most heartwarming thing
   for Emily to hear everyone answer,
   "Of course."

"I can tell this story," Emily said,
   "but I'd like help from a particular three…"
   she gave a knowing look to
   Avorne, then Valéon, and Darkon.

"You're pulling me into this?"
   Avorne held up his hands in protest.

"The whole story starts with you,"
   Emily pointed out.

"I'm not saying tell the whole thing –
   just the first part.
   And then we can take turns.
   Valéon can be next,
   and then Darkon,
   and then me."

"How come you're last
   in the rounds of storytelling?" Darkon asked.

"Because I came in latest into this whole thing," Emily insisted.
   "Just ask Valéon. He came and got me, and it took a while before I came
in to join you all."
   "What about Ionthann then?" Valéon asked as a last effort to pull someone
else into this endeavor. He flew down to land beside her and gave her a
quick side hug.

"I offer my full support," the captain of the guard laughed.

"I'll chip in here and there if it makes you all feel better. Why are you all getting cold feet? If you all dragged Emily into speaking for the second peace treaty, you should have expected her to do something similar in return."

"That's right," Emily grinned.

"But lucky for you, this is a lot less people and a lot less pressure."

And to Mirae, she said,

"No speaker's platform this time, Mirae.

Just comfy couches for everyone.

Oh, and the food.

We should let people eat when they want

so they don't go hungry

while we tell them what happened."

"I'm on it," Mirae nodded and then skipped off to take care of the minor adjustments to the King's Heart.

Well, the only thing left now was to start. Emily prompted Avorne to begin, and once he had told a sufficient portion of his story, she had Valéon speak, and then Darkon. When he finished, she picked up the story and told her part. They went in rounds, and Emily was glad that she suggested this method. For one thing, everyone got a chance to add what made an impact on them the most. For another, they all got to learn things they didn't know. No one knew all the details, and so when Avorne, Valéon, Darkon and Emily spoke, they kept finding out new facts amidst their shared common knowledge.

There were many interruptions

as they stopped each other and said,

"I didn't know that,"

and "How come you never brought this up?"

and "That's new – since when?!"

Emily felt it was like playing a game where you and a close friend told the other something they didn't know about you. But more than that, she felt like it was better with all four of them telling this long and interwoven story. Emily knew she could have taken the whole spotlight; everyone was more than willing to give it to her.

But Emily loved the feeling of sitting by the roaring fireplaces in the great reception hall on the most comfortable couches with her dear friends. She wasn't sure how Mirae had pulled off a design like this, but the young architect had made it so easy to be present and content. Emily didn't feel even the slightest shadow of worry the entire time she was there, and by looking at the faces of everyone around her, she could tell the peace that she felt had settled around the whole room.

It was like round two of the second peace treaty attempt, Emily thought. Only instead of speaking on an epic and large scale, they spoke on a much more intimate and smaller scale. Both ways were quite different, and spoke to different audiences, but Emily liked them both. She also thought that this was the perfect Christmas present for her and those who had come to listen. This would do everyone's hearts good – hers included.

As if to confirm her sentiment, her blue and gold deck of cards appeared in her hands as she listened to Avorne speaking. Emily curled her fingers around that deck of cards and felt the coolness and familiar weight and heft.

She peeked at the top card
and read one word:
HEALING.

How fitting. Emily smiled.
It described this Christmas in the King's Heart perfectly.

Epilogue

A week after meeting Emily at the King's Heart for Christmas, as if to usher in the new year, Avorne was visited by Crystal, Ryan, Vincent, and Emily.

The King of Eld Mané had gone for his usual walk outside on the parapet to get some fresh air, a bit of exercise, and gaze at the King's Heart which still stood in the Inkstone Mountains. Whether they had sun, rain, or snow, the King's Heart remained bright and beautiful. Always open and available to any who needed it or wished to come inside.

While admiring the stained glass work, which he did every time he saw the ever-changing masterpiece, Avorne considered what work needed to be done – both in the immediate and distant future. There were plenty of further negotiations that needed to be made between individual countries and kingdoms. And the nightmare outbreaks were still a sore spot they needed to deal with on a case by case basis. But offers for help were flooding into the palace every day through the mail system.

Did someone need help with a particular problem? Such and such a kingdom had a solution to offer. Was someone in need of a particular service? It could come free of charge from the north or south, depending on the situation and need. Avorne had delegated the task of pairing up the problems and solutions to Uncle Vandek, who had a knack for pairing up the perfect combination of people or places. Avorne was convinced it was the double affinity for perception and influence hard at work.

Somewhere in the middle of his musings, Avorne was interrupted by an invisible door that opened right beside him. He nearly had a heart attack, but composed himself enough to welcome the four Legends who stepped from Emily's apartment onto his palace parapet and greeted him warmly. What brought them here so soon? Avorne thought they had plenty to take care of in their domains. Was there a problem? Some issue?

No problem, they reassured him. No issue. They just wanted to see how everything was going. Avorne raised an eyebrow at this admission. Everything was going fine. Plenty of problems still to be addressed, but they were making headway. He might not have had an affinity for perception, but Avorne still picked up on an unspoken wistfulness among Crystal, Ryan, Vincent, and Emily.

"Well?" He asked.
"Contrary to popular belief,
I cannot read minds. What is it?"

There was a good deal of hemming and hawing.

Avorne was amused at the collective shyness that fell across the foursome. Emily spoke up for the others in an attempt to help them out. Ever the leader, that Emily, Avorne was pleased to note that she had kept her confidence and looked energized instead of exhausted. What Crystal, Ryan, and Vincent wanted to say, Emily began to explain, was that they had a request. They wanted to hear his story from the beginning.

The beginning? Avorne studied these young Legends, wondering if they were aware of the implications of what they had just requested in their enthusiasm. Did they even know what had taken place? The enormous struggle that had brought his country and others to this place and the King's Heart? He knew that they didn't. The four of them had come near the end, with no knowledge of the peace efforts. They had spurred on many a conflict and many a resolution in their arrival. Avorne knew this, but his younger friends didn't know.

But he patiently waited for clarification. Emily explained for Crystal, Ryan, and Vincent, who could barely contain their excitement:
They wanted to hear his story
from the beginning,
to know how it all started,
and how it became the journey

that led to the King's Heart.
And they wanted to write it down for him,
so he'd have a record of it
and have something for posterity
to share with future generations.

Emily added as a side note,
   "These three really want to try their hand at a collaboration, writing-wise.
They wanted something challenging, meaningful, and worthwhile."

Avorne just shook his head.
   "You're asking to hear twenty years' worth
   of political endeavors and failures
   for over a dozen countries
   and countless people.
   That in itself would take a very long time."

It didn't matter –
   they kept telling him over and over.
   They wanted to be the first ones
   to write everything down for him.

Would he let them?
   Please?

Avorne fought the urge to heave a huge sigh.

Well…he tried to think of what that would require,
   if he broke it down into more manageable pieces.

"There are a lot of people who were involved,"
   Avorne started, thinking of the countless individuals
   who helped this enormous effort come to fruition.

"I'll keep track of them,"
　　Crystal volunteered.

"And many places,"
　　Avorne went on, thinking of
　　all the kingdoms and countries
　　this peace effort had spanned.

"I can keep track of them,"
　　Ryan nodded this time.

"And many complicated events…"
　　Avorne said, wondering how he could
　　even begin to retell what had happened
　　and weave them into a coherent narrative.

"I love a complex plot with good intertwining subplots!"
　　Vince grinned.

"They're the best kind.
　　You can never get bored.
　　Things are always changing up.
　　Every time you go back,
　　you find a connection you missed."

"Who would even want to take on such an endeavor?"
　　Avorne asked, his mind already beginning to hurt
　　from considering the enormity of what was being asked of him.

"Who would care?
　　Why would they want to tell my story?"

"We would," Emily said.

"Partly because we're Legends.
Mostly because we're friends."

"What would you call it?"
Avorne asked.

Emily smiled.
"The Chronicles of Promise."

"It would be long," Avorne warned.
"To put it all in one volume would be..."

"Madness," Vince clapped Avorne on the back in good cheer.
"But not to worry, Majesty," He flashed a smile.
"We can split it up into multiple volumes. Like a trilogy."

"From the way Avorne's describing it,
there might need to be another volume,"
Ryan pointed out thoughtfully.
"It could be a four book deal."

"What do you even call that?"
Crystal was saying. "A quadrilogy?"

"Or tetralogy," Vince said.
"Or quartet.
But that makes me think of music."

"What's wrong with music?"
Crystal asked then.

"Nothing," Vince said blithely.
"But let's be honest;

calling it the Promise Quartet would be awkward."

"How is that more awkward than
   the Promise Tetralogy
   or Promise Quadrilogy?"
   Ryan asked.

"That's why we should stick with The Chronicles of Promise," Crystal insisted.

"What if it's more than the estimated four?"
   Avorne lowered his voice so only Emily could hear.

"Does it matter?"
   Emily was amused with all of this speculation
   before they even got started
   on pulling Avorne's stories together.

"You can have multiple chronicles; it sounds better."

She turned to Avorne and said.
   "Your story is an important one.
   And you've been here from the beginning.
   It's something that should be recorded
   and passed down for posterity.
   Who knows how it will influence
   those who come in the future?"

Avorne was impossibly moved by this. He had been thinking of the generations that would follow him and wondering how he could leave them the foundation that had been built over the years.

"Oh, wait, wait, wait!" Crystal interrupted his musings.

"Before we start, we should totally do this in the King's Heart!"

"You mean Emily's place?" Vince asked.
　"But we just came from there."

"No," Crystal said,
　"I mean, *that* one,"
　she pointed to the King's Heart that Mirae had designed
　that still remained in the Inkstone Mountains.

"Valéon's in the library,
　so I bet he could help us look up everything we need.
　Plus, it's so much more comfortable over there."

"It's like a giant retreat center," Ryan nodded in agreement.
　"Dad said so when we were driving home from Emily's get-together on Christmas."
　"Who's in charge?" Vince asked.
　"I bet we could ask to borrow the space."
　Avorne laughed.
　"That would be Mirae, and she'd be thrilled to know that there are people who are interested in using her space for something like this."
　Avorne finally caved in and took the four to the King's Heart. Any regret he felt regarding this decision melted away as soon as he saw Mirae's delight at being asked to borrow the King's Heart for an extensive recording session to document the history of the peace treaty efforts.
　"Why didn't *I* think of that?" She said, getting all excited.
　"That's brilliant!"
　Vince gave a light-hearted bow. Ryan nodded his acknowledgement. Crystal beamed. Emily just looked at Avorne as if to say, "See? I told you so."
　"Can I stay and listen?" Mirae asked then.
　"I can help you with the visual effects."

"What visual effects?" Avorne asked then.

"Just watch,"
   the young architect stood taller
   and her chest swelled ever so slightly with pride.
"You'll see."

Touched by the enthusiasm that surrounded him, Avorne was moved by this and thought back twenty years to how it all started.
   "Well, it all started with an ink sign..."
The King's Heart, which had been composed of the familiar stained glass patterns all along its floor, walls, and ceiling, shifted, each tile changing color, turning into a white, gray, or black. All of a sudden, the King's Heart revealed a scene in the Inkstone Mountains, the white mountains holding an ink sign that reached for the bleak sky like an ebony claw.
   Avorne jumped. So did Crystal, Ryan, Vincent, and Emily. Well, that certainly was a very convincing visual effect. When Avorne found his voice again, he managed to ask Mirae,
   "Why did we not have these visual effects for Christmas?"

Mirae just shrugged.
   "This is a new challenge.
   Maybe the King's Heart
   is making accommodations
   for your new need."

As if to emphasize that point, the ink sign in the mountains now grew farther and farther away, and then they could see the palace of Eld Mané to the left, and to the right, in the foothills, two people walking. Avorne was blown away to see himself walking side by side with Uncle Vandek, both of them twenty years younger. He was shocked that everything down to the clothing they wore that day was accurate.
   "How did you get it down to the tiniest detail? The weather was exactly

386

like that. It had just rained. The ink sign looked like that ebony claw. I don't know how you knew about what we wore either; I've never told anyone."

"I didn't; the King's Heart did," Mirae shrugged.

"But if you ask me, if you want Crystal, Ryan, and Vincent to really understand what you went through, you should show them what it looked like as much as possible.

This was a good point. Avorne had to agree.

"Well, if you really want an epic retelling, you'll need to grab more people and bring them here. Valéon's in the library right? He was there from the start. Where's Halas? He helped quite a bit. He could get in touch with mother and ask her to add in her part. It should be easy to pull Iris from the gardens; she was the one who took me up North. Ionthann played a very important role as well. It might be hard to get Sylasienne to come over, but we could always ask. Theia and Crescens will be easier to reach, since they're in the Healing Wards. Oh, and Uncle Vandek. He won't like retelling this part, but wait until you see what he did for us later. Darkon should be here for this too."

Avorne realized his list of people he wanted present was getting longer and longer. He was amazed that Crystal's level of excitement was proportional to the list of individuals he kept naming. Avorne added a side thought.

"I wonder if Tal and Raehn are available; they came up to visit Renadé after hearing that she's pregnant."

"I didn't know you're going to have a baby!"

Crystal was delighted. "Boy or a girl?"

Avorne chuckled. "We don't know.

Ren thinks that it's a boy. I think it's a girl."

He wasn't surprised that everyone was now curious to know about the name choices. Avorne divulged the information willingly.

"We're still thinking of the names. We want it to be a surprise for everyone. Now," he cleared his throat.

"Where were we?"

"Trying to decide if you're really going to ask all the people you just mentioned to the King's Heart," Mirae offered, helpful as always.

"Right." Avorne looked at
Crystal, Ryan, and Vincent
with a skeptical eye.

"How serious are you three about this?
Do you have the time to stay a while?
Do you mind waiting?"

"Very serious," Ryan said.
He held up his notebook and pen.

"We're still on Christmas break," Vince added.
"We can stay the whole month."

"We don't mind waiting," Crystal said.
"You waited for me all those years ago."

All this time, Emily had said nothing, clearly content to remain to the side and let Avorne do business with the other three. After asking Mirae to see if she could reach as many people as she could to see who wanted in on this new endeavor, Avorne took a minute to speak with Emily. He pulled her aside and bent down to speak into her ear.

"And what do you say?"

"You mean as Emily or Ribbon Princess?" She glanced at him uncertainly.

"As an up and coming leader," Avorne corrected her. He saw the way she held herself taller at that and the sweet smile that came upon her lips.

"Well, it's challenging, meaningful, and worthwhile," she began.

"In your own words," Avorne said, not taking that as a satisfactory answer.

"Oh, well if you put it that way," Emily grinned then.

"I think having this for posterity would be a treasure that we can all share. I won't ever forget it. It gives me an excuse to spend more time with you and everyone else, so I'm not saying 'no' to this. Are you okay with the idea though?"

Avorne laughed.

"I can't compete with four young, very ambitious Legends. How can I compare?"

"What's to compare?" Emily asked.

"After all, we can't compete
with a King who's nothing without his people."

For some reason, Avorne felt himself get choked up over that unexpected compliment. Emily patted him on the back to let him know it was all right. He noticed a thoughtful look come upon her face then.

"Avorne, does that phrase have a history too?"

"Very much so," Avorne said.

"You'll hear all about it. With Mirae's help, no doubt you'll see it too."

"I can't wait," Emily said then.

"Even if I'm not writing it."

"Same," Avorne admitted.

"It'll be a miracle if we manage to pull it all together."

"Oh, we'll pull it all together," Emily reassured him.

"For the sake of the future generations,
we'll do it and do it well."

Avorne had never felt so comforted in his life to hear that reassurance. He considered his child who was yet to be born, and all the other children who were yet to be born as well, who the future would depend upon in just another generation. What legacy would he leave them? Avorne wondered. An example of what had been done, and a promise of what could be done. A vision of the King's Heart that might change its form and function to fit the next need, but at its core remained the same. Above all else, that was the legacy he wished to leave as a father and a king.

And realizing that Emily still waited for his response,
   Avorne nodded in agreement.
   "Right. Well said."

He glanced around at the King's Heart
   that surrounded him
   and murmured softly,

"For the sake of our
   future generations…"

About the Author

Sarah Choi has loved writing and drawing since she was young. That childhood passion grew into a lifelong effort that still continues today, albeit through different worlds and stories as of late. In her spare time, Sarah enjoys dreaming up new story ideas, learning bullet journaling, and improving her drawing skills.

Also by Sarah Choi

The King's Secret (Book 1)
Upon returning home, Avorne, fourth Prince of Eld Mané, finds an ominous "ink sign" looming above the back of the palace from the Inkstone Mountains. The ebony claw rising from the mountains disturbs Avorne, especially once he learns that a peace treaty he had no knowledge of is to take place that day between the North and South.

When the peace treaty efforts go wrong, however, Avorne finds himself in a situation that requires him to overcome his fear of the North and insecurity in his own abilities. With the help of Iris, his tutor; Halas, his half-brother from the sky; and Valéon, an attendant of a house of nobility, Avorne embarks on a journey to not only right the failed effort between the nations, but also step into his calling and claim his kingship.

The King's Crown (Book 2)

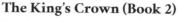

Twelve years after the first peace treaty attempt, Avorne is crowned King of Eld Mané. Before peace efforts among the North and South can be restored, certain amends must be made, such as rescuing Valéon — the keeper of the original peace treaty draft — from the Ribbon Fortress in Silkairen.

But when his crown is stolen the night after his coronation, Avorne falls seriously ill. The new King of Eld Mané must find and reclaim his crown before time runs out. Though circumstances become increasingly bleak, Avorne is helped by Ionthann, the captain of the guard; Halas, his half-brother; and Renadé, an ink enchantress and prodigy.

The King's Legends (Book 3)

As King of Eld Mané, Avorne seeks to restore peace between the North and South. The most pressing needs include relocating Tal, a friend gone missing; restoring Eles Teare, the capital city of a neighboring southern country along with its ruler, Raehn; and rescuing Valéon, the holder of the original peace treaty draft, still captive in the Ribbon Fortress up north. Even with the aid of Avorne's half-brother, Halas, it all seems insurmountable.

Enter Ryan and Crystal. They know nothing of the peace efforts; they barely know each other. But Ryan and Crystal soon find themselves involved with the events of the places and lives around them, attaining the title of Legends in Avorne's world. When circumstances become worse in the years that follow, Ryan and Crystal are joined by Vincent and Emily.

The four new and unexpected allies may be just what Avorne needs to realize the long-delayed second peace treaty attempt.

The King's Promise (Book 4)

A nightmare has taken over the Ink Prince, and the Sky Maiden has given up her light to save him. Ryan and Crystal are trapped in the Written World they once loved. Yet despite their noble efforts, the shadow grows and the nightmare darkens the land.

A new team arises as Vincent and Emily rather unwittingly and unwillingly enter Avorne's world to rescue Ryan and Crystal and help the King of Eld Mané subdue the terrible nightmare that threatens many realms and nations.

What seems to be a hopeless and impossible situation is met with the message that Avorne carries with him wherever he goes engraved on the inside of his crown: A KING IS NOTHING WITHOUT HIS PEOPLE. And so it is that without fail, the King of Eld Mané finds allies and friends to uphold this promise wherever he goes in his efforts to restore peace.

The King's Heart (Book 5)

Twenty years after the first peace treaty attempt, Avorne, the King of Eld Mané, searches for a way to usher in the new peace efforts. The most difficult obstacles have been overcome, and reconciliation has begun between the North and South. However, Avorne feels the weight of silent expectation; everyone waits for him to somehow procure the second peace treaty single-handedly. On top of this, Avorne notices an ink sign in the Inkstone Mountains that only he can see. What could it signify?

Thankfully, Avorne is not alone. Many allies come to stand by his side and help him to reach his vision of peace. There is Valéon, the living legacy of the first peace treaty attempt; Darkon, the King of Kites from the North; and Emily, the Ribbon Princess and Legend of Silkairen. Together they reach for the peace that has remained unattainable until now.